CURRAWALLI STREET

CHRISTOPHER MORGAN

CURRAWALLI STREET

ALLEN&UNWIN
SYDNEY·MELBOURNE·AUCKLAND·LONDON

Australian Government

Australia Council
for the Arts

This project has been assisted by the Australian
Government through the Australia Council, its arts
funding and advisory body.

First published in 2012

Allen & Unwin
Sydney, Melbourne, Auckland, London

83 Alexander Street
Crows Nest NSW 2065
Australia
Phone: (61 2) 8425 0100
Fax: (61 2) 9906 2218
Email: info@allenandunwin.com
Web: www.allenandunwin.com

Cataloguing-in-Publication details are available
from the National Library of Australia
www.trove.nla.gov.au

ISBN 978 1 74237 710 0

Internal design by Darian Causby
Set in 11/20 pt Berkeley by Post Pre-press Group, Australia
Printed in Australia by McPherson's Printing Group

10 9 8 7 6 5 4 3 2 1

For June Morgan

1914

❧ Chapter One ❧

Always there has been this funny little hill. Always there has been a crooked path of some sort running along its crown. Sometimes it could not be called a path; sometimes it was just a break in the growth of the tree trunks where the wind had pushed them aside when they were saplings, like the part in a head of hair, for the wind always liked to run up this rise and sail over the crest; and it has always been a place to stop and be still for a moment. Wallabies climbed the gentle slope to reach the top and always looked around, for it was a good place to see if safety was still a companion. Dingoes used the top of this slight hill to look back down the track in case there was anything small thinking it was safe to move. Kangaroos looked about from this spot to decide which way to go next; men stood here and looked for where there might be shelter. It isn't a big rise, not really a hill, but the illusion of height is fundamentally important to all animals.

Now there is a gravel road running east to west where the track once was, but the rivulets that the rainwater makes in the gravel look exactly the same as when there were only tree roots and branches bending in opposite directions in that spot. At the crest where the break in the vegetation was and where animals stopped to look about, there now is a church. Its spire is higher than the currawalli trees, even though some of them are two hundred years old. The gravel road is called Currawalli Street.

On either side of this road are houses with people inside living their lives sometimes quietly and sometimes loudly. And they are not houses that will be blown down by the next mighty wind; they are structures built to last, with young gardens that will grow. To the west, beyond the smaller road that adjoins the street, is deserted farm land. Forgotten paddocks of long grass. To the east behind the church is a patch of scrub and then another line of almost identical houses sitting along an almost identical street.

Running alongside Currawalli Street, behind the houses on the north side, is a train line. It is built up high to keep the tracks as level as possible. Trains run along there almost every day, making enough disturbing sounds to take up the space once filled by the cockatoos and silence.

Look at this young man, John Clarence Oatley, known as Johnny. He has finished picking the plum skin out of his teeth and he walks up to the wire fence at the back of his yard. The number five train from North Melbourne is due in three minutes. He and Kathleen have lived here in this house for ten months now and this train has been struggling slowly past with its one passenger carriage, two goods wagons and a mail-laden conductor's van every day, except Sundays. It is hardly ever late.

The plums are from next door. Eric gave him a bag. Johnny knew they would taste different to the ones Nancy, Eric's wife, had given to Kathleen, even though they are from the same tree. A man is much more careful about the quality of produce he gives as a gift to another man. That's why Johnny didn't give Eric any of his tomatoes. They just weren't good enough.

'Johnny, the photographer's here,' Kathleen calls from the open window of the kitchen.

'Coming. I'm just waiting for the train.' He turns towards the house to look at her as he speaks. She smiles at him. He can hear the train in the distance as it pulls itself up the rise.

Beyond the wire fence is a dry grass embankment thirty feet high. At the top of this are the train tracks. Johnny likes the moment when the vibration of the approaching train makes the tracks and the wire fence sing. At the very point where the rails reach Johnny and Kathleen's land, they stop climbing and run level for twenty yards before beginning to descend. And the train's journey becomes easier.

As the sound of the steam engine grows louder, Johnny also hears the photographer setting up his equipment by the side of the house. Kathleen is about to call Johnny again but she sees the steam engine appear through the currawalli trees and so she waits.

As the black engine struggles past as slowly as ever, belching oily smoke, the driver leans out of the cabin and waves to Johnny. As he always does. Johnny nods back and waits till the conductor, looking out of the open window in the van at the rear of the train, waves as well; then he turns and marches awkwardly round to the side of the house. He is wearing his good Sunday boots, not yet worn in. He prefers his other pair but Kathleen has insisted. She doesn't insist about very much generally. She wants him to wear these boots for the photograph. He doesn't tell her that these uncomfortable boots aggravate the pain in his back.

She has set a chair in the dirt next to the weatherboard wall of the house and the photographer invites Johnny to sit down. When he is seated, he kicks away a few clods of clay then looks up at the camera. Kathleen is standing behind him, looking so comfortable in her high-necked blue dress that everything else—the dirt, the newly stained wooden fence, the cockatoo in the branches above, the bright-red gumnut flowers trodden into the ground, even the photographer—looks out of place. The photographer, a tall, painfully thin man with long dark hair streaked across his forehead, has on a modern suit more appropriate for the evening than this time of day. He ducks under a black cloth behind the camera and Johnny feels Kathleen's hand on his shoulder.

From under the cloth, the muffled voice of the photographer. 'Don't smile. Sit still.'

Johnny looks at the lens, content to wait until it is all over. He wants to say that the photographer doesn't have to worry about any smiling because Johnny doesn't smile very often. It isn't that he is ever miserable or sad, it's just that his face doesn't fall to smiling. Instead, he says nothing. He sits still.

Just as he has asked others to sit still. He has gone from farmer to portrait painter without really knowing how. Life does these tiny little toe movements and before you know it you are doing an entire dance. An aunt gave him some oil paints as a gift; a horse threw him and then trampled him. He can't do farm work anymore. So he ends up painting forgettable pictures of forgettable people instead of mending wire fences and leading sheep to watering holes.

Aunt Beth, who gave him the paints one Christmas, was known in the family as a 'strange woman' because she took regular umbrage at the mildest of things. She was hardly ever invited to the farm because she always made people around her feel uncomfortable so he never saw her much.

'I'm not grumpy,' she told him once. 'I just expect people to do better than they think they have to.'

But everyone else assumed she was a permanently angry person. His father didn't like his own sister at all, and the times she did come to the farm, there would always be a crisis. The eggs weren't fresh enough; there were bull ants in her bed; the yard was a Chinese mess.

Johnny liked her. She told him about the fine art of belonging. Not necessarily belonging where you were. But belonging somewhere. Everybody belonged somewhere. There's an art to it.

'I still haven't found where I belong. But I will,' she told him.

And she did. In a grimy hotel surrounded by prostitutes and flash-by-night drifters. She never returned to the farm and he saw her only once more.

He and Kathleen had just arrived in the city. Aunt Beth was walking with a group of five fancily dressed people down a street of restaurants and bars. She came over to him.

'I can't talk now.' She moved to touch him on the cheek but she stopped as she reached out. He was an adult. No longer a marooned farm boy. She walked away to rejoin her friends.

An art teacher had come to the farm to buy some sheep from his father, saw Johnny's paintings and suddenly Johnny was attending an art school, seeing the city for the first time and everything that came with it. Noisy crowds, busy streets, painted women, men who preferred other men, gutters full of rubbish, the sands of an ocean.

And back home again to an unwelcoming farm. Then the accident and the terrible pain in his back. At first he couldn't bend over. And a farmer has to be able to bend his back. Johnny could only sit straight. On a horse or in front of a canvas.

A farmer bends his back. But a portrait painter doesn't.

A portrait painter has to deal with bank manager's wives, retiring lord mayors, spoiled children, dubious sportsmen. A farmer doesn't.

And that's one of the reasons his face doesn't fall to smiling.

Kathleen's hand grows heavier on his shoulder. He smells a perfume in the air. Honeysuckle. She must have picked some from the bush that grows along the front fence. He assumes that she is wearing her bracelet with the locket. Her sisters sent that over to her and this photograph will be sent back to them. In fact, it will travel to many places, across land, across seas, across years. He doesn't know how many people will look at it. He imagines Kathleen's family will put their copy on the mantelpiece in their sitting room. Who will see it there? Who will know what it really shows? England is such a long way away. When you apply that distance to a photograph, that photograph becomes only the flimsiest of depictions. It won't reveal anything other than a hazy outline of Johnny and Kathleen's life.

It won't show that it has been too hot for five days in a row; it won't show that you are tired of brushing away flies; it won't show that there is too much dust in the air because they are building another new home up the street or that the rain is long overdue. All it says is that you are sitting on a kitchen chair amid a pile of clay by the side of a new wooden house, and that you and your wife are still together. And you are wearing new boots.

He wants to yawn.

The photographer extends his hand, holding a square tray filled with a powder. Johnny has to concentrate not to look at it because the sun is reflecting off it like a kaleidoscope. There is a sudden flash and resulting puff of smoke, and then the photographer's head emerges from under the cloth. He is smiling as he slides a plate out of the camera box without looking at what his hand is doing, as if he is performing a magic trick.

'That's it. I think it will look good. You were both still enough.' He gathers up his equipment, says a quick goodbye and carries it all back to his waiting buggy. He is in a hurry to be somewhere else. Johnny wonders how anybody can survive such a hectic pace of life. He stands and Kathleen picks up the chair behind him and carries it back around the corner. He looks down to the honeysuckle lying in the clay.

After he has watched the photographer slap his horse with the reins and move off, he walks around the corner and inside to find that Kathleen has already changed. Her bracelet is nowhere to be seen, safely returned to the Chinese lacquered jewellery box. She has put back on her bread-baking dress, as she calls it. Plain calico with no frills.

Johnny looks at her hands while she moves about the kitchen, preparing the ingredients. They are big hands, but not so big as to be noticed as such by everybody. Kathleen sometimes says to him, when the sun has gone down and it is not yet time to go to bed, that she thinks her hands are too large. Johnny always disagrees. He holds one of them and makes a point of turning it over, considering it before answering. Then they always laugh. This is one of their scripted scenes. If the photographer was there at that time with his camera, then he would have to be concerned with smiling.

But the photographer wouldn't be there. Because they are the hours that are not meant to be shared with anyone else. Johnny remembers as a boy being confused by this time of night because there didn't seem to be anything appropriate to do. Now that he is married to Kathleen, these hours shine.

'Why don't we go for a walk after tea tonight?' Kathleen suggests as she sifts the flour.

Johnny likes to walk out and look at the end of the day. The light sits differently on the gravel road, and in the dusty trees, and on the clouds.

Dinner is a boiled chicken that Kathleen has bought from Maria three doors up. What they don't eat she will try to keep for tomorrow night, but Johnny is fussy about fresh food. They have a meat safe but the ice man hasn't come for three days because his wife is ill. Influenza. A strange word.

They tend to make their evening walk along the same route. Out of the front gate, turn left past Eric and Nancy's house next door, under the tree that is home to a family of apostle birds, on past number fourteen, the empty house. Johnny remembers what Aunt Beth said: 'An empty house is never finished.' Kathleen always gives the tiniest of shivers when they walk past. Then by William and Maria's, heading towards the church at the end of the street. They cross the short grass beside the church to reach an old kangaroo track that runs behind the houses on the opposite side of the road. They follow the path all the way down the slight slope until they meet the little road at the other end of Currawalli Street, coming out opposite the hotel. Sometimes on summer nights they walk around to the private entrance that leads to the lounge. They then have a drink each. It is against the law to drink in a pub after hours but there is always someone local in there, someone who has been invited to use the private entrance; sometimes the local constable can be found in there too. After the drink, they walk back up Currawalli Street past the empty blocks to their house. There are currently seven houses in the street, one under construction, and plans to build more. Johnny's mother would have said that the seven houses are sheltering under the shadow of the church spire. That's the sort of thing she said. He shakes his head when he hears her voice. He knows that the houses are just built where they are because that's where the best land is; the best part of the hill. And it happens to be close to the church. But she would have assumed that the people in the houses wanted to be close to God.

Tonight, at their front gate, the air full of the scent of evening honeysuckle, Johnny stops to look across the street at the empty yard beside number nine. The yard is already known as number seven even though all that stands there is a shed and a lean-to for the horses to shelter under. The framework for the house that Alfred and his wife Rose are going to build for their daughter one day is lying on the ground, ready to be erected.

Eric told Johnny about their building plans. Eric knows about them because Rose told Nancy.

On the other side of Alfred's house is a block of land that would be number eleven. Sometimes Johnny finds himself looking at it without having noticed that it has drawn his attention. He doesn't like it. He knows land like this. Nothing grows there. It is barren as if from a drier part of the country. Kathleen has said that she gets a cold feeling from looking at it. He doesn't tell her that most likely something bad happened there. He knew a spot like this near the farm where he grew up. The Aboriginal people wouldn't walk across it, they wouldn't eat anything that grew near it; they wouldn't drink water from the creek that ran nearby. It was a place where something evil had happened. Number eleven feels like that.

The wagons still aren't home. They are overdue by a week now. Johnny knows that Alfred, the owner of the wagons, is worried. Alfred's daughter, Elizabeth, has taken charge of an expedition for the first time. It has been a point of bitter contention between Alfred and Rose. Rose didn't think Elizabeth was ready. Alfred did. Johnny knows all about this too. Once again, Eric told him.

But the thing about these sorts of disagreements is that the point of bitter contention is not often what the real argument is about.

Johnny's mother and father were like this. They would argue about the direction of the fences, the colour the bedroom was painted, whether Johnny should go away to boarding school, whether Grandmother should stay with them, but never about the real issue. The issue even Johnny could see when he was still a child.

They were two completely different adults, unhappy together.

Currawalli Street in 1914 is on the outskirts of the city. Thirty years before, the area was easily an afternoon's cart ride away through rough bush, but the need for new homes grew and continues to grow and so houses and streets have replaced the scrubby bush. The city of Melbourne sits at the top of a long bay; if Melbourne was a woman at a church picnic with her skirts spread over the grass, then Currawalli Street is just at the hem of those skirts. There is still a surrounding band of deserted fields that farmers don't need to use and beyond that some dry bushland. On occasion the scent of wild country blows gaily in with the soft westerly wind and sometimes it creeps in surreptitiously like unwanted smoke with the hot north wind. But more often than not nowadays, the wild country isn't in the air at all.

From his front yard that afternoon Alfred Covey throws another apricot stone towards the little road and then watches the train driver wave down to Johnny. He sees the event as regularly as Johnny stands there and as regularly as the train goes past. Johnny doesn't know that. Soon after, Alfred—his hands eternally in his pockets like a country cricketer deep out in the field—watches as the photographer speeds away. Alfred is the type of man who is happiest leaning on the fence looking into the distance, looking down the street or looking over at the railway line. He finds it uncomfortable talking to most people. Not for the obvious reasons that you'd expect but because people can't help but stand in front of the view when they talk to you. And it is the view that always draws his attention.

Animals like him, especially horses. This is because they hold the same preference for a view as he does. Very rarely does he look a horse in the eye and he has never stood in front of one. He is convinced that horses respect him for that.

Alfred is the owner of the empty yard next door and, in spite of his reluctance to talk, he confided to Johnny two nights ago about his daughter and the wagons.

'It isn't as if she is incapable,' he explained. 'I wouldn't let her do something like this if she was. I was happy for her to go. Working these wagons is the only way that I can earn a living. I wouldn't risk that if I didn't think she was good enough. And she's got the bloke who's worked for me for years with her. She'll be alright.'

Johnny watched as Alfred spoke. The older man's chest heaved, and he had to force nearly every word out of his mouth. When his hands came out of his pockets, they balled into fists. He was exhausted by the conversation.

Alfred still oils his remaining hair and it glistened in the evening light. Hair is the sort of thing that you don't pay any attention to until it goes. It is the same with water. Johnny remembered on the farm that when there was plenty of water it was used with no care for its conservation. When the dams had dried up and the sky remained cloudless for weeks on end, it was treated with the sort of reverence usually accorded to paper money. Everyone acted as if they had always been careful and economical about its use.

Alfred's scalp was pale and looked too exposed to the evening air, like the bottom of a dam.

'Why didn't you go yourself this time?' asked Johnny.

'My health. I needed to rest and not worry. That's what the doctor said. That worries me more. But I should have known that I'd worry more being stuck here at home than I would if I was out there in charge. My doctor says that worrying has the capacity to kill me.' Alfred touched

Johnny's elbow and guided him to the front fence, away from the house so that they could talk out of earshot of his wife. 'I think I will ride out and find them. Just in case they're in trouble.'

'I wonder if your doctor would think that a good idea?'

'Perhaps not. And I promised Rose that I would listen to him this time.' Alfred coughed a tiny cough and then smiled at Johnny. 'He doesn't know everything. He only talks as if he does. Rose believes every word he says.'

He coughed that small cough again and walked over to the apricot tree. He picked two from a low branch and handed one to Johnny. 'Ah well, can't do much about it. That's my story. Enough. Let me ask about you. Do you mind my asking how you came to own a home so soon? Most couples have to do it rough for the first couple of years.'

'No, I don't mind. My parents died and left me a farm and some money. A few years before I had had an accident with a young horse and I wasn't really able to do farm work anymore. There were people wanting to buy the farm, so I sold it. Kathleen's parents sent some money over from England as a wedding gift. To make up for them not being at the wedding, I suppose. And we decided to buy a house closer to the city. That's why we're here. It's a long way from anything I know. Except for the train.'

'You know trains?'

'There was a railway line that ran past our property. I have always known trains.'

'So you're a farm boy from the bush?'

'I am. Kathleen comes from London.'

Alfred jingled the coins in his pockets. 'London. I lived there for a while. But I had to come home. It was the people walking in all directions that got to me. At least here people tend to walk the same way. But

15

over there! This way. That way. It started to confuse me. I didn't know where I was. I ended up staying in my room all day. You met your wife over there?'

'No, here. I've never been there. We'll go one day, I suppose.'

Both men looked out over the fence as they talked. They watched the day's last willy-willy wheel down the street, drawing up the grey dust into its dance. Men rarely look at each other until they are putting a full stop on the conversation, saying goodbye or about to start fighting. You sometimes need good ears to be a man. Johnny thought that was why his dad's ears were so big—because none of his father's friends looked at each other when they spoke and so his dad's listening had to be acute.

Johnny waited until he thought Alfred had finished this topic, and then changed the direction of the conversation. 'What do you do with the wagons?'

'Nothing special. Map making.'

'You make maps? Who for?'

'No, I don't make them myself. I used to be able to. But now everything is too crowded. I employ someone to do the actual map making for me. I gather the information that he needs. Sometimes a map is intended for the local shire, sometimes it is for the government, sometimes for the farmer who works the land. But this one is for the army. That's why it is a worry that the wagons haven't returned yet. This map needs to be made quickly and made well. That's what I'm known for. That's why they came to me.'

Johnny watched Alfred's eyes furtively return to the head of the street. He was still jingling the pennies in his pocket. He had been in his front yard until the sun went down every night for the last week.

'What's the next step?' asked Johnny.

'You mean if they don't return soon?'

'Yes. What will you do?'

'As I said, I will have to go out and find them. Make sure everything is alright.'

'Maybe I could go for you?'

This time Alfred turned and faced him, indicating that Johnny had made an important offer. 'No, it's too big a job, I couldn't . . . although you would be perfect, I must say. You can ride and you know the bush. But it does feel like a job I should do myself.'

'But your health . . .'

'That's right. That doctor says that I have to slow everything down if I want to see Christmas.'

'Blimey! Well, the offer is there. If you want me to go, tell me. I am ready at any time.'

'It would take a load off my mind . . . I'll let you know when it's the right time to go. If you don't mind. If your wife doesn't mind.'

Johnny shook his head. 'She won't mind.'

Alfred had turned away again so that both men stood side by side looking into the distance. The willy-willy blew itself out and the dust settled itself back on the street to wait for a hard rain to lodge it firmly to the earth.

Johnny and Alfred talked about other things for a few minutes longer. Then they both threw their apricot stones towards the setting sun, turned to face each other and said goodnight.

Johnny felt a little excited at the thought of heading out into the bush, especially with a purpose. It was getting harder to justify to himself his occasional expeditions. He never had a destination, or a time limit. And Kathleen never demurred; she was more tolerant of his need to wander than he was. But he had begun to think that a man needed to be at home looking after his family.

By the time he reached the front door of his house, he was resolved to try to push Alfred to let him go soon—in the next few days. And as he turned the door handle, he could hear Kathleen singing. He likes to hear her singing; it means that she is happy. He knows that sometimes she misses her family and friends in London and it is in those times that she stays quiet. She answers him when he asks her a question and she is pleasant in her responses but she stares out the window without looking at anything. She sits with a cup of tea without drinking until it has gone cold and he has to gently prise it from her hand. But when she is singing it is different. It means that those particular demons are asleep.

When they come back up the street after their evening walk, Johnny sees that the wagons still aren't in the yard. Alfred is pacing along his front fence.

Kathleen asks after his health.

'As good as can be expected.' He shrugs and changes the subject. 'I will take you up on your offer, Johnny. Can you go tomorrow morning?'

'I can.'

'Good. Thank you. I'll have everything ready for you. Come over here at first light. I'll be waiting.'

After they have walked on, Johnny asks Kathleen if she wants to accompany him but she declines. He doesn't try to change her mind:

he travels much more quickly on his own. Yet he likes her company on a journey. She is a good travelling companion, asking questions about the trees and other things that he knows about. She rides a horse reasonably well, given that there wasn't much cause for it in the part of London where she lived. He always borrows a horse for her that is gentle and forgiving.

They return to the house so that Johnny can prepare what he will need for the journey. Not that he needs much. His horse is ready to travel. He needs hardly any clothes and he will collect food on the way. He opens the cupboard above the icebox, takes down the silver cash box and transfers to it almost all of the money from his wallet. Cash is one thing that he won't be using in the bush, and Kathleen may need it.

There is something comforting about having a travelling bag once more sitting beside the back door. He sleeps better knowing it is there and ready. He and Kathleen lie together in a half light, where silhouettes take on degrees of substance.

He wakes at four thirty, just before the sun and the roosters. The waning moon still reflects in the windows. He quietly gets out of bed and walks from the room. By the time he is pulling on his favourite boots, Kathleen is in the kitchen with him, organising the small amount of supplies he is going to take. Within minutes he is ready and after a small kiss, he has slipped out of the back door.

His horse has sensed that there will be travel today; she is ready at the side gate, and stands still while Johnny tightens the saddle straps. Once he has climbed with some difficulty onto her back, she begins to walk slowly down the path. The sound of the four hooves on the gravel always makes him want to cry. It is a song from his childhood. After he settles into the saddle he looks back. Kathleen, touched by the moonlight, is standing at the bedroom window watching him. She doesn't wave. She is tightly holding the book that her sister sent her, open at the first page.

As he had said he would be, Alfred is waiting for him in his front yard. The sun is just beginning to climb, but it is still under the line of currawalli trees. The two men greet each other, and Alfred pats a small leather bag before reaching over the fence and passing it up.

'A map, a compass, and the route they were planning to travel. There and back. You do know my daughter, don't you?'

'Yes, I have talked to her at church a few times.'

'Ah yes. Church. Of course.' Alfred doesn't go to church. It won't be too long before Johnny doesn't go either. He feels like he is wasting time there. His time and the church's time.

'If you travel their route the opposite way then you should make contact with them . . . soon, I hope. And would you pass this to my daughter when you see her?' Alfred hands Johnny a slip of paper. 'It's a note from me. Telling her to come home. To give up on the map.'

'I'll give it to her. Will she obey it?'

'No. But give it to her anyway.'

By the time Johnny turns his horse to face the direction they are going to travel, Alfred has come out onto the street. Both men nod without looking at each other. The sound of the horse's hooves fills the early morning.

At the end of the street, he turns to the left and heads along the little road towards Choppingblock Road up ahead. He is tempted to cross over the creek and enter the bush there, joining up with the road a few miles further on, but he decides not to in case he misses the wagons.

Johnny always likes being on a road at this time of day. The air is clear and the horse keen to move. Johnny's mind is fresh too. He rides steadily underneath the flowering gums that hang over the road. At the corner of the little road where the Choppingblock Hotel stands, he sees Arthur the publican splitting some firewood for the stove. Arthur nods between axe strokes and Johnny lifts his hat. Arthur is usually too busy to stop; he's always working on either the pub or his garden. Sure enough, Johnny sees a partially built arch for training roses lying on its side at the back of the pub, much like the one his mother used to have in her kitchen garden.

He looks back at the road he has turned out of. It doesn't have a name but everyone knows it as the little road. It runs past the railway station. Choppingblock Road soon begins to climb the first of many hills. Johnny gives the horse her head for a moment so she can stretch her legs a little. She breaks into a gallop and the increased speed fills him with a tiny tremor of excitement. He pulls her up after a few hundred yards and she falls back into an easy walk.

He is travelling underneath a continuous cloud of dust that sits still in the air. A bullock dray must be travelling along the road, going north. Johnny judges that it has passed about five minutes before and he will come up to it soon.

He sits back in the saddle and begins to think out the day ahead. He is used to planning like this. It is also how he paints a portrait. The blank canvas is like the road to be travelled; he maps out which direction to take, which lines need to be drawn first as references, just as he looks for landmarks to keep himself riding in the right direction.

Only fifty years ago this road was frequented by bushrangers, waiting for a lone traveller like himself to come along. But old age, a better police force and the threat of the noose has thinned the ranks of the bushrangers and now they are virtually non-existent. Only the light of mind or the savage at heart venture into that profession nowadays.

He can soon see the outline of the bullock dray up ahead. Most of the time its wheels run smoothly in the ruts worn into the road by earlier traffic; the dust rises up in clouds only when the wheels veer towards the side of the road where the dirt has been displaced. But there is still enough for Johnny to taste it in his mouth.

By the time he reaches the back of the dray he can see that it is full of supplies and probably heading back to one of the logging camps. A company chops down the trees near Mount Sterling and brings them to the city docks where they are loaded as ballast on the ships leaving for Europe. So even before the insects have come to their senses and realised that their home is now dead, they are likely to be deep in the belly of a ship steaming to Portsmouth or Marseilles.

As he draws abreast of the dray, Johnny nods to the driver, who nods back. They look at each other for a while, neither feeling like engaging in the standard exchange about the weather. The driver sits forward on his bench, his hat pulled down close to his eyes, a cigarette drooping out of the corner of his mouth. Eventually he tilts his head in the direction of the storm clouds brewing, and Johnny nods again before lifting up his chin and spurring his horse on.

He pulls the horse back to a walk when he is two hundred yards further up the road, at the crest of a hill. Before him he can see the lay of the land, the twists and turns of the creeks and gullies. Behind him are the bullock dray, struggling up the hill, and the land he has already seen and is content not to see again until he returns home.

Before him Choppingblock Road dips and turns as it climbs small hills, drops down into tiny green valleys, runs alongside creeks and squeezes around rocky outcrops. The predominant feature of the panorama is the vast choppy sea of grey-green eucalypts. Gum trees that bend to no wind and grow straight and tall towards the clouds. He stops longer to take it all in.

Johnny hears the hooves and the clink of saddling gear as another horseman comes up behind him. Without looking he can tell that the rider expects to be in the saddle for a long while, as the ring of the saddle buckles are quickly deadened with each step by the weight of a heavy load. By the ease of the horse's steps he can also tell that this is a journey beginning, not coming to its conclusion.

'Hello, travelling well?' he asks, his eyes still surveying the horizon. He turns as the other horseman comes up beside him and stops. The face is familiar.

'Yes. I believe I am travelling well. And I hope, all things considered, I will continue to do so.'

Johnny sees a man of his own age. But whereas Johnny is dressed for the road, with a broad straw hat, solid boots and a heavy coat that will keep out the coming rain and the wind, this man is dressed in a town man's suit of the current fashion: expensive heavy tweed cut to sit close to the body, and a matching hat with a thin brim. A pair of two-toned button-up shoes that look as if they have never seen mud completes the picture of a city man on his way to being lost in the country.

Johnny looks briefly at the man's horse. There is the difference.

The animal looks as if it has travelled great distances before, and all of the saddling gear looks well used. It shapes the horse. The man is at ease, his back comfortably straight and his legs well accustomed to their position. The stirrups have been drawn up closer to the saddle in the old stockman's trick. By lunchtime, when the opportunity for faster riding is gone, the stranger will drop them into a more standard relaxed position. Johnny did the same thing in the morning. It adds speed to a journey by giving the fresh horse more freedom to run. The trick is to know when to drop them down; in that position, stirrups become very tiring for the rider.

'You're headed a fair way?' Johnny guesses.

'Yep. All the way to Sydney. Will take me fifteen days, I believe.'

Johnny nods and looks thoughtfully at the dirt between them. 'Could be more. Don't think it will be less.'

'Me neither. But I'm hoping. I've done it a few times before. It's a good ride.'

'I've done it only once before. Good farm country. Worth seeing.' Johnny continues to look away when he says, 'I know you. I've seen your face somewhere.'

A trace of suspicion and what sounds like exhaustion creep into the stranger's voice. 'I've been living at the Choppingblock Hotel for a few years. You know it? Perhaps you've seen me in there.' He scratches his chin, and Johnny notices that he has shaved this morning. It says something about a man when he takes the time to shave his face even though he will be alone on a country road for most of the day.

'Maybe, but I don't go into the bar often. I live around the corner in Currawalli Street. Perhaps I've seen you walking about.'

'Perhaps that's it. Where are you headed?' the stranger says as his horse drops its head to investigate a scarlet beetle crawling across the gravel.

'Up a ways. I'm cutting across at Weather Hill. Heading to Wensleydale.'

'We're going in the same direction. Let's travel together a bit.'

Without another word both men direct their horses towards the centre of the dirt road and encourage them to walk on down the hill. Both men ride in silence and only begin talking again when they dismount for a cup of tea by a creek.

'That was a big snake back there,' says the stranger.

Johnny nods. 'Yep. Keep my eyes open for them this time of year. Never know when I'm going to come between the mother and her babies.'

'It's not a good place to be. My horse previous to this was bitten because I hadn't been paying attention and wandered into a nest area. Horse died. Left me out in the bush for a few days.'

'Same thing happened to me. Can't blame the mother snake. Who wants a horse stepping on your babies?'

While they are talking they build a small fire and fill a billy with water from the creek. When it boils, Johnny drops in a handful of Ceylonese tea-leaves and both men retrieve their cups from their saddlebags.

'What's your name?' Johnny asks.

The man looks him up and down, suddenly serious. 'You know, I don't like to tell people my name. But I assume you're asking me so that we can talk better?'

'That's right. Why else would I ask?' Johnny is surprised.

There is suddenly something dangerous in the air. If not for the easiness of the stranger's manner previously, Johnny would be getting ready to protect himself.

'Alright. My name is Alfred Brady . . . Bert Brady.'

'The gangster that everybody talks about? The one who robbed that big department store in the city? The one who goes out with actresses?'

'Yep, that's me. I'm the gangster. Although I don't have a gang or a girlfriend.'

'Pleased to meet you, Bert. My name is Johnny Oatley.' The sense of danger blows away as Johnny stretches out to shake hands.

'Pleased to meet you, Johnny. What do you do?'

'I was a farmer. Now I paint pictures of people.'

'You mean a court painter? That bloke who sits up the back of the courtroom and draws pictures of the people on trial?'

'No. People pay me to paint their portrait. They sit in a chair and I do an oil painting of them.'

'Leaving out the rough bits.' Bert grins.

'That's right. That's if I want to get paid. People don't judge a portrait painter on how good his paintings are. They judge him on how good they look in the painting.'

Bert laughs.

'People. You can't beat them. Why are you going to Wensleydale?'

'Helping a neighbour. He's trying to find his daughter and their two wagons. They're late back.'

'How late?'

'Three weeks. A bit more.'

'That's not long. My dad was three years overdue once.'

'I don't think this neighbour would be able to wait that long.'

'Shall we ride a bit more?'

They stamp out the fire and rinse their cups in the creek. The horses are standing together under a currawalli tree; its branches hang down low to the ground. They are standing on either side of the tree, scratching their flanks against its trunk. Johnny likes the look of the currawalli tree. Its leaves always seem too big for its branches, giving it a top-heavy look. The men draw the horses away from the trunk of the tree and are soon on their way.

Bert is tall and thin. When he pushes his hat back on his head he looks even taller. He has a face that makes him look like a hard man. Johnny realises now that he has seen photographs of him in the daily paper; he assumes that they received those photographs from the police. They looked like they were police-style photographs. Except for one he saw of Bert as he sat exhausted in a tram shelter after being jostled, according to the newspaper, by a group of drunken thugs. One trouser leg was up his calf as he looked into the camera, evidently too tired to look away or complain about the photographer's intrusion.

'Why are you going to Sydney?' asks Johnny.

Bert sits back in the saddle. He looks into the scrub by the side of the road for a few moments. 'Well, Johnny, I am going to join the army. I have been trying for a long time to abandon the way I have been living. I want to do something, I don't know . . . decent, something worthwhile. I fell into my life just like anyone falls into anything. I don't feel I had much say in it. And now I am Melbourne's favourite career criminal. Everyone knows me or about me so it doesn't matter anymore whether I commit a crime or not, if I can be stitched for something then everybody is happy. Except me. The papers, the police, the politicians, the man in the street, they're all happy. It doesn't matter that I didn't commit the crime or that the real criminal is still free. Doesn't matter at all.'

He looks over at Johnny. 'I figure I am a sure bet for the hangman's noose one of these days. I'll be charged with a murder and they'll be happy to wrap it around me. That's why I left in a hurry this morning; word is that I'm about to be set up for something. So I had to move quick. Hence the city clothes. I'm going to join the army in Sydney where I'm not known. The way things are looking, there will soon be a war and we'll all be going over to Europe to help out the mother country.'

'A war? But I thought they were talking their way out of it?'

Fatigue comes into Bert's voice again. 'They're not even trying to talk their way out of it. The papers just say they are. We'll be at war before the year is finished. And if we are, then that means most of the world will be.'

'Why?' Johnny asks, dismayed at the idea.

'One word. Progress.' Bert makes it sound like a sad word.

'I don't understand.'

'The world is in the process of changing from the old to the new. If you sent a letter to London thirty years ago it would have taken sixteen weeks to get there. Now it takes only six. Everything works at such a faster speed now. Your children will think our pace of life is slow. But to us it is very fast. To our parents it would be an unbelievable miracle.'

Johnny notices that the road up ahead begins to climb. He feels the horses pick up speed as they sense the incline. He leans forward in the saddle. So does Bert. Johnny hasn't thought about war much before. It is something the old men in the public bars of hotels talk about but only when they have run out of other things to say. Old men like to sink their teeth into something that they feel unhappy or uncomfortable about. What they say isn't to be taken seriously. It is just the ramblings of spent brains. This is the first time he has heard someone of his own age talk about it with such conviction and surety. As if it is going to happen, no matter what.

Bert continues, 'There will be a war to speed up this progress. To shake the tree and clear the dead wood out. To get rid of the old and give the new growth plenty of room.' He pauses and turns in the saddle to look for a moment at the road behind. 'To live accustomed to such speed has some advantages but it also brings some bad things with it.'

'Like what?'

'We can now find out what is happening in London in six weeks. We respond straightaway. They receive our response in six weeks. That's only twelve weeks. It used to be eight months before they could receive any reaction from us. By then tempers could have cooled, fights could have been fought. The chances were it would be all over. Now we can be involved almost immediately.'

'Is that a bad thing?'

'Sometimes it is. The leaders we have are suited to this country, suited to being far away from anywhere else. But now they can throw their hats into the ring and say things that they have no idea about. It could be dangerous to give them so much power.'

Johnny pulls tobacco out of his pocket. The horse knows that he has dropped the reins and that they rest on her neck but she doesn't change her pace. Johnny begins to roll up a cigarette and passes the packet over to Bert who also lets go of his reins. His horse doesn't react either. Bert lights his cigarette, draws deeply on it and then resumes talking. Johnny is happy to listen.

'One thing that has to be considered about the men in this country is that most of us are descendants of English convicts and have a very healthy disrespect for English ways—all that pomp, the aristocracy, the class system. Without a doubt, Johnny, when the war comes the leaders of our little country will hand over control of our army to the British generals. Apparently most of them come from the upper classes and there is some serious concern that they might not be smart enough. I reckon that our army may end up having to fend for itself or else it may be sacrificed.'

'Bert, how do you know all of this?'

'Look at what Calway has written about the English. Look at Bally-money. They're not hotheads, angry at everything. Calway's a professor. Ballymoney's a bishop. It's all there if you look. The Irish talk about it. I read lots. And I have learned to read between the lines. That's where the truth lies.'

He stretches in his saddle and looks at Johnny. 'The world is changing. Have you seen one of these flying machines?'

'Yes. There is a field near where I live . . . where you have been living. They take off and land there. I went over to have a look at them.'

'Me too. I made a point of going to see them. I'll tell you this. Being able to fly isn't the most amazing thing about them. Rather, it's the speed at which they can cross the countryside—almost as fast as you can turn your head to follow them. If one flies overhead when you start to puff on that cigarette, it will be almost gone from your view by the time you blow the smoke out of your mouth. That's what's remarkable about them. And who knows what they will do in a war? See where troops are hidden? Drop bombs?'

Johnny flinches involuntarily. He hasn't considered this at all. But it makes sense.

Bert pushes his hat back on his head and wipes his brow. The sun is starting to climb and the heat is building, even while the storm clouds are getting closer. 'The British army have experimented with these flying machines in South Africa. Seeing how accurate they can be and how much damage they can do.'

'And how were they?' Johnny asks quietly.

'Very effective. The bombs killed more people than shells fired from cannon. The army was very pleased with the experiment.'

'Who was killed?'

'Some villagers that the British could see no need for.'

'How do you know all this?' Johnny asks again.

'That's one of the good things about being a notorious gangster. The nicest people are more than happy to rub shoulders with you. If you can help them. A judge just back from London told me about the experiments at dinner at the archbishop's one night. He had seen the report himself. The English want us to start producing these flying machines. The judge thinks it might be a good idea. He wanted me to talk to a few people I know in the carriage-building business.'

The day continues to get hotter, and Bert pulls off his coat and undoes the buttons on his vest. Johnny takes off his own coat and straps it to the back of his saddle.

'I plan on buying some more appropriate clothes in Euroa,' says Bert. 'City clothes are only good for one thing.'

'What's that?'

'The city.'

They both laugh. The road is rockier now and the horses' hooves ring out loudly through the scrub.

'I think it's time to drop the stirrups down,' Johnny says.

The men steer the horses into a glade by the side of the road. Johnny stretches his back before he jumps down out of the saddle. Bert riffles through his saddlebag and pulls out a loaf of bread.

'Lunchtime,' he says.

Johnny comes up with a block of cheese. The men stand under a ghost gum while they eat, then take a few careful steps across the open ground and return to the horses. If there are any snakes about, they will attack only if threatened. Johnny and Bert know enough to stay out of their way by avoiding the long grass where the snakes like to hide. Johnny has sat by the side of a friend as he lay dying from snakebite almost this far away from a town. Seeing it once is enough.

'You've got a bad back?' Bert observes.

'Yeah, I have.'

'Getting better?'

'No, this is it, I'm afraid.'

'How did it happen?'

Johnny bends down stiffly to check that his horse's shins are okay. He says nothing until he has felt all four legs. Then he straightens, making sure his face doesn't register the pain. 'Funny thing. We had a really gentle mare on the farm. And a quiet stallion. We got her to foal. The foal turned out to be the opposite of its mother and father. Threw me when I wasn't expecting it and trampled me after I had gone down. A nastier horse I have never met. We sold it on as quickly as we could but the injuries I suffered wouldn't go away. And so now I am limited in what I can do. Funny though. Just because both parents were calm and quiet I expected the foal would be the same. But it wasn't. If I didn't know horses better I would have almost said it was vindictive.'

'Born bad.'

'Yeah. I suppose that's it.'

'It happens. In humans as well.'

Both men lengthen their stirrups and climb back onto their horses. They head off up the road, which is still climbing. It has been for half an hour now. The crest looks as if it is about a mile ahead. Johnny can sense that his horse is starting to feel the effect of this hill. The time between each step is minutely slower and the hooves come down heavier. Her head hasn't dropped yet. When it does, Johnny will look for a place to camp for the night. He relies on this horse and she relies on him. He could work her into the ground but he would be able to do so only once. She would never recover properly.

He makes himself comfortable in the saddle, looks about, and asks Bert, 'So where did you learn to ride?'

'The same place as you, I imagine. My parents had a farm down by the Llewellyn River. I spent all my childhood on the back of a horse. You too?'

'My folks had a farm up near Strathbogie.'

'Sheep farm?'

'Yep. Most of the time. And you? Wheat?'

'Mainly wheat. Sometimes sheep.' Bert looks ahead. 'You'll be leaving the road up here?'

'Yes. There's a good track that runs off to the left along that ridge. That will take me to Wensleydale.'

'Johnny, I did enjoy talking to you. I'd like to ask you two favours.'

'Of course. What are they?'

'Don't tell anybody you have seen me. And write out your address for me so I can send you a letter.'

'Why do you want to send me a letter?'

'I have no one else to write to. I don't know whether I will write at all, but I don't know what is going to happen and what I'll feel like doing. And you seem like a decent person to write a letter to.'

Instantly Johnny feels a tiny degree of suspicion but that is quickly overtaken by the honesty of Bert's request. Two farm boys, a long way from home.

'I'd be pleased to get one.'

They come to the top of the hill and the track across the ridge emerges. Johnny writes out *number 10 Currawalli street* on a page torn from his notebook, hands it to Bert and then looks along the road that he is about to turn off. 'I hope you stay safe, Bert. Good luck to you.'

'Good luck to you too, Johnny. See you in the heather!'

They both lean forward across their horses' necks and shake hands. The horses step back and the men part. Johnny can hear the hooves of Bert's horse for a few minutes but then the track is swallowed up by a stand of thick trees and with the colder air comes silence.

As Johnny adjusts his position in the saddle and rubs the small of his back, he recalls the many fellow travellers he has met before on many different roads. It was always an encounter that could not be replicated in any other situation. Two people, content to fill in some time with conversation, intent on a destination, after having spent hours or maybe days alone with their thoughts reflected by an untouched bush landscape.

But this meeting with Bert stands out more than any of the others. It is the first time Johnny has seen the light of the future on someone's face, and he is left with a more defined picture of what is to come. A few other men have mentioned to him 'the rumblings of war' as if it is nothing but a slogan; this is the first time he has felt a real presence on the horizon. When he wished Bert to stay safe, he really meant it.

He settles down into the saddle and leans forward so that his weight sits more on the shoulders of his horse. She responds by moving faster, the rhythm of the hooves picking up. When they emerge from the trees Johnny can see that thunderclouds have passed over him, heading to where he has come from.

ℜ Chapter Two ℜ

Alfred Covey from number nine Currawalli Street has a map shop in the centre of the city. His maps are highly sought after: anybody travelling across the southern part of the country knows that a Covey map will be the best aid to have on hand when heading into such a vast unknown. And a Vast Unknown is exactly what most of the country is. So Alfred's business, begun in the last ten years of the nineteenth century, is booming as more people arrive and are paralysed by what they see: black mountains sitting in the distance that change colour and shape; trees that hold out the sunlight and bend stiffly in a wind that is unrelenting and unwelcoming; weather that can be hot enough one day to start a monstrous fire and also, without warning, bring enough rain to send a sudden flood roaring down from the hills; animals and reptiles that are aggressive and deadly; and natives who are assumed to be treacherous. Finally, there is the distance: everything is so far away from everything else. No one wants to be lost. It is a horrible thought.

And Alfred Covey's map-making business has enabled him to buy a home on the outskirts of the city and pay for a good education for his daughter.

His wife, Rose, started her working life in Alfred's shop. That's how she met him. She responded to an advertisement placed in the window. Eventually she left to go and work in a delicatessen. He followed her and courted her over the counter. They were married and chose a block of land out at the edge of town among the currawalli trees. They lived in a tent and watched as their house was built. Rose was pregnant by the time she sat in their new felt armchair, and Elizabeth was two weeks away from being born when Alfred planted the apricot tree in the front yard and thought, for the first time, about buying the land next door.

Now the apricot tree hangs over the front fence and they are having a house built for Elizabeth at number seven. It doesn't occur to Alfred that she might want to be somewhere else.

On the other side of Currawalli Street at number sixteen stands Maria Conte who emigrated from Italy after her heart was stolen by a wandering Englishman. That's what her family decided had happened. From the oldest habitable part of Rome, she came with him to this new country. William's wanderlust evaporated as Maria's grew, and she settled down only reluctantly. They haven't moved from Currawalli Street since. She and William produced two children and eventually she didn't feel the loss of her original family quite as strongly.

Her grandmother had told her what would eventuate—it was something the old people in her village said: the wandering man will eventually put down roots deeper than anybody else. And that's exactly how it turned out. William, who once saw new countries to explore, new horizons to head for, new borders to cross, now doesn't see beyond the front fence, and he is happy. Still, when Maria describes him to other women, she says simply, 'He is a good man.' And when she looks at her children, she knows that's what he is. It wasn't he who stole her from her family in Rome; it was that uncaring moment called love.

Maria's mother and father are now dead, victims of a famine and a life of hard work. Under a mantel clock that she and William bought in the city, Maria keeps the letter from her brother telling her of the sad news.

And if playing on the crowded streets of her childhood, watching, as she grew, all the different types of people around her family, has shown her anything it is that everybody has an affinity with something. For her father, it was rope; her brother, donkeys; her friend, cooking fish. And Maria has an affinity with chickens. Ever since she was little she was able to manage the hens and roosters her family owned and make them do the things that chickens have to do to make them worth keeping: lay eggs and get fat.

Maria's chickens were fatter than they should have been considering the small amount of food that could be put aside for them, and they laid more eggs than any other chooks in the street. No one knew for certain why this was so, but her mother was convinced it was because Maria made them happy. And it was true that they liked to be around her, even when she was sleeping. There is now a chook pen at the back of number sixteen and the chooks supply enough eggs for her family, and for the general store near the railway station to become known as a place to get good eggs.

William must have always had a sleeping passion for geraniums and now that he has settled down they are planted all around the chook pen. The chooks like to eat the buds just before the flowers bloom. The chooks are happy and so is Maria. William doesn't say anything.

At number thirteen lives Morrie Lloyd, the son of the once-celebrated Melbourne theatre impresario H.G. Lloyd. Morrie is a widower who buried all of his plans, all of his dreams, with his wife Gwen. He was once an elegant man, a barrister who walked the floors of many established city houses with his head held high. Now he walks the streets dishevelled, with his dog, head down.

Where once he rolled glamour and success around on the tips of his fingers, walked into a room assuming there would be a woman or a man present who was in love with him, expected to always be heard when he spoke, and where once he sailed before a strong steady wind, he now leaves glamour and success in a back drawer in the kitchen; he looks at the radiogram without turning it on, tries to avoid speaking to too many people.

The woman he loved died.

Gwen was one of those people he had read about; he had seen theatre shows about them, he had heard clients talk about them. The sort of person who turns your life upside down quite easily. He met Gwen without meaning to; he wasn't looking for anybody, certainly not in the reception room of his office. She was the sister of one of his clients. A lost cause certainly but for a reason Morrie could not identify at the time, he found himself working harder than he ever had to successfully defend this man. In the end, he didn't succeed but by then the distant view of Gwen had become a fixture in his life that he did not want to lose.

He didn't know how to win her heart, which was a result of never having to do it before. Therefore he accepted and gave up a lot more than he probably had to. She was younger than him but he was used to walking out with younger women.

But he had to shed a lot of his habits and manners before he impressed her. His reserved seat at Flemington races, his enjoyment of late-night dinner parties, many friendships that were good for a single man to have, the flippant amusing responses that he used instead of saying what he felt. Finally he gave up his Savoy Hotel suite to move into a thinly built wooden house on a street at the edge of the city when they married.

Gwen loved him and understood that, just as the Italian woman across the street was living in a foreign country, so was he. She taught him how to speak the language of the street, how to be discreet about how much and how little he knew, and the extraordinary value of being anonymous.

He happily gave away most of his work so that he could spend more time with her and together they enjoyed a honeymoon that lasted seven years.

But then she died.

The Reverend Thomas Tierson and his sister Janet live beside the church at number fifteen. In reality their home is only a small weatherboard house, but in church records it is always referred to as a manse, and so the siblings have adopted the term with a certain amount of humour.

It is Thomas's second church. His first was in a little country town called Leongatha where the congregation was never very big. People worked so hard that they generally slept right through the ringing of the Sunday church bell. Thomas couldn't blame them; he saw how solidly they worked and so he performed most of his duties by going out into the paddocks and onto the factory floors. A farmer would say more in a field than if he was sitting in a church office tugging at a stiff collar; a worker in the town's drainage-pipe factory would be more inclined to talk about his darker concerns at work, where he could be sure that his wife and children and neighbours weren't somewhere about.

But eventually Thomas was called into the city. The church authorities felt that he could be of more help in a place where there were more people. He was sad to leave Leongatha but he knew that this nomadic lifestyle came with the job. When he left the little town he shook hands with the same amount of quiet enthusiasm as when he met his new parishioners in Currawalli Street.

Janet Tierson had been with her brother in the damp old house in Leongatha. She had swept nests of bush rats from her armoire, and a black snake from the kitchen that appeared just as she was about to remove scones from the oven. There were other assorted animals and insects too. She was happy to come to the city, although she discovered it was a lot harder to find a way in among the women of Currawalli Street than she had in the country town. She suspects that it has something to do with Thomas's delicate manner. The men don't seem worried by it but it is a great concern to the women—she can tell by the way they look at the pulpit and talk to each other after the service ends on Sundays. Janet deduces that women in the city like their connection to God to be masculine and rugged—the things that Thomas isn't.

And she doesn't mind the spinster connotations that come with being a sister looking after her reverend brother. In fact she welcomes them; the situation gives her much more freedom than she expected and she makes good use of that freedom. She has learned to look for and cultivate discretion. She finds it very enriching to be able to see another view of the world from the window of a lover's bedroom. And so she is happy to appear to be the sad sister who has no other interest in life than her brother's welfare. It works well for her.

Currently she is entertained by a gentleman of wig and gown on the other side of the city. James has his own world and his own life to contend with and she wants no part of it. Nor does he want her to be a part of it. They meet with a subtleness that he, as a lawyer, is used to. He has no interest in finding out who she is or where she sits in society and it is enough for him that she wants him to lie by her side. He knows their relationship is transitory and will last only as long as his conversations hold her interest and the view from his window is fresh and enticing.

James expects her to leave him as lightly as they met; in this instance, it was with the brush of a hand at an after-show dinner. She looked at him, he at her, and the rules of engagement were silently established. He is used to cultivating this type of relationship, and always surprised by how many women are willing to accept the terms. There are many people in this society who can't fit into the confines created by the mores of the day but who have no inclination to stand up and rail against them. They prefer to just quietly ignore them and go about their business with their own notions of morality and decency.

And there is in this type of lovemaking something powerful and exciting that Janet thinks might fade in marriage. She doesn't know that for sure but she does harbour strong suspicions. The thought of being with one partner for the rest of her life fills her with enough dread to give her a steel spine that will not bend. She does not want that kind of life.

James is a good man, strong and interesting, but she feels they are reaching their end. She expects that he feels it too.

She knows that the time to leave is coming because they have stopped meeting as two individuals who each bring a scent of mystery with them. That scent has evaporated into the night air. She knows that the time to leave is coming because they no longer talk of abstract visions but speak, with a type of familiarity, mainly of things that will see them through the next moment in their life together. She knows that the time to leave is coming because she has realised that they are just two everyday people who like being in each other's company. One night they sit together on the side of his bed and swap small gifts. They didn't plan to do this together. They arrived at this exchange individually. He has a pair of delicate pearl earrings for her to remember him by, as she has a thin silk scarf that she hopes he will keep in the drawer by the bed. The thought of him being blindfolded by a lover with this scarf gives her a delicious feeling that she keeps secret from him.

And they both have the same words: 'I hope you remember me.'

But the leaving is not quite for now. They still have a few nights of passion to share.

Returning to Currawalli Street on the train the next morning after giving the gifts, Janet looks out at the ever-expanding rows of houses spreading across the paddocks, and thinks about the reasons she wants to move on from James. Time has left them exposed as the people they really are. And she doesn't like that she can see that.

By the time she opens the front gate of the manse, her mind is made up. Happy that Thomas is still at church, she walks through the house, pushes open the back door and without stopping sweeps up Thomas's trowel. The high heels of her shoes make it hard to dig in the damp soil and so the process takes a while and she has time to reconsider her decision. They are beautiful earrings; they give off a blue glow in sunlight and a greenish tint when in shadow. She has never owned pearls like these but she thinks her decision is the right one. She puts the earrings back in their embroidered red box and places the box in the bottom of the hole. She sees for the first time that across the top of the box are her initials, embroidered in gold thread: *JT*. Replacing the soil is easier than the digging was, and as she walks back inside she decides that she will ask Rose Covey for a clipping of some bush or flower to plant there. She will do that tomorrow.

No one has ever moved into number fourteen. Finished, its door was never crossed. The garden and lawn are maintained by a stranger who knows nothing of its owner. He is employed by a solicitors office in the city.

The house stands among its young trees and bushes yet there is no mistaking that it is empty. No one in the street knows why. But that doesn't stop rumours, some of which develop a life and energy of their own. And in the end, that can be mistaken for the truth. For example, Rose believes that a gangster has had the house built and plans to move there after he is released from prison. But his parole request has been rejected yet again and so the house remains empty as he serves more time. Whereas Maria believes that a rich family have built it for their lunatic son, who they plan to move in there when he is stable enough.

Next door to the empty house live Eric and Nancy Dunold at number twelve. On the other side are Johnny and Kathleen. Johnny was at first very concerned about having people living this close to him, until Kathleen explained to him that just because neighbours can look, that does not mean that they won't look away. They know that you will, and you learn to know that they will. It's a kind of privacy and discretion that everybody shares. For her part, she is used to having neighbours live much closer to her than this, and she explained to him what London was like.

Eric Dunold had been a junior crewman aboard the thirtieth steamship that sailed from the shipworks on the Clyde River. He finished his sea-going career as the first officer of a large cargo ship plying the South Seas route, bringing strong tropical timber and fibres to this country. He gave up the sea because he was tired of saying goodbye to Nancy and she was tired of seeing his chair empty at the dining table.

He had walked down the gangway for the last time when the ship docked in Melbourne and then watched it sail away without him. He had brought all of his worldly possessions with him on this voyage. He also brought Nancy, and they set up a home in Currawalli Street almost before the ship had disappeared over the horizon.

As with Johnny, it took some time for Eric to grow accustomed to living like this. In Eric's case, he wasn't used to having so much earth around him. He was used to his landscape being fluid. Nancy helped to reacquaint him with the ways of the land and eventually he saw that most things in this landlocked life rose and fell like water and were swirled around by a deep current. The waves that were around him now looked different and moved slower, that's all—waves of new feelings, people's faces, strange animals, unfinished conversations and tides of struggles, joys, confusions and contentments. Once he was able to see that, he no longer looked for masts and furled sails among the currawalli trees. The way to judge the land and all that was on and in it was exactly the same as the way he had judged the ocean and all that was on and in it.

The thing that was the same in both environments was time, and he was well versed in watching its passage. After he realised that, he found his land legs for good.

Nancy Dunold had left behind her home in a medium-sized Scottish village where she was used to living largely alone. Eric had gone away each time for at least three months, sometimes for a year. And now she had travelled with him to a new land. She too is learning how to live again. Not just to be in a new country with new ways but to have someone by her side every day. It is a new experience for her but she remembers all the times she had wished that Eric was with her. And now he is.

Before, the ocean had been like a mistress that he kept, and Nancy knew about. A third party in their relationship. Nancy would never ask Eric to give up the sea because she knew that the love he felt for it was vast enough to stretch beyond any horizon that she could imagine. It might even have been deeper than what he felt for her. But he has walked away from this love to be with her. As far as she is concerned, that is something more golden than a ring.

He is a good man. And she sometimes hadn't minded being on her own. She had become good at it. She had found a type of comfort in adhering to a routine, finding companionship in odd places: the ticking of a clock on the mantelpiece, the turning of a leaf, the ageing of the bristles on a broom. But more often she had wanted his arms to hold her and hide her face from the world. Now she spends every night in them listening to the night pour itself into the morning.

On Currawalli Street, these people are slowly forging the type of friendship that only neighbours can have.

❧ Chapter Three ❧

It is the tenth of April. This year the summer came late, later than ever before. Currawalli Street lies in the sun like a sleeping lizard. The heat pushes down gently at first, but after a few hours the trees, the bushes, the dirt and the houses with their unpainted corrugated-iron roofs will be brutalised by its fierceness. And by the end of the day they will look beaten. There are a few weeks in the height of summer when even the birds stay still in the branches all day, hidden from the hot rays and only venturing out at first and last light. And these are hardier birds than any Kathleen has known in England. They are tougher, brighter, louder.

When she first heard the sulphur-crested cockatoo call out it sounded like someone screaming in pain, but Johnny explained to her where the sound came from. And when one of the builders working on the house two doors up was crushed by timber that fell from an overturning dray pulled by an ox, she knew what a scream of pain really sounded like. She arrived in the front yard of number fourteen at the same time as

Maria from number sixteen. The other workmen were trying to move the load of timber from the man's bloodied body and had just lifted the dray off him. The ox had fallen down dead, a victim of the heat. The man screamed as each piece of timber was lifted. Both women knelt beside him and Maria held his face in her hands as Kathleen wiped the perspiration from his forehead. She kept one hand on the timbers that still sat on his abdomen and legs, hoping that she might be able to stop them from falling further across his chest. As each length of timber was removed the smell of fresh blood grew stronger. Eventually enough timber had been taken away that she could see that the remaining lengths closest to his body were soaked in it.

As the load on his body lightened, the man's screams became fainter. He began to tremble and suddenly his eyes focused on something behind Kathleen's head. Then he slipped away. At exactly that moment, a strand of her hair freed itself from the bun it was tied in and fell, touching him on the cheek. She brushed it away. Maria told the workmen that there was no need to rush anymore, and those words were more devastating than the man's screams had been.

Kathleen has since come to be fond of the sulphur-crested cockatoo and its shriek. No bird has ever made her laugh in delight before. Cockatoos fly together in a large gang like drunken wharf workers and they live to cause trouble. They pick orchards clean in a day, bite through veranda posts, slide down iron roofs until the inhabitants inside can't take the noise anymore. Twenty could be slaughtered but forty would be back tomorrow with the very knowledge that the dead twenty had learned the day before. There is in these birds something at play that walks in step with the land. Some communion that doesn't make sense in the way

Kathleen knows things. There are stories of some cockatoos living for over two hundred years and so they may have seen the first white settlers coming ashore, struggling with wooden barrels that smelled of the pickling oil inside mixed with sea water that had soaked through the wood; seen the ropes from canvas tents fanned out like the legs of a thin octopus that was uncomfortable on the land, and wondered at the pathetic scratching in the dirt into which frail seeds were tossed, destined to rot away. No wonder cockatoos scream wickedly like they do.

If Kathleen is to be honest, this country scares her. The darkness here belongs to someone else. And it is at night that she feels it the strongest, that she is a stranger in a strange land. A few times late in the evening she has seen something indistinguishable moving in the distance among the currawalli trees; occasionally too she has smelled a strangely beautiful aroma in the air first thing in the morning. Something beyond what she knows. Sometimes she feels what might be the soft feathers of bulrushes touching her arm. When she first arrived at the farm to take up her teaching position and she was standing a little away from the house, trying to comprehend a sky so big, a local Aboriginal woman appeared in front of her, holding out her hand curled up in a ball. When she was sure that Kathleen was looking at the hand, she uncurled her fingers and revealed a ball of white bulrush tops. She leant forward and lifted Kathleen's hand, guiding it onto the top of the bulrushes so that both women were enclosing the flowers. They held that clasp for two minutes until the moment was broken by a gang of cockatoos landing a few yards from them.

And though they spoke no words, Kathleen was suddenly sure that this woman was offering to help guide her through this strange world.

And although she never saw this woman again, Kathleen still feels the same. In Currawalli Street she found a pink and grey galah feather in a small ball of mud and grass on her front path. It looked as if it had been constructed by hand, not by nature.

Kathleen looks up from the half-moon table where she is rereading a letter from her younger sister. She knows just where Louisa will have written this: at the mother-of-pearl table by the piano where the warmth of the fire comes across the room and makes the velvet curtains tremble slightly. She remembers the view that is behind those curtains.

As she looks out her own front window now over the honeysuckle that is growing along the front fence she can hear the apostle birds calling to each other in the tree next door. Across the street at number nine, Rose Covey is looking at her flowers, one hand reaching up to idly caress a leaf on the apricot tree. Kathleen decides to walk over and say hello.

Many different things have made Rose a stronger woman and a sadder woman than she wanted to be. She says she has been beaten by the sun and hammered by life, and she looks already to have begun the steep descent into old age. Her voice cracks when she speaks and a small hump has appeared between her shoulder blades; when she leans forward she looks as if she is trying to get away from it. As she bends over a flowerbed you can see that her hair is silver in the body and black on the tips. It is striking enough for some children to be frightened of her. Her face is lined in the way of someone who has grown used to not having much sleep and she constantly looks to have a haze of bother floating around her. She is always mildly troubled by something that runs deeper than any normal concern. Whenever she stops moving, a cloud of some kind of abstract desperation catches her up and shadows her face. Sometimes the cloud of desperation will be thick like smoke swirling around her legs as she walks. The reflection of it is in her eyes. That is when she falls silent and her face looks drawn as if she has just witnessed something unpleasant.

Rose Covey was eight years old when she had her first vision. She was looking up and, in the dirty thin clouds that always blew across the sky on windy days, she saw a picture of the man who lived down the road falling off his roof. At that moment the only thing she thought was that his scream sounded funny and so she smiled. But as she was alone she could share it with no one and so she forgot about it until three days later when her father, who had been fixing the front gate, burst into the kitchen and yelled to her mother that Jack had fallen off his roof and was dead.

The second vision happened when she was sixteen, on the very last day of her school holidays. She was sitting on the back step trying to attract the magpies to the crumbs of bread she was holding when she saw the river rise over its banks very quickly. The water dislodged all her father's work sheds, the house cow was carried away, the flowerbeds and the washing line with her new yellow blouse disappeared into the muddy swirl. But above all she heard the noise, a roaring as if a giant was bellowing mightily over the hill. When she blinked, the water was gone. There was no noise other than the sound of the magpies coming tentatively closer. Her blouse was still blowing gently on the line in the morning wind, the flowers were bending their red and pink heads, the sheds were untouched, Daphne the cow was at the fence gazing into the distance, and the river looked to be as lazy as it always did. She kept this vision to herself. She locked it away with the other things she was beginning to lock away.

In the afternoon she returned reluctantly to boarding school. That night a big flood raced down from the hills and the river broke its banks. Contact with her parents became irregular for a while. When she returned home for the Easter break, things felt the same even though they looked a bit different. There was only one big shed now where there had been three smaller ones. The flowers had gone, as flowers do, but the bed looked to have been freshly dug; the clothesline was strung up between different trees but Daphne the cow was still standing at the fence, staring into the distance. The debris of the flood remained in the lower branches of all the trees: long strands of sapling bark, clumps of bush grass, torn leaves from trees far away, all packed and squeezed into tight elbows of the branches just above Rose's head.

And now, at fifty-one, she is having a third vision.

After wiping away the dust that has accumulated overnight on the side table Kathleen walks from her front room, thinking how sad Rose looks most of the time. It occurs to her that maybe Rose hasn't had worse experiences than anybody else; maybe she is only cursed with remembering them better. Kathleen shakes her head at a thought so sad.

She has not known Rose for long but she has heard her vividly recount incidents from her childhood. The taste of apples from her uncle's tree, the colours of wool displayed in a shop window one Christmas, the smells of the bush after a strong rain that washed away the dust and dryness the day her grandfather left on the drove he didn't return from, a childhood visit to the city and the sound of a tram loaded high with vegetables being drawn up the main street outside her bedroom window on its way to an early morning market: Rose remembers everything.

By the time Kathleen has closed the front door and reached the gate, Rose is standing up straight, looking down at her feet. Kathleen begins walking across the street, calling hello. Rose takes a moment before she looks up. She begins to respond, and Kathleen sees that her face is like a stone mask of sadness.

As Kathleen walks out of the shadows that fall halfway across the street, the morning sun slaps her and its warmth brings a freshness into her body. The currawalli trees that grow behind her house look best in this kind of light, when the sun is not yet hot enough to burn, and the leaves look as if they are trying to reach out towards it. The wind is picking up. The breeze carries the scent of the gum trees and as the breeze gets stronger so does the perfume.

Concentration spreads across Rose's face as she says, 'I was just thinking about you, Kathleen.'

A gust of wind, suddenly cold. Rose waits until Kathleen has walked in through the gate before she comes over and puts her arms strongly around the younger woman. Kathleen is taller than Rose by a head and does not normally embrace anybody other than members of her family. Rose senses her discomfort and tells her that she wanted to hug someone; she apologises for making Kathleen uneasy.

'Still hot,' Kathleen says, to change the subject. It is an unneeded observation.

'Too hot for this time of year. It should be gone by now. Or at least showing signs of going.' Rose touches the dry brown leaves of a plant. 'But it's not showing any signs at all.'

'What do you think it means?' Kathleen asks. Rose looks at her seriously for a moment. Then she smiles.

'I don't know. I don't know.'

They walk over to a bed of yellow foxgloves and talk of the condition of the soil and how it affects the colour of the flower. Rose knows about these things and Kathleen is eager to learn as much as she can about this strange dry soil that she lives and walks on, digs, sweeps out of the house and plants vegetables in.

Rose leans down as they talk and turns over the dirt with an old bent fork from the cutlery set that Alfred's parents gave them as a wedding gift. She sinks to her knees as she sifts through the clumps of dirt. Kathleen can't make out all of Rose's words and so she drops down next to her. Rose smiles at her. The clump she is holding breaks up under her thumb and leaves a large red worm lying on her palm, exposed and wriggling. She puts it back on the ground and covers it over with the dirt.

Her daughter, Elizabeth, has never shown any interest in her garden. Rose knows that Elizabeth can live easily without Alfred and Rose but they can't live without their daughter. And now that Elizabeth has fallen in love with a man up north, Rose also knows there is a chance that once she has returned from this trip she may not stay for long. All Rose can do about it is dig her garden and grow her flowers, so she works at the dirt with the fork, turning over each clump, working her way along the bed.

'Hello!'

Kathleen and Rose know without looking that it is the reverend's sister. Her voice is husky, with a night-time echo, and it makes Kathleen think of someone talking through a curl of perfumed smoke. When they turn they see her looking down at them from the fence.

Rose invites her into the garden; as always, Janet walks with more confidence than she rightly should for a spinster in her twenties, looking after her reverend brother. Her auburn hair is set as if she is about to leave for the races; a Chinese shell pin holds a sweep of curls in place. Her dress makes her look broader in the shoulders than she really is and has the effect of highlighting her long and elegant neck. Her soft Italian shoes have clearly never been near freshly turned soil before; they were made more for dancing than walking. She steps onto the stone path and stands between the two married women, who are still on their knees. Looking at the foxgloves, she tells Rose that they are too good to pick. Then she bends and picks one.

Kathleen stands up, dusting her knees; as she helps Rose to her feet, she asks after the reverend. Janet waves her hand as if she is dismissing the question and says that Thomas is always fine. Then she adds that he is relentless like a machine. Neither Kathleen nor Rose know what she might mean by this and their faces betray their confusion.

Janet smiles to herself.

Rose steals a look at Kathleen as Janet tries to explain. 'It's as if he turns it on at the start of the day and then turns it off at the end of the day. Like a machine.'

'Oh, I understand. Turns what on?' Rose asks.

'His faith.'

'Ah,' Kathleen and Rose say at the same time. Janet turns away from the two women for a moment to look down the street. They wander away from the foxgloves to the apricot tree. Janet mentions that she saw Johnny riding out of the street this morning, looking as if he was going on a long trip.

'Yes. I was just about to talk to Kathleen about it,' says Rose. 'He has gone on behalf of Alfred to find his wagons and see if they need any help.'

Janet looks at her. 'Alfred is still sick?'

'Yes. I think he's worried that Elizabeth is not back by now. Not that he says anything. And you know how men get. Like a machine.' The other two laugh.

If ever there was a time for Rose to openly talk about her marriage, this would be that time. But she is not going to. She doesn't even consider it, although she has spoken of it in her head plenty of times.

At first, Alfred never worried about anything. He was so happy and content and always had fresh ideas in his head. Then about ten years ago he started to brood and mope around the house. He wouldn't say what was wrong and he hasn't offered any explanation since. Some men are good at hiding what they are thinking about. Some, like Alfred, aren't.

And marriages don't need physical distance to separate. The house and the necessities that come with it may be shared but interests can go in opposite directions. More often than not these separations aren't sudden; they grow and grow over the years as more things fall into the tiny cracks of a marriage and open them further.

Rose looks over at the rose bush she and Alfred planted when they first moved here. Its flowers are still as beautiful as when it first bloomed but it is now untended and its thorns turn inwards and scratch its own strangled branches. She comments, as if to herself, 'I have been meaning to prune that rose for two years. Now I will have to wait till August.'

The wind has turned around; it is now coming in from the north and carries with it strange scents. Janet looks at the line of currawalli trees in the distance.

Rose stands up straight and stretches her back. She invites both women to dine with her tonight. Alfred is going down to the pub, Johnny has gone into the bush. Janet will be alone because Thomas is attending a dinner at the bishop's house. On the strength of their new communion and because they accept that Rose is more at home in a landscape like this than either of them are and because they have their own dread for the night's isolation, both the younger women accept the invitation. All three are mildly surprised by what they just agreed to.

'Are you not invited to the bishop's house?' Rose asks.

'Of course. I am always invited. But I choose not to go.' Janet shakes her head slightly as she speaks. 'Do you know the bishop? No, of course not. How could you? He is a strange little man. Quite horrible.'

She turns again to watch a willy-willy dance down the street. This bishop, whom Thomas has to rely on for so much, makes depraved suggestions to her without using any words, his leering eyes, his overly wet mouth, his lifted eyebrows proposing retreats into the shadows. Holding a spoon to her mouth or wiping her lips with a napkin seems to give him some kind of perverted pleasure that he barely conceals.

She turns back to the others and they see that her cheeks have reddened. She shakes herself and tries to smile. Kathleen and Rose don't smile back.

'The bishop has made inappropriate suggestions to me,' she finally says.

'Does your brother know about this?' Rose asks.

Janet begins pulling at the foxglove she has picked. The petals float down to the ground. 'Oh yes. He knows very well. I keep nothing from him. I imagine that my non-attendances at those dinner parties will eventually work the bishop into a frustrated fury. And then he will send Thomas somewhere far away as punishment. The bishop will blame me for the way he feels.'

Kathleen thinks, how much further could far away be?

Rose thinks of her vision, and of the grass next to the church.

Looking out the window of number twelve, Nancy sees Rose chatting to Kathleen and the reverend's sister and decides to join them. She walks across the street to Rose's front fence, leans over and smiles at the three women. Each is happy to see her, in varying degrees.

For Kathleen it is only a little, for although Nancy brings with her a sense of Britain that Kathleen has not otherwise been able to find this far away from London, she talks too much and too loudly about things that aren't really important.

Janet is a little more pleased to see her, because Nancy evokes a kind of earthy sensuality that isn't common with the other women of the street. Except Maria. But if Janet is ever going to confess her adventures to anyone it will probably be Nancy, for she feels that Nancy will understand without needing an explanation whereas Maria will need one. And she sometimes thinks that Nancy already knows, which is a sort of comfort.

Rose is the happiest at Nancy's presence, because the Scottish woman knows how to allow life to throw itself at her and never loses her resolve in the face of it. It is good to have someone like that close by.

'Will you come over for dinner tonight?' Rose asks her.

Nancy doesn't have to consider for long. Eric is going down to Station Pier tonight to have dinner with an old friend of his whose ship is in port for only one day. He will spend the night on board. She accepts.

'Good. These two are coming also.'

Nancy promises to bring over a bottle of Eric's apple brandy, as long as the other women agree to drink too much of it. After all, this will be their first dinner together. She claps the top rail of the fence with both hands and heads home with a sense of purpose. The things that she was going to do tonight will need to be done now instead.

Janet takes her leave soon after. Kathleen walks around the garden with Rose for a while longer, without speaking. Both women are happy in the silence. When Kathleen turns out the front gate, Rose goes inside.

That evening, after Thomas has ridden off down the street to have dinner with the bishop and his minions, armed with a plausible excuse for his sister's absence, Janet closes the front door of the manse behind her and walks down to number nine. Kathleen is already sitting at the table, laughing at something Rose has said. By the time Nancy arrives with the brandy, Janet is laughing too. And that is the way most of the night goes.

There is a freedom in the atmosphere, not because of the liberal drinking of the apple brandy but because there is no man there to pour it. Standing in the hallway beside the front door at the end of the night, they all agree men are to be banned from the following dinners. As they say goodnight, they all sense a change in the air. A man might dismiss it as a sudden sea breeze sprung up, but to these women it is something else. A twisting, of sorts. Alfred returns through the front gate but goes straight out to the stable and listens to the women's receding footsteps.

❧ Chapter Four ❧

The next morning, Alfred walks slowly down Currawalli Street and along the little road to the store opposite the railway station and buys a copy of the daily newspaper. He is planning to scour it in case there is any news of his wagons but he doesn't get past the front page before forgetting about them. Rather than returning straight home, he walks across the road, greets the stationmaster, sits down in the station waiting room and reads through the whole paper.

He reads every article concerning the front-page story. *War Ahead. Conflict Coming, says Prime Minister . . . Europe has gone quiet as if preparing herself . . .* He is alarmed by what he reads. Previous news of the potential crisis in Europe has always stressed just that: its potential. This is the first time he has seen it presented as an inevitable event. And not just as a small 'colonial' type war but something bigger; something that might drag in the whole world. Even though Alfred is a mapmaker, the concept of the whole world is still unimaginable to him.

And no politician in Europe seems to be talking anymore about a way to stop it from happening; they are now asking how its effects can be minimised. That is unnerving because it means an acceptance has already been reached that many people are going to die. Things like war seem such an easy thing for certain people to accept. Alfred turns the pages and reads more.

Relationships between many countries in Europe are in tatters, the damage is irreparable and so a war beyond anything ever seen is going to occur. England is beating its chest loudly, confident that young men from all over the Empire will answer her call to arms. And that means Australia. That means Melbourne. That means Currawalli Street.

Alfred folds the paper closed and puts it down on the seat next to him. He is old enough not to go but of course he will. Men of his experience in making maps will be needed. Rose won't try to stop him.

He leaves the paper on the seat at the railway station and walks home. His feet are suddenly heavy. He doesn't know why. He wishes his wagons were home. Turning into Currawalli Street he can see the church at the opposite end. In front of the church is a manicured garden and beside it is a square of lawn. In the centre of the lawn is Rose, standing still and looking down the street towards him. He looks at her and, for a moment, remembers how far they have come together. She has said he's become distant in recent years but that is the exact word he would use to describe her. He laughs to himself then walks along the street towards her. He calls out a greeting but still she doesn't respond. It is only when he is a few steps away that she seems to emerge from her oblivious state and see him. She smiles.

He smiles back and says, 'You look good standing there. Very pretty. Standing still like a statue.' He knows how to lift Rose out of these black holes she falls into.

'There will be a statue here. It will be put here soon.'

'And who will it be of? The mayor? The bishop? The prime minister? Me?' He stops laughing when he sees the effect his words have on her. She has stopped smiling. 'What's the matter?'

'I hope it's not of you.'

'Why not?'

'I just don't know. That's the thing, Fred. I just don't know.'

'Let's go home and have a cup of tea. I should have made you one before I went out. I don't do that for you these days. I don't know why. I'm sorry. I only wanted to get the paper. I forgot to bring it home, after all that.'

'A cup of tea would be good. Let's go home. I wish Elizabeth was back,' says Rose, already tired.

'So do I. So do I.'

Eric Dunold walks jauntily home from the railway station. He always feels good after sleeping onboard a ship. The rhythm of a ship tied to a wharf sends him into different type of sleep, different from on land and different from at sea. It has been good to see Jacob. Last time they ran into each other, they were both rushing to leave Hong Kong harbour and neither could spare any time for real conversation. So last night they talked into the small hours and then started again when they awoke. The train left from a platform opposite the wharf and the smoke from the steam engine mixed with the smoke from Jacob's ship as it manoeuvred away from the wharf to begin its journey back to Portsmouth. Eric hadn't bothered waving from the window at first; he assumed that Jacob would be concentrating on the logistics of leaving the harbour and wouldn't be looking at a train steaming off into the distance. But then he saw a capped figure emerge from the door on the side of the bridge and raise his hand, and he leaned out the carriage window and did the same thing in return.

And as he walks into Currawalli Street, he sees Alfred and Rose Covey standing together in front of the church. As they begin to walk away from the church towards him, he raises his arm again in a half-wave. Alfred waves back.

Eric doesn't know Alfred that well yet; shore life is not like being on a ship where friendships are forged very quickly. On land it is different; everything gets soaked up by the earth or blown away by the bushfire wind and friendships are slow to grow. But Eric has seen Alfred's maps and they are clearly made by a man who knows the mechanics of travel, even though land maps to Eric have always seemed crowded, over-blown, and overly detailed. However, one of the reliable ways to judge a man, besides whether he can pack a bag and sit still on a journey, is whether he knows the workings of a map.

Nancy opens the door when she hears his footsteps on the front porch. She embraces him long and hard as if he has returned from sea. He comments aloud on this and she pulls back and looks at him.

'You silly man. It is because you are *not* coming home from sea that I hug you so. It makes sense, doesn't it?'

'Yes, it does. Perfect sense. What shall we do today, my sweet? Any-thing you desire.'

Nancy thinks for a moment. 'Well. I do believe I would like to spend the rest of the morning lying in your arms in our bed, and then I would like to go into the city and have lunch at the Savoy Hotel.'

'I can do all of that.'

That is how they spend the morning. Eric thinks that there are two kinds of light that a woman's body looks best in: candlelight and morning light. Through the open window, they can smell distant smoke. A bushfire somewhere miles away.

Johnny Oatley watches his horse sniff the air. He knows what it means. He looks for a gap in the trees by the side of the road, and when he finds one he steers the horse off, lets her wander away through the bracken. Then he looks ahead to the horizon and sees a line of smoke. Bushfire.

It is his second day on this track and he is well into the rhythm of travel. His mind works better in a setting like this. He watches the smoke for five minutes to see how quickly it is being lifted away from the flames and whether there is any irregular movement. He decides to continue, knowing that he will have to be alert from now on. Many times he has seen a bushfire at this distance; the first time was when he and his father sat on the big hill above their home and watched a line of fire eat its way through the scrub; he stood with local Aboriginals and watched another, knowing he wouldn't have to retreat until they did. He and bushfires aren't strangers. The fire is about twenty miles away but the tiniest change in the wind direction or speed can amplify a fire's passage and alter its path in seconds. Fire has a mind of its own: that's what his father told him on that hilltop. People of that generation knew it was best to stay away from these fires. They could never be tethered or fenced in or cut down or controlled.

He is glad now that Kathleen hasn't accompanied him. He doesn't want her to see him frightened. Of all the things in the bush, it is bush-fire that scares him the most. You can sense what a wild horse or an angry snake will do. You can estimate how much water is around when you're going to need a drink under a relentless sun. You can see where the high spots are when a flood is coming. But the only thing you can know for certain about a bushfire is that it will burn. You can't tell where, or for how long, or at what speed. But you can be sure that it will be absolute and without mercy.

Suddenly he sees a carriage travelling quickly along the track towards him. It is pulled by two horses and another two riders are behind it. Johnny doesn't like this. Even from a distance, he can see that they are fleeing something. He decides to go no further and wait to hear their story.

The retreating group is upon him in a few minutes. He lifts his hat to them. The carriage, loaded with furniture, is being driven by a woman in her forties with a child on either side. The pair on horseback, an older man in his fifties and a youth, ride over to the gap in the trees at the side of the road to look back at the smoke before turning their attention to Johnny.

'The fire's coming,' the older man says. He waves the carriage and the boy on and they continue up the track.

'It doesn't look too fast.'

'We have been travelling for two days now. This is the furthest it has been behind us. It burned through our land and has been chasing us ever since.'

'Maybe it will burn itself out soon,' says Johnny.

'You would think so. There's a railway line up the track, is there not?'

'It's at least a day away, probably two with a carriage.'

'I know. It can't be helped. We can't go in any other direction. We're going to leave the carriage behind and catch a train to the city. I'm not confident that this fire *will* burn itself out.'

The man looks exhausted and frightened. He knows and Johnny knows that there is nothing that any human can do to help. A bushfire answers to no one's logic. It burns down cathedrals and orphanages as readily as brothels and sly grog shanties.

It is not the first time that Johnny has heard of a bushfire chasing a person or a group of people. It is a tale of horror that he remembers being told around the kitchen table at the farm. Then, when Johnny was a boy, his father took him in the middle of the night to a lonely crossroads in the deep blue-gum forest. They travelled for two hours to get there and stopped in the undergrowth back from the road. Johnny smelled smoke. It was summer. The horses were uneasy. Suddenly there was the sound of hooves on the road coming quickly towards them. A rider tucked into his mount galloped past. Johnny glimpsed the look of terror on the rider and horse. The sweat from the horse glistened in the moonlight. Johnny and his father waited until the sound of the hooves had disappeared, then they wheeled about and galloped in a diagonal direction back towards home. Johnny saw out of the corner of his eye the red glow that they were riding across the face of.

They had ridden out of the path of the fire and slowed down. Still they did no talking until they had unhitched the gate to the house paddock.

Johnny asked his father, 'So who was that? He looked scared.'

'That man was chosen by the fire. It is the worst thing that can happen to a human being. He has been riding for over a week. The fire is catching him. It will consume him.'

'Could we not have helped him?'

'No. There is nothing anybody can do. The fire has selected him and nothing is able to stand in its way. We could do nothing.'

'Why did the fire pick him?' asked Johnny.

'No one knows why. Every man hopes it is never him. That man we saw tonight is a dead man.'

'That's why we went to see him?'

Johnny's father looked down at his boots before he spoke. It was something Johnny had never seen him do before. When he lifted his head, he looked fully into Johnny's eyes. 'We went because it is something, I hope, you will never forget all your life. You will remember the look on his face, the sound of the hooves, the smell of the smoke, the strange light. If you do forget, then I'm afraid your life is not worth living. Not that you will know.'

For a few years, Johnny didn't understand what his father meant by this. But when he did understand, it made the sort of sense that he had come to expect from a man who had seen the powerful drama of midnight thunderstorms brewing, the beauty of soft running rivers, the sudden excitement of hundreds of kangaroos hopping over the crest of a hill, the views of miles and miles of gum trees, as an unremarkable matter of course.

His father added, 'Of course, the horse will throw him soon. Its own survival instincts will take over from any control that man may have over it. The fire won't come after it.'

'Will it be alright?'

'Yes, we'll go and find it in a few days. It will be somewhere close, probably down in the gully near where we were.'

'How did you know that he would be riding along that road? How did you know that the fire would be chasing him?' Johnny persisted.

'I just knew. I don't know how. You live in this land long enough, strange things start to come into your head. You'll find that out,' his father said quietly.

Johnny sees again that man's face from long ago as he watches the older rider talk to him now, eyes darting from side to side. They are not the furtive looks of a man expecting danger but the exhausted glances of a man expecting death. There is resignation in his voice, only a hint of it, but Johnny can tell that he has almost given up.

Johnny asks, 'Is the fire after you?' Their horses move in a very subtle, fluid dance.

The man looks at him, evidently finding some comfort in knowing that Johnny understands what is happening. 'I don't know for sure. We have been travelling as a group. I assume it is me because my horse has been growing tenser. Normally she is calm around fire. It could be my wife or one of the children but I don't think so. They know nothing of this element of fire. My understanding is that a fire only ever comes after someone who is aware of what it is doing. But, who knows?' He smiles grimly in the reddening light.

Johnny leans forward. 'Then you must keep travelling. I hope you reach the train line.'

'I hope so too. I'll put them on a train and then ride the other way. Maybe I will be able to find a fresh horse at the station. Hopefully the fire will follow me and not the train.' He wheels his horse about and looks at the carriage that has thundered up the track ahead of him.

'Good luck to you,' Johnny says softly. The man nods even though he could not have heard the words. He and his horse are bathed in the red light of the distant fire. They disappear into the dust.

Johnny quickly turns off the track and heads out across the line of flames that he can now see clearly in the distance. There are bushes and trees for a few miles but then he comes onto a sandy embankment that runs the same way he is headed. This is a riverbed, usually dry, that periodically fills with water and appears as if the river has been running strongly for years. He follows it past the skeletons of tree trunks and large rocks that look like the smooth skulls of giants. The line of flames is now behind him, headed away, and so he slows the horse to a walk.

Up ahead he soon sees a road sitting in the afternoon light. Johnny breathes a sigh of relief when he hears the hooves striking gravel again. The feeling surprises him. He looks back at where he has just come from—the dry riverbed, the unbending gum trees, the still smoke—and then he thinks of the people trying to escape the fire. The memory of that night ride with his father, and then of that riderless horse, with its weary head bowed, standing in the ashes. He breathes out again. It is behind him.

He looks on down the road in the direction he will ride. There is dust ahead that indicates travellers. He keeps moving forward and tries to make out what is throwing up the cloud of dust. Then he pulls the horse to a standstill. He looks again and smiles.

Coming towards him are two wagons.

❧ Chapter Five ❧

The smell of the bush is in the air. Nancy, walking down the front path at number twelve, stumbles unexpectedly. She curses, using a phrase of her mother's; in fact she sounds like her mother when she says it.

Three years ago her left leg started to stiffen up and now she favours the right. She is getting used to not standing straight. Sometimes she doesn't notice anymore. Eric says he can't tell at all. Whether he is telling the truth or not, she doesn't know. Although standing crooked in itself doesn't anger her, she finds that she is now prone to sudden bursts of fury and sometimes tears. The tears are inexplicable. In the past, her anger would always evaporate unspoken with the wind, but now it demands that she give it form. And Eric, who nearly always takes the brunt of her rages, suffers it patiently and with a quiet dignity.

She is forty-two years old and has, for most of her life, been accustomed to people saying she is, at the very least, pleasant-looking, if not beautiful. At about the same time as her leg stiffened, the compliments began to dry up. She wasn't worried at first. And truth be told, worry is not the right word; it is a concern that this part of her life has arrived too early. There are many shining gifts that come with age, her mother had said. Wisdom, patience, dignity. But worry, concern, anxiety also arrive. And they are certainly not shining gifts, Nancy thinks.

She walks out the gate and slowly across the street. The gravel sounds like shallow water under her shoes. The sun is hot again, gum leaves are blowing down the street. Halfway across, she turns to look at her house.

Hume and Hovell ivy, that has runners like thin fingers and leaves like tiny green hearts, thrives in this type of weather and has grown quickly across the top of the veranda. The corrugated-iron roof is painted red. Long strips of thin board painted yellow cover the exterior walls and keep out the wind. The window frames are white. The most impressive things about the house are the ornamental struts that vertically connect the eaves of the roof to the walls. Each one has been individually carved by Eric into the silhouette of a face in profile.

When the wind isn't blowing, he sits in his wooden chair on the back veranda and carves. Slowly he is working his way around the house, taking down and working on each strut in turn. There is one strut every ten feet and so far there are five faces staring out at the world. They are the faces of people who lived in the village where she and Eric were born and where they continued to live after they were married. As she passes she always nods hello to Michael the baker and blows imaginary kisses to Colin the brickmaker's son, who left the village to make his name as an actor. He was easily the most handsome boy in the county and that made him a figure of derision and ridicule with the other boys. Before he left, he kissed her. Colin was her first love. He joined a repertory theatre company and became exactly what he wanted to be: a famous actor.

Wattle trees lean against the front windows and their branches scrape gently at the glass when the wind blows. Eric likes this because he is used to sea winds creating a noise. That is how he measures its strength. It is information that he no longer needs to know but doesn't like to live without. He is used to the music of canvas rippling and swelling or the whistling of the wind rushing around a funnel or bulkhead. Nancy knows that it gives him comfort to hear it. On still days, he becomes lethargic, but when the wind blows strongly he walks more quickly, achieves a lot more, talks louder, gets more excited about things. So Nancy doesn't mind the branches brushing against the windows.

The front yard is shaded by an old currawalli tree, the home of the indistinct grey apostle birds. Johnny from next door has told her about these birds. They are all of the same family, and they stay in the one tree for generations and make it their family home. They love to play together and make lots of noise and their behaviour keeps Eric and Nancy amused and enchanted—they have even given four of the birds the names of their parents, all long gone in a land far away. Saying their names out loud is a comforting thing to do. She especially likes to hear her mother's name on Eric's lips. Jean. It touches her in a way that she will not allow anything else to touch her.

As much as Eric had been hardened by the sea, so had she, but not in the same way. Not by a cold North Sea wind but by a cold Scottish bed. Not by an endless, landless horizon but by an empty chair opposite her. She kept herself to herself, the same as any sailor does. But it was not Nancy's manner. Now she has become one of those people who is so warm and natural that you would assume she is an old family friend. You may be surprised to find that not many people know her very well at all. That's the way she prefers it.

Rose is standing in her garden staring down the street at the church. From across the street Nancy can see that she is crying and she calls out so that Rose might have an opportunity to wipe her eyes before she comes close. As she walks through the front gate of number nine, Rose is dabbing her cheeks with the corner of the yellow apron she is wearing.

'I'm sorry, Nancy. I've got something in my eye.'

Nancy holds her arm so that they are wiping the tears together. 'Rose, can I be telling you something while we are alone? It won't go any further and you can take it for what it's worth.'

Rose looks at her closely and nods.

Nancy tells her about the woman who lived ten houses away when Nancy was a child. 'She could do nothing right: she cried all the time; she had no husband, no family to speak of, but she could see things. It was the one thing that she did well.'

'What do you mean?' Rose asks guardedly. Nancy lowers her voice.

'She had premonitions, pictures of things that were going to happen that she saw in the clouds, in cups of tea, in fruit that had rotted and split open.'

'Why are you telling me about her?'

'You remind me of her in some ways. I just thought . . .'

'I don't see things in tea-leaves, if that is what you mean.'

In fact, Rose has thought about telling Nancy or even the reverend from church about her vision, but she thinks neither would be ready for the torrent of words that would flow out of her mouth once she began to speak. She has made the cold decision to stay silent for now.

Nancy releases Rose's arm and drops her hand away. 'No. Of course not. I'm not saying that you do. You remind me of her, that's all. This woman told me that my father would die on a Tuesday morning after chopping firewood. He did, leaning over to light his pipe, resting on the axe.'

'How old were you?'

'Seven.'

'That's young.'

'Not really. Not in our country. My mother had a proper job by the time she was seven. She started out sweeping the steps for the post office when she was four. So I wasn't expected to be a child for too long. I was carrying my weight by six. At seven, I was old enough to understand the principles involved in visions. It was part of our lives. We talked about it the same way we would talk about the river rising or the apples ripening.'

'Thank you, Nancy, for explaining all that to me,' Rose says briskly. 'Now, I don't want to talk about these things anymore. Tell me something else.'

'Um . . . let's see. Eric and I went to the Savoy Hotel and had a piece of coronation cake. It was very nice. Have you tried it?'

Rose shakes her head. 'No, but Kathleen's mother has sent her out the recipe from London. She said it was in all the newspapers over there at the time to help celebrate the king's coronation. I promised Kathleen that we would make it together. Will you help? You're the only one to have seen it.'

Nancy laughs. 'Yes, of course I would like to help. When?'

'Come over this afternoon and we can look at the recipe to see if it needs something exotic. I'll ask Kathleen. I think she is getting a bit concerned for her husband. He has been away three days now.'

Nancy shrugs and then says, 'Tell me again about those bulbs you showed me.'

The truth is that Kathleen isn't worried about Johnny's safety. But there is a portrait that has to be finished in six weeks' time, and a letter has come from the bishop's attaché asking about the painting's progress and whether the bishop will be needed for another sitting. Kathleen knows that Johnny will have it finished in time, but she is always anxious when there is a date looming in the distance.

Johnny works on his paintings in the spare bedroom. When Kathleen goes in each day and looks at the canvas, she is always struck by how incomplete it looks. But it is always the same. She always worries and Johnny always finishes in plenty of time.

Now she walks into the room again and over to the canvas. This is Johnny's biggest painting yet. Not in size; in the importance of the sitter. The bishop is the same man that Janet talks of with such abhorrence and from the few things that Johnny has said about the sittings, Janet seems to be right to want to set the dogs on him.

Not that Johnny says much to her. He keeps his work to himself. As a man who grew up working on the land, finding himself earning most of his money sitting still with a paintbrush in his hand does not rest very easily on him. And so he tends to leave it in this room as much as possible.

But one evening a month ago while she was massaging his back, he mentioned to her with a shadow in his voice that the bishop wanted another painting done. One that the Church didn't need to know about. As the sittings for the official portrait progressed, the bishop explained to Johnny the type of painting he wanted. Johnny would tell Kathleen only that it was grand and very strange. She assumed it was something he did not want to share with her. But if he did the painting as the bishop asked, they would have enough money to think about visiting her family in London.

Kathleen looks out the window at the street. She and Johnny go to church every Sunday as much to support the reverend as anything else. Thomas is a new friend and they don't like to think of the church being empty. Johnny has a fairly solid picture of God and he suspects that a church isn't necessarily the place God is going to be on a Sunday. Kathleen has always gone to church, and questioning God has never come into it. Church was just something you did before Sunday lunch. It gave you a chance to think about the night before without being disturbed.

This room is the cleanest in the house. Its walls are white and the window is large and looks out to the west. Johnny needs the dust to be kept away because it sticks to the oil paint and darkens the colours, so Kathleen comes in twice a day and wipes all the surfaces. And it gives her a chance to look at the progress of the current painting.

She likes the smell of the paint. She likes the smell of turpentine on the rags; it gives the room an atmosphere of industry and reminds her of her father's back shed, where he keeps all his woodworking tools.

The floors throughout the house are Baltic pine and drenched in linseed oil. They run the length of the room from the back wall to the fireplace. Johnny always sits while he paints and his chair is made of black snakewood. It is a straight chair, thin like an old man is thin, and strong like a young man is strong.

The easel is covered in smeared and dripped paint which sometimes shows a strange beauty and mystery, elements that Kathleen cannot define in words. Johnny said to her once that a teacher at art school had told him that there are things much deeper than what can be seen or spoken of. Things that can only be measured by what is felt. He didn't know what that meant. Neither does Kathleen. She likes to have an explanation of the things she appreciates. She is uncomfortable with the unknown.

Thinking she hears a noise at the front door, she walks out of the room and up the hallway. The sun is coming in strongly through the glass panel above the front door. Without pausing she pulls the door open. There is no one there. Across the street she can see Nancy standing with Rose. She thinks about what chores she has left to do and whether she can leave the house unattended for a while; deciding that she can, she goes back to the sideboard in the dining room, moves aside the folded embroidered tablecloth that Johnny's mother used for best, and takes the recipe for King George the Fifth's coronation cake out of the celebratory coronation mug that her mother sent her. Queen Mary watches her stonily from the side of the mug. At the front gate, Kathleen sees Maria coming down the road from number sixteen, leading her horse.

'Hello, Maria,' Kathleen calls.

'Hello, Kathleen,' says Maria. 'Do you know if Alfred is about?'

'I don't. Is there something wrong with Margaret?'

'Who can tell? There may well be. I don't understand her. I've never had an animal like her. *Mannaggia*! I'm more used to donkeys. At least you can tell what they're thinking.' As she comes closer to Kathleen, she lowers her voice and becomes conspiratorial. 'Ever since William borrowed an automobile from work and brought it home last week, she has been strange. He put it in the backyard next to her for the night. I don't think she liked it.'

'Perhaps she thinks it will take her job?'

'As if it could. Although after the day I have spent with her I wouldn't mind if it did.'

Kathleen pats Margaret's flank. 'Alfred will know. He has a way with horses. Do you think it's strange, how he seems to know what they're thinking?'

'No. Some people have an affinity with things.' Maria smiles. 'Look at me with my chooks.'

'Yes, you're right. I wonder what I have an affinity with.'

Maria drops her left arm to her side and catches the reins in her right hand. 'Maybe it's cockatoos. You always look up at them when they fly past and you always talk about them.'

'Oh dear. Do I? Perhaps I do.'

They both laugh as they cross the street, but halfway across Maria looks back up the street towards the house next to the manse.

'How is he going?' Kathleen asks.

'Morrie?'

'Yes. I don't know him that well.'

'He doesn't say much. He's up and down. He's a hard man to know.' Maria looks at Kathleen. 'You know that he has dinner at our place? Sometimes everything will be okay but then he will drop his head onto his chest and stay like that for a long time. We have learned that the best thing to do is to carry on the conversation around him. After a while he will lift his head, there will be tears in his eyes, but he will rejoin the conversation as if nothing has happened.'

'I hardly got to know Gwen before she . . . passed away,' Kathleen says.

'She was a nice woman. She was good for Morrie. I don't think he is an easy man. You know how some people need someone else to help them get through their . . .'

'. . . day,' Kathleen nods, finishing Maria's sentence.

'I was going to say life. But day is better.'

'I've known people like that.'

'Me too. I think I might be married to one,' Maria adds.

'Really?'

'He's a bit of a closed book. About some things. But then he's open about other things. I don't know. He's a good man. He and Morrie seem to get on fine. Until William starts to talk about his geraniums. Jesu Maria! He goes on and on, and finally Morrie has to go home. I can't blame him.'

Margaret jostles Maria, pushing her gently back on her heels.

'Yes, you're right, Margaret. We had better get out of the middle of the road in case William drives up in that automobile contraption and runs us all over.'

Maria hasn't finished speaking before Kathleen starts to laugh. As the two women and the horse move off the street, Rose and Nancy hear their laughter and look over. Rose calls out to Alfred, who emerges from around the back straightaway as if he has been standing still waiting for the call. When he sees Margaret he smiles. The horse tries to walk towards him but Maria holds her reins.

'Let her go, Maria. She won't run away,' Alfred says. He walks back around the side of the house and Maria drops the reins. Sure enough, Margaret quietly follows him. Nancy, smiling, shakes her head and Kathleen looks at Maria who is raising her eyebrows, and says, 'Margaret loves him.'

Rose walks towards the two women. 'We were just talking about coronation cake. Do you have that recipe, Kathleen?'

'Here. I've read through it. It calls for . . . let's see if my memory is still working . . .' She holds the newspaper clipping behind her back and looks up at the sky. 'Drambuie and oat flour from Scotland, dates from East Africa, cardamom seeds from India, maple syrup from Canada, sultanas from . . . Australia, I suppose, plain flour from . . . somewhere. And of course eggs from England. English eggs because eggs bind all the other ingredients together. As does England bind all the other countries together. That's what the recipe says; I remember that. We can get those ingredients easily enough, can't we?'

She hands the recipe to Rose who says, 'Sort of. I don't think the oat flour will be from Scotland, nor do I think that the dates are going to be from East Africa, but the sultanas will definitely be from Australia.'

'This will be an Australian coronation cake,' Kathleen says.

They move inside. As the wind picks up and pushes darker clouds across the sky, Alfred and Margaret come back around to the front and watch them as they sail over. Alfred is absently holding an old horseshoe that he found in the grass. He tosses it into the paddock next door, just missing the wooden frame that the builders have erected.

Johnny reins in his horse when the wagons are still twenty yards away. He can see Elizabeth controlling the first. Riding forward to meet Johnny is a young man. His body sits still in the saddle, his eyes on Johnny's, no emotion showing on his face, or at least none that Johnny can read. He sits tall in the saddle and lets his left foot fall from the stirrup as he closes up.

'My name is Walter Cummings,' he says before Johnny can begin his own greetings. 'Beth says that you are her neighbour . . .'

'That I am.'

'. . . and that her father most likely sent you to look for her.'

'He did. My name is Johnny Oatley.'

Walter holds out his hand. Johnny reaches forward and shakes it firmly. The young man turns his head back to the wagons. 'Beth needed to stay away this long. She had to do what she did.'

'What did she do?'

'Married me.'

'Oh.' Johnny answers quickly, surprised.

'Now we are headed back to Currawalli Street to meet her parents.'

'I promised Alfred that I would assist her to come home if that's what she needed . . .'

'She doesn't need it.'

Walter Cummings's face is darkened by the sun and hardened by the wind. He has a striking moustache that brushes his cheeks, and even though it curls downwards it highlights his eyes, which are clear and alert.

Elizabeth pulls the wagon to a stop level with Johnny. His horse skitters sideways as the wagon creaks to a standstill between Johnny and Walter, who encourages his own horse forward. Johnny looks over at Elizabeth; holding the reins. He knows from Kathleen that she is twenty-five but she looks older. Her dark hair normally falls over her shoulders but today it is pulled back. Her arms are bare and Johnny can see the strain in her muscles as she holds the reins tight.

'Hello, Elizabeth. And congratulations,' Johnny says.

'Thank you, Johnny. Father sent you?'

'He did. He started to get a bit worried. But I don't mind having a bit of a ride out here, so I suppose I may have encouraged him to send me. He probably would have waited a few more days if it had been left up to him.'

'The silly old man. What did he say? Did he tell you I was incapable?'

'No, not at all. He told me you would be fine. That this job would hardly tax you at all. I think doing nothing is what is affecting him. He doesn't come across as a man used to sitting still.'

'I would wager that he and my mother are at each other.'

'I don't know. I'm not a good judge in matters like that, but I would say probably.'

'We're headed home now. Will you travel with us or will you go on home and tell them that we are coming?'

Johnny thinks for a moment. 'A bit of both, I suppose.'

'Good. It'll be nice to have someone new to talk to,' she answers, but aims the words at her new husband. 'Walter? Is that alright with you?' Johnny looks Elizabeth's husband full in the face.

The young man looks back at him for a moment, then up at the clouds. 'It'll be fine,' he says stiffly.

Johnny moves in behind the wagon and waits. Elizabeth flicks the two old wagon horses into action and after a few yards Johnny comes up by her side. Walter stays on the other side. It is clear that he doesn't like the sudden company. Not at all.

The wagon behind is driven by Cedric Jones. Johnny knows him only to nod to. He sees him when he is working with Alfred repairing the wagons. He looks about forty but is probably not that old. Alfred says that even though Cedric has been with him since the early days, he still doesn't know where he lives. He is as slow as a bear when nobody is posing a threat, but as quick as a snake striking when someone does. He offers more company than Elizabeth and Walter, who have launched into a heated discussion. Johnny reins back until he falls level with the second wagon.

Cedric looks at him. 'They're having a fight.'

Johnny nods. 'I figured that. Then I'll stay back here.'

'It's best. They throw around words like stones. They don't care who gets hit.'

'You sound as if you have been.'

'I have. But not for much longer. When we get back, I'm off. Alfred doesn't pay me enough to take that sort of treatment. I work for him, not anybody else. My father once said to me, "It doesn't matter how old you get, a woman's words will still sting." He would know—my stepmother had a tongue like a whip.'

'So where will you go?'

'The army. I think that is the place for me.'

'I was talking to a fellow who thinks there will be a big war.'

'I talked to a bloke who said that too. He said that Australian troops will be needed. It might be hard to get into the army when it starts up.'

'Maybe. Depends on how many soldiers they are going to send. Lots of blokes will want to join up. Sounds like a great adventure,' Johnny says, thinking about Bert Brady.

They talk above the rumble of the wheels on the track but they can still hear the shouting from the first wagon. Cedric lifts his eyebrows and then continues. 'My father went to South Africa to fight the Boers the first time. He said it was great fun. Once you got used to the bullets and the killing.'

Johnny looks away from the track, which runs along the ridge of a slight hill, at the farmland in the valley beside them. A wattle and daub hut has smoke coming from the chimney. He has a momentary urge to ride down there and invite himself in. He nods to Cedric. 'I wonder what they're cooking.'

Cedric smiles and Johnny sees that smiling is something that doesn't sit comfortably on his face. It makes him look slightly misshapen. 'I reckon they're having a potato and mutton stew.'

'With peas and cabbage?' asks Johnny.

'No, all the cabbage is used already.' Cedric looks at Johnny and says, 'I grew up in a place just like that. That's what we ate every day. For lunch and then for dinner. It was a winter meal but we only had winter vegetables in our garden. That's all that would grow, no matter what the season.'

Johnny knows rural poverty. The spine of this country is made up of people living in similar conditions. 'We only had silver beet,' he says. 'That was our vegetable.'

Cedric nods towards the house. 'So you know what it's like under that roof?'

'Yes, I think I do. It looks much the same as the place I grew up in too. We were lucky; the land turned us some money and my dad was able to build us something bigger. We began to eat more than mutton.'

Cedric shrugs. 'Good for you. My parents fought the land every year of their lives. It was the drought in the nineties that killed them. Now the shire has flooded our land to make a lake. My dad would have laughed.'

Johnny pulls out his tobacco and offers it to Cedric, who declines. 'Besides arguing, how are the newlyweds going?' Johnny asks.

'Alright I suppose, if you count fighting as a good thing for a young couple to do. They seem to relish it. My brother and his wife are like that. They have argued every day of their married life. They will probably still be arguing in heaven when they get there. I suppose they love each other though. It is the same with these two. You see it in their eyes, but they need only to look at each other to argue about something.'

Johnny thinks about this. 'I don't argue with my wife. Are you married, Cedric?'

'I was once. For a short while. I have stopped saying that she took off with a travelling salesman. I don't know who she took off with. I came home from a trip and she was just gone, that's all. Took everything. But you know what, Johnny? I look back over the way I was with her and the way I was in general, and I have to say I can't blame her. If I ever talk to her again, I'll tell her that.'

'Do you know where she is now?'

'Oh yes, I found her. But when I saw her, I knew it wouldn't be right to go up and say hello. She lives in a big town. I saw her with her new family. She was picking out a dress for her daughter, I suppose it was. She looked happy. She had never been happy with me. Yes, I will take some of that tobacco.' He waits until Johnny passes it over. 'But some couples argue; some don't have to. There is only one way to judge how good your marriage is.'

'What's that?' Johnny asks, looking at the trees growing by the side of the road. Their trunks have been blackened by fire.

'At the end of the day, when the lights are out and you have given up your prayers and are about to fall asleep, if you are happy to be lying next to the person you are lying next to, then it is a good marriage.' Cedric rolls his cigarette with one hand. 'Companionship. That's the thing a man needs more than anything else. To be able to sit comfortably with someone in silence. I worked that out after my wife left me and I was looking at what I missed her for. Everything else—the food, the loving—was replaceable. The companionship wasn't.' He flicks the reins across the back of the horses. 'Of course, I worked most of that out while standing at the bar of a pub on my own. When everyone went home to their families, I stayed there.'

Johnny glances over at him. 'You don't look like a big drinker.'

'Oh, I'm not. I drink slow. I don't have the thirst. My old man had it and gave it to my brother. The need to keep drinking when everyone else has stopped. When drink is not the thing needed anymore but the urge remains. A horrible type of thirst. I have been frightened all my life that I will wake up one day with it. I haven't so far.'

The wagon up ahead has stopped. Johnny and Cedric stop about fifty yards behind and Johnny can no longer hear the raised voices.

'This is why the trip has taken so long,' Cedric explains. 'They stop every time after they have argued. Another hour is gone. I sit back here and smoke.' He lifts up his cigarette and looks at the burning end.

The next day, after an early morning visit to the Victoria Markets, the ingredients are all laid out on the bench behind Rose's kitchen table. The four women are sitting around the table discussing whether to have a cup of tea or a glass of Eric's apple brandy. They decide on tea.

Rose pulls a mixing bowl from the cupboard and Kathleen grabs a wooden spoon from a drawer.

Janet draws the unfolded newspaper clipping close to her and starts to read aloud: 'A Coronation Cake to celebrate the Coronation of George the Fifth, 22 June 1911, created by Sir Stephen Bolton, Master Chef to our Royal Family.'

The women begin measuring out the ingredients, and Janet reads the recipe's explanatory paragraph with a flourish: 'Drambuie from Scotland to bring a flavour of the Highlands, oats from Wales to give a blood-warming body to the cake. East African dates, Australian sultanas, Canadian maple syrup, Rhodesian sugar to add a rich sweetness. Cardamom seeds from the jungles of India to give a hint of spice, Palestinian nuts to give a taste of the Northern African climate, coconut from the Solomon Islands to add some tropical sunshine, Irish butter to smooth everything, the flour of New Zealand to offer a firm base, chemicals from Hong Kong to embrace the evolving twentieth century, and finally the eggs of England to bind everything together. The cake is covered all over with Royal Icing.

'Firstly, the dates, cardamom seeds and sultanas are soaked overnight in the Drambuie . . .'

'We don't have Drambuie so we have to make do with Eric's apple brandy. Eric is Scottish so it's pretty close,' Rose says.

'The butter is melted, blended with the maple syrup then added to the dates,' Janet continues. 'The dates should be soft enough to break up into the butter mixture . . .'

Kathleen brings over a saucepan from the stove. The melted butter turns golden brown as it mixes with the dates and the maple syrup. The bowl is passed around the table as they take turns with the wooden spoon and mix the ingredients vigorously to break up the dates. As she mixes, Maria is talking about the benefits of folk dancing as an aid to childbirth. She had learned an Arabian dance in the third month of her second pregnancy and is all for it. Kathleen listens with some interest, Janet with none at all.

'In another bowl, place the walnuts, almonds and coconut and pound into a powder. Add the sifted flours and sugar to the butter mixture . . .'

Nancy is keen to see New Zealand because she met someone from her corner of Scotland who said that parts of it are very similar to where she comes from. She is interested to see what it might look like. Not at all because she is homesick, she adds a little too stridently. She shakes her head when asked about family still in Scotland. All surviving family members have gone to South Africa.

Maria would like to return to Italy because she misses something she calls 'the babble' and wants her children to have the experience of it. She describes it as a mixture of every noise from every street, from every room, from every voice in Italy. Something so overpowering that even the white cockatoos in the trees around Currawalli Street would not be able to hear themselves screech over it.

'Add the baking powder and the walnut, almond, coconut powder . . .'

Maria smiles when she talks of the babble. It is a cacophony, she says, that gets in the blood, the muscles, in every thought, every dream, every conversation.

Janet interrupts. 'How is this Arabian dancing done?'

Maria, who didn't think Janet had been listening, stands and lifts her dress above her knees. She begins to hum a discordant tune and repeatedly bends and straightens her knees, which makes her hips sway. Before too long, Kathleen and Nancy are trying it. Maria's humming grows louder. Janet has put down the spoon and joins in, moving with the others.

'Back to the bowl!' Rose orders and the women sit down, laughing.

Janel continues. 'Beat the eggs and add to the mixture which should then be mixed thoroughly . . .'

It takes forty minutes for the bowl to go around the table twice. By the time it is in Rose's hands the second time, she has a cake tin ready, greased with butter. She turns and opens the oven door, checking the temperature by splashing a small amount of water onto the oven wall. She can judge what the temperature is by how far down the wall the water runs before it evaporates. If it isn't hot enough, she puts some more wood in the fire; if it's too hot, she closes the vent that lets in oxygen for the fire to breathe so it dies down a bit.

She spoons the mixture into the cake tin and then bangs it once on the table in front of Maria to dispel any air bubbles. Maria blinks. Rose then places the tin in the oven. As she closes the door, she sighs happily and is smiling by the time she stands.

Nancy and Kathleen have already gathered the dishes and spoons and are washing them in the sink.

'Time for apple brandy?' asks Rose.

'Definitely,' Nancy answers. They all fill their glasses and raise them to toast the monarchy and apple brandy.

Thomas is weeding the church garden. He works harder at this than he does at delivering his sermons. There is an orange cat walking about his feet, watching what he is doing, and Thomas's friend Robert Parsome is sitting reading on the bench under the currawalli tree.

A few months ago Thomas had been trying to formulate a sermon while working in the garden. He was struggling to find the right words as he pulled out weeds. The more he struggled, the more weeds he pulled out. It was early on a Friday morning, sunny but not yet hot; the air carried the scent of gum flowers and bushfire smoke, and he could hear the bleating of sheep in the paddocks beyond the trees. He was so caught up in wondering what to talk about on Sunday that, without being aware of it, he began to weed his way down the street. Once he realised what he was doing, it occurred to him that the sermon should be about taking things too seriously and the danger of obsession. He then threw down his trowel and went to look through the Bible for a suitable passage.

The more he looked, the more it seemed that the whole book was about obsession and so he went and lay down on his bed.

He didn't doubt that he was writing a sermon about obsession that he himself should listen to. Janet had said that he was getting obsessive but he thought she might only be joking. She obviously wasn't. It wasn't just things like the weeding. It was the punishing prayer times that he devoutly adhered to, the large amount of Bibles that he kept throughout the house—in every room, in fact—the regular cleansing of every crucifix in the house, even the blessing of the eggs that he made Janet suffer through.

He sat up in bed. The thing he didn't like about self-reflection was that he often saw things he didn't like seeing.

That night he ate only a bread roll for dinner as penance, and as the sun began to go down he walked out the front door. The owner of the Choppingblock Hotel had given him a standing invitation to come down to the bar for a drink and this is what he decided to do. He knew about going to the side entrance and by the time he walked into the half-full bar, he was ready to abandon whatever needed to be abandoned. He was given a tin mug with his name written on the side of it and he began to drink, listening to the people around him talking. The more he drank, the happier he became. He was invited to express his thoughts on many subjects in a number of conversations and was surprised to find that he actually had a healthy body of opinions that weren't necessarily the Church's. The people around the bar seemed to recognise that too and the talk became freer as the night progressed.

At about the time that he gave up trying to climb onto the bar to marry the barmaid to the owner of a wheat farm down the road, he was coaxed home gently by a quiet man named Robert. Inside the manse, Robert made him a cup of tea and began to feed him slices of dry toast.

Soon Thomas was sober enough to realise where he was and what was happening. Robert and he eventually became tasters of an exquisite kind of love. And they have been tasting it ever since. Robert Parsome, a lost man from a strongly Catholic home in Sydney, the place where his mother's God was cold and his father's faith was cruel was finally finished with sitting alone in a room above the Choppingblock Hotel and moved into the manse effortlessly. And as if they had always been together, the three became one of those families who aren't really families. The sermon that was to be about obsession became about finding love in unexpected places.

But today the weeding isn't helping to find the subject of Sunday's sermon; Thomas's mind keeps wandering off. The orange cat is now sitting by the front gate, still watching him. Robert, deep in his book, has become enough of a comfortable companion to be left to entertain himself.

Thomas hears the sound of an engine and looks up. A biplane is crawling uneasily across the sky. Thomas watches as it disappears into a bank of cloud and then emerges, going in a different direction. The pilot must have been so disorientated by being inside the clouds that he didn't know in which direction he was going. Thomas likes the idea of that; it is very appealing. He wonders why he finds it so. The plane quickly returns to its original direction and soon the sound of its engine fades into the distance.

He looks down at a weed he is about to pull out of the earth and thinks about that plane lost in the cloud. It strikes him that what disappoints him sometimes about the Bible is that it never gets lost in a cloud. The words and the stories are always the same. They always go in the same direction. Sometimes he would like to tell a different story, using different words, and not know what the ending is. Not know where he is heading with it. It's not about faith. He certainly doesn't question his faith any more than the next man does. Sometimes that's a lot. Sometimes that's hardly ever. What he questions is the validity of the path his faith leads him down. It is well trodden, probably over-used. He knows that on this path he will never see or touch anything new because everything has been examined, turned over, patted, crumpled and stroked already. And is new no longer.

On a whim he decides that he will walk down Choppingblock Road to the field where the planes are kept and see if he can be taught to fly one. He will go right now. The sermon can wait. Robert looks up from his book as the gate closes. He smiles at Thomas's retreating figure.

Eric is stretching his legs near the side fence, having a break from carving another silhouette. This one will be Burns the grocer. He is happy to be thinking about idle things, such as how Burns had a withered arm but was stronger than most and able to carry heavy boxes from the carts into his store better than any man who worked for him.

Eric's day started out well enough but now this strange cough has come back. He remembers the night three months ago at the Mozart concert in the town hall; that was the last time it appeared. It is a cough like no other he has ever had. It seems to rip the skin from his lungs and his throat each time it comes on. And always in gaggles of three.

He is leaning against the house with the side fence three feet in front of him. It still smells of the tar that the builders have daubed on it to protect it from the termites. He can hear Johnny moving on the other side of the fence; it sounds as if he is gardening. He must be back from the bush, Eric notes. But then he hears hammering and the fence begins to vibrate. Funny, he thinks, Johnny must be just home from chasing Alfred's wagons—why is he doing repairs around the house so soon? A sulphur-crested cockatoo sits in a tree above the fence, head turned sideways, looking down at him.

A paling in front of him is torn away and then the one next to it. The afternoon sunlight bursts in and for a moment Eric is blinded. In front of him is a man he's never seen before, about twenty-five, with short cropped black hair like an onboard Chinese coal shoveller, unshaven but not bearded. He is wearing a strange red shirt and blue trousers, the shirt so bright it makes Eric blink. What is this man doing attacking Johnny and Kathleen's fence? They lock eyes for only a moment. Then the stranger quickly replaces the palings where they were and Eric hears him step back from the fence, which appears completely untouched. That strange man certainly wasn't Johnny but there was something in his face that did remind Eric of him.

Eric pushes himself away from the house wall and walks inside to find Nancy.

'Is there a man staying with Kathleen?' he asks. 'If there isn't then I think I have just seen a ghost. I might have a brandy.'

Nancy comes straight over to him, sensing in his voice that something has happened. 'What's come over you? You must have seen many, many ghosts at sea.'

'I did,' says Eric nervously. 'Plenty. But they all made sense. I don't know—they were always doing something symbolic . . . something operatic.'

'What does that mean?'

The words come tumbling out of Eric's mouth. 'They were wrapped in sails and ropes, being dragged just under the surface of the water. Or rising above the waves of a storm. Or standing at the end of a pier waving goodbye. But never like this. He was just fixing the fence. With a hammer and a red shirt.' Nancy can tell that Eric has been shaken by this.

'But the fence doesn't need repairing,' she says, as she touches his cheek.

'No. And I can't see where he has been. He ripped off two of the palings but they look untouched now. And the red was . . . so bright. So . . .' He lifts the glass to his lips and drinks.

'Are you frightened?' Nancy asks.

'No, of course not. I'm concerned, more than anything. You know how I am with things I don't understand. I hope Johnny and Kathleen are alright.'

'I saw her before but why don't you go in there and see?'

'I'd rather not. Kathleen might think I'm a stupid man who has spent too long at sea.'

Nancy kisses him on the cheek. 'Too long for me. I'll go see if Kathleen wants anything from the shop.'

'I'll come with you. We'll go to the shop together. A walk will be good.'

Nancy looks at him. 'Oh, but I'm not going to the shop. It's just an excuse to knock on the door. Everybody in the street does it.'

'You mean the women?'

'Oh yes. The women. It keeps everybody in touch—I mean the women. Nobody gets lonely. Nobody gets swamped by too many visits.' She smiles. 'If Kathleen wants company, she'll say that she needs nothing and she'll invite me in for a cup of tea. If she wants to be on her own, she will tell me she needs something inconsequential and I will forget to get it for her. As a system it works well.'

'Does it? Maybe I should try it with the men.'

She touches Eric on the arm and looks at him seriously. 'You can give it a try. It won't work though.'

'Why not?'

'The system only succeeds because all the women know what its real purpose is. I don't know that the men in this street are clever enough to work it out.'

'Really? You might be wrong. Maybe I'll give it a try.' Eric looks down at his glass and remembers the face of the ghost. 'Yes, I will give it a try.'

❧ Chapter Six ❧

Morrie Lloyd looks out the front window of number thirteen. He likes to stand here. The currents of the wind are strangely different directly outside his house compared to anywhere else. It blusters and swirls in all directions, and it is here that the willy-willies gather themselves for their boisterous run down the street.

He looks down at the rumpled clothes hanging from him like rags on a clothesline. Before, he always dressed well. It was the thing that set him apart from other men. He had suits of fine European material and his hats were just that little bit broader in the brim so as to be noticed but unobtrusive enough that no one knew why they had noticed. He had a figure that a suit hung on well. Not now though.

He wonders if the willy-willies have anything to do with the funerals held at the church. They could be ghosts trying to escape from the funeral service and the reality of being dead. He shakes his head. It sounds like his father talking. His father. God rest his soul. It was he who taught Morrie to always dress well.

He turns from the window and looks around the room; it is comfortably full of furniture, but empty. His wife died on that couch in his tired arms.

Sometimes Morrie thinks that the most profound and immediate debilitation that her death brought to him was that suddenly he had no one to talk to. It's not talking about the grand things he misses—the things that he thinks long about, clearing his throat before he speaks. He can write to the paper about those things, talk to the greengrocer, speak to someone in the office. It is the idle musings: the lemon tree growing another two inches, an itch on his elbow all day, a new bird's nest in the tree outside the back porch. They were good at that level of communication; not every couple is.

There had never been any need for him to go deeper because Gwen understood that when he talked about the puddle in the road or the train being late, the child's scarf lying on the path or the limping dog that wagged its tail at him, he was also saying he was a little angry. Or a little bit pleased. Or a little bit excited. Or a little bit . . .

Now there is no one to know what he is feeling, and that's what is really sad. For a while after she died he always finished the evening by calling out a goodnight to her and hearing it echo down the empty hallway. But the silence that followed became something he despised.

Then Lazarus came along. As if his wife had sent him to give Morrie someone to talk to. Lazarus is a dog. A stray dog. A dog that no one likes. He took up residence at thirteen Currawalli Street exactly three months after Gwen died. Morrie opened the front door because he had heard movement on the porch, and Lazarus walked straight in and sat himself down on the lounge-room rug. After a while he looked over to

Morrie as if to say hello and from then on that was where Lazarus lived. He eats with Morrie, sleeps in the same room as Morrie, walks with Morrie whenever he goes out. They are companions. A dog is good to share things with. Exercise. Conversation. Silence. Out walking, Morrie has stopped lifting his head when he passes people. Instead he pretends to fuss around Lazarus. No one really notices him, when he does this.

Except for the Italian chook woman, who ignores his funny ways. She speaks easily to him. Her name is Maria. These days, when Lazarus disappears, Morrie will usually find him with Maria, sitting under her table while she does something in the kitchen or out the back keeping an eye on the chooks. When they aren't in their pen, they peck around Lazarus but he never snaps at them. He likes to put his chin on the ground and follow the wandering chooks with his eyes. The little chicks sometimes walk over the top of him.

Before Gwen died, Morrie had little to do with his neighbours. Only once did he ever sit around a table with them, at Christmas, next door in the reverend's house for afternoon tea. He remembers because he had a heavy cold. The religious business was dispensed with very discreetly as if everybody, including the reverend, was slightly embarrassed by it, then the tea was poured. And, as if he was having some sort of attack, or perhaps because he had taken too much brandy for his head cold, Morrie talked freely to everyone and had a contribution to every subject that the conversations covered. Suddenly he became the controlling personality at the table. All interruptions were presented with the inter-jector's eyes on his face.

When he and Gwen went home he had to lie down for the rest of the afternoon. But he remembered something he had said at the table to that map-making fellow from number nine who was tying a piece of string to his fork and then untying it as the conversation washed around him: 'I don't want to rust away.'

'What did you mean, you don't want to rust away?' Gwen asked when they were having a cup of tea after dinner that night.

Morrie answered after a long pause. 'I don't want us to get old and stop thinking—stop wondering about things, stop doing things, stop being curious. When he retired my grandfather sat down in an armchair and never really got up again. The world changed around him but he didn't change with it. That's where he died. In that chair.'

'People have to die sometime.'

'Of course everyone has to die, but not necessarily because they've retired from work and think they have no other purpose. In effect, they retire from living. There are plenty of things that my grandfather could have done if he let his mind stay active.'

Gwen didn't rust before she died; she didn't even get old. Thirty-seven. *What sort of a life was that?* Morrie thought as he watched her coffin being carried from the Currawalli Street church. At first he wondered what he was going to do with all the plans and proposals they'd had together. He expected to have trouble getting them out of his head, and he was right. He couldn't sit still. And he couldn't move. These things began to tumble his thoughts around. The long trips on slow ships, going to restaurants in London, the exploration of Tasmanian caves, mountains in the Grampians they were going to climb, where they would live in Switzerland so that Gwen could finally see snow, the camel rides through the outback, the general store they were going to open in that country town they visited once—and of course, the children they were going to have.

So he was trapped, unable to express his grief because his mind was already filled up with plans suddenly made pointless and irrelevant. And every day it seemed as if one more emerged that he had forgotten about. After a while he wondered if this was what grief really was: a study in frustration, trying to tie up the loose ends of pieces of string that he kept finding.

But then one night about three weeks after she died, a great pain hit him. A pain in his soul, strong enough to make him stop using any of his senses. Strong enough to make him give up.

He sat still for two days until someone knocked on the door. And kept on knocking. He struggled over to the door, a little scared at how weak he was. On the veranda stood Maria, the woman with the chooks. At that time he only really knew her to nod to in passing. She held a basket covered by a cloth, and she looked at him for a moment then stepped into the house and escorted him back to his armchair. To this day he can't remember whether she pushed him aside to come into the house that first time, but he thinks she probably did. He heard clattering in the kitchen and she returned with a hot bowl of tomato soup and some bread. She didn't talk to him other than to say she would come back in an hour. She did that, and then continued to come three times a day for the next two weeks. Eventually he gave her a key and she came and went as she pleased. She didn't talk much, which suited Morrie, for he had nothing to say and no strength to listen. The food changed with every day and he assumed he was eating what she fed her family.

One day she found him in the kitchen, making a cup of tea. Taking it as the beginning of recovery—a sign she had been waiting for—she came over most days and took him back to her own kitchen where there was a chair around the table waiting for him. He and Maria's husband William began their friendship around that table. Between them on the table there is always food being eaten, a newspaper being read, an atlas being explored, or a chess board being stared at. Theirs is that particular type of male friendship, one that needs a subject or a project. When they are left alone with nothing to do or talk about, the relationship falters. At those times Morrie generally goes home. He doesn't mind. William wants to talk all the time about geraniums. Morrie gets dizzy when William starts on about them.

Maria and William have two children, Irene and James, aged thirteen and sixteen. At first James had no time for Morrie. At sixteen, he found grief to be a stupid indulgence, something it was best not to cater to; instead he felt it should be trampled on and ground into the dirt. Morrie respected that because he sometimes thought along those lines himself.

Then Lazarus turned up, and started to follow Morrie to the Contès's house each day. He sought out James with a wagging tail and a long tongue on arrival and picked him as the person to sit below at the table. And that was what finally broke the ice between Morrie and James.

There is smoke in the air today. Lazarus smells it and looks up at Morrie, who looks to the end of the street. There is a dirty brown cloud on the horizon. It is a long way away.

Morrie turns out of the front gate and begins to walk fast. The wagons still aren't back at number nine. He can see Alfred's legs pacing up and down the front yard. He keeps his gaze downwards and almost walks straight into Maria, who is coming towards him, also without looking, talking to the woman from number ten.

'Morrie, you know Kathleen, don't you?' Maria hastens to perform the introductions.

Kathleen takes a quick step forward. 'Of course he does. How are you, Morrie?'

Morrie looks up at the tall woman standing next to Maria and tries a smile. 'Ah . . . good, yes . . . how are you, Kathleen?'

'I'm very well, thank you, Morrie. Where are you going on such a fine day?'

'I was just going for a walk to break in the day. Although when I smell smoke I don't feel like going too far.'

'But the fire must be a long, long way away.'

'Of course. But it still makes me want to stay at home.'

'Yes, I know what you mean,' says Kathleen. She turns to Maria. 'I hope Johnny comes home soon.'

'He knows what he's doing,' Maria replies. 'This is his land. Are you worried?'

'Oh no, he'll be fine. He knows the bush better than anybody.'

The two women don't notice that Morrie has dropped his head and continued walking. Lazarus, wagging his tail, is sniffing the orange cat asleep under the daisy bush, trying to make it react.

After only one day Johnny is considering riding on ahead. Yet another domestic drama at the first wagon. Elizabeth and Walter are trying to whisper but their whispers soon end up as yells. Johnny rides next to

Cedric's wagon. Cedric holds the reins loosely, looking at the land-scape to the left side of the road. Johnny's eyes are drawn in the same direction. The road still runs along the ridge of a hill and through the trees he can see green ferns running down to the river. The water is running quickly and the thought of washing off the dust of the road is enticing.

Cedric is thinking along the same lines. 'A wash would be good.'

Johnny thinks better of it. 'Yes. But that will put paid to the day's travel. We won't want to continue on.'

'That's true. And yet that is probably one of the attractions of the river; I'm sick of this wagon.'

'So this really will be your last trip?'

'Too right. As I said, I'm going to enlist in the army. Make sure I get over in time. I want to be there for the start.'

Johnny thinks about what Cedric is saying. He watches the flow of the river. A parrot flies up from the edge of the water and screeches at the sky. The echo of the screech mixes in his mind with the echo of Cedric's words.

Going to war is an adventure for a single man, not for one married. He assumes he probably won't be needed. But if he ever is, he will have to think seriously about going.

Actually, Kathleen and he will have to think seriously about whether he should go. That is one of the hard things about marriage: there are now two people to make one person's decision.

Up ahead, Elizabeth stops her wagon. Walter waits until Johnny is abreast of him. 'Elizabeth and I are going to stay here for a few days. You and Cedric can keep going. Cedric has in his wagon all of the information that Alfred needs. We should be a day or two behind you. Tell Alfred we're fine,' Walter announces.

'Fair enough.' Johnny is surprised that he feels so much relief. 'We'll see you in Currawalli Street when you get back. Watch out for the fire. It seems to be moving away from where we are, but you never know . . .'

'You don't have to tell me, Johnny,' says Walter sharply. 'I know bushfires.'

'Sorry. Well, Cedric and I will keep moving.'

Cedric scratches at his beard. 'I might not be there when you arrive, Walter, and so I'll say good luck to you.'

'And to you,' Walter answers. They shake hands.

Cedric urges the horses on around the lead wagon. As he draws level to where Elizabeth is sitting, he takes off his hat. 'Good luck to you too, Elizabeth. I hope it all works out.'

'Thanks Cedric. I'll see you back there.'

'Maybe.' He waits until he is past and then mutters to himself, 'Maybe not.'

Cedric's wagon makes good speed now. He is a better driver than Elizabeth and his horses know the road ahead will take them back to Currawalli Street.

'Home by tomorrow, do you think?' Johnny asks in a voice suddenly light.

'I reckon. Probably we'll turn into Currawalli Street late afternoon.' Cedric smiles at Johnny. 'Maybe earlier.' He keeps smiling as he looks beyond the heads of the horses.

Johnny rides alongside the wagon. He looks back and sees Elizabeth steering her wagon onto a track that goes down to the river.

*

Elizabeth draws in a breath. The wagon rolls down the embankment to a flat grassy area that Walter has singled out by the river. It will be the first place to flood if the river rises and Elizabeth doesn't like it. She indicates further along the embankment to another flat section that is much higher. She urges the horses on. Two well-trained animals. She looks over at Walter, who lifts his eyebrows.

'It's okay,' she says as she grips the brake handle tightly just in case the wagon begins slipping. The ground becomes a bowl and dips before rising to the site she has selected. She applies and then releases the brake at the right time and the horses begin to pull again. Only for a few steps and then the wagon is on flat ground. The horses stop without being ordered. Elizabeth's arms are sore from the reins and she straightens them a few times to stretch the muscles.

Walter has dismounted and is now unhitching the horses, who know the procedure well enough to wait for the last leather strap to slap against the wood and then they walk down to the water. Elizabeth watches them drink as Walter unbuckles his saddle. His horse follows the others and they stand side by side with their heads bowed into the water.

'Swim?' asks Walter. Elizabeth nods.

Clothes come off easily; in the heat of the day, most of the buttons are already undone. The water is cold around Elizabeth's feet at first but as she steps forward and the riverbed falls away, she doesn't notice it.

Travelling by wagon is a brutal, dusty business. The horses disturb a lot of dirt and then the wagon upsets the rhythm of the wind and the dust tends to circle around the driver. Elizabeth only has to sink underwater once before her body feels hers again. She stops to reacquaint herself with her stomach and hips and shoulders.

Her feet no longer touch the bottom and she has to swim to reach Walter. She treads water, watching a banksia branch dip into the water and then rise hurriedly. Gently it dips back into the water again, as if it is equally attracted to and repelled by the water. She looks at Walter again.

Standing on a submerged rock, he overbalances slowly and falls back into the water. Elizabeth laughs and feels around with her feet for the rock. She slips on the slimy algae, falling forward into Walter's arms. The previous days have been long and hot. It is good to wash them off. Good to rid themselves of the echoes of empty words that should never have been spoken. Elizabeth puts her arms around Walter's neck and together they slip under the surface and then rise up for a moment only to sink back under. They are relaxed enough to allow breathing to become a secondary issue, both drifting along in a sleepy moment as if they are in the same dream, and as though the sounds of the bush around them are part of it.

Walter slides under her once more and Elizabeth lets him go. He rises to the surface and holds her feet. She lies back in the water, moves her arms to stay afloat and bends her neck forward, strands of her hair across her face.

She has to push only a little for Walter to let her feet go. She is pleased that he lets go easily. She realises that, about some things, she doesn't know him that well. About others, she feels that she has known him all her life. She assumes that he feels the same about her.

They swim side by side down the centre of the river, then pause while a long red-bellied black snake glides from bank to bank ahead of them. It disappears into the ferns above the waterline and they swim gently back to the wagon, their heads above the surface, taking in mouthfuls of the other's splashes. Once inside, they make love easily; each has become versed in the movements and reactions of the other and so the pleasure has reached a higher level.

Walter is running on a decision he made. About to marry someone else, the manager's daughter at the farm where he worked, he first met Elizabeth and her father on their initial map survey. When they left to return to where they came from, Walter found that he couldn't get her out of his mind. He broke off his engagement and when Elizabeth came back the next time, they both declared themselves and decided to embark on a life together. They were passing a little church in a small country town, the reverend was out the front weeding the garden and, on the spur of the moment, they decided to go in and get married. Cedric was the best man, and from then on Walter started sleeping in the front wagon. But since leaving that little country town, he and Elizabeth have been arguing about every little thing, so much so that Walter sometimes looks at the wheel tracks in the dust and wonders about the wisdom of the decision he made. But there is no going back. The wheel tracks always get blown away by the wind and now his heart burns like never before when Elizabeth touches him.

He thinks of their plans. A house is being built for Elizabeth in the same street as her parents. Next door, in fact. He is reserving his judgement on that until he sees the street, the house and the mother. The impending decision about these living arrangements looming before them is one of the reasons they are quick to break into an argument over anything.

Elizabeth tries to stop him thinking too much about the future and he tries to stop himself from thinking too much about the past. That only leaves the current moment. He doesn't mind too much, quite liking what he is becoming. Gentleness was never required in his old life because Annette was happy for him to be as rough with her as he was with the men on the farm. But already he can see that being gentle is going to have its own value with Elizabeth. There seems to be a new sun shining and he is beginning to see things in its new light.

As he walks out of his front gate and onto Currawalli Street the Reverend Thomas Tierson looks up at the afternoon sky. He then steadily lowers his head until he is looking at the horizon beyond the treetops. He takes a deep breath and holds it, a little apprehensive. When he visited the airfield, it had only a shed and three cows on it. The man inside the shed turned out to be a parishioner and was happy to oblige Thomas with a flying lesson. Tomorrow at dawn. He lets the breath out and wonders what time the man meant by dawn. He didn't want to ask; for some reason it is a piece of knowledge that he doesn't want to confess he doesn't have.

Tomorrow morning he will see the world from a new perspective. The street. The manse. The church. Maybe he will even have a new view of God?

The Word of God is something that hasn't come very easily to him ever since he watched his father die five years before. If ever there was a reason for him not to believe in the existence of God then that was it. The old man, who had devoted his whole life to the work of the Lord, died in an agony of uncertainty. Every man has his moment of crisis, so the bishop says, and unfortunately his father had his just before he died. Thomas didn't have any words to comfort him because, like him, the old man needed more than the obscure ramblings that both of them used at times like this. He wanted to know where the logic was in his final moments and whether it would offer the comfort he wanted. Faith and Logic. They go side by side like unsettled brothers. If a man desires one, he will love the other. If faith is the root of a man's distress, then logic will be his comfort. And if logic is his well-founded system of belief then faith will be his unfounded passion.

Thomas knew this. He had learned it by observing that most men of faith had what was close to an obsession with logic. Their lines are always straight; their sums are always correct. If a clergyman has retired to his office, it is most likely not to study the Bible, but to study his book keeping. His father certainly had this obsession.

But at the time of death, logic is left standing at the door and a man has to rely on faith by his bedside. Most men are able to surrender to their faith at that moment. But Thomas could see that his father wasn't able to.

He had no words when his father asked him for certainty about God. He had none when his father asked him if a lifetime of belief was enough. He had none when his father asked him if heaven was a reality.

He didn't know.

But then he remembered something he had witnessed four years before in an Aboriginal settlement near Leongatha. An old man was dying and, although Thomas could not understand the words, he knew that the man was scared about what he would find on the other side. The daughter, kneeling by his side, leant down and held him to her breast. The man's uncertainty and fear had left his mind long before he died, rising above the clearing, drifting into the currawalli trees. Thomas felt it go.

And so that is what Thomas did. As an answer to his father's questions, he held the old man's head to his chest and rocked him like a baby until he stopped breathing. Thomas continued to rock him for ten minutes afterwards. It was there that he and his father had finally learned about the logic of faith.

Thomas thinks a lot about the issue of faith. He has spent most of his life unsure about the decisions he has already made: the clothes he has bought, the meals he has chosen from the menu, the books he has decided to read. And yet he has undertaken to devote his whole life to something of which he has no proof, something on which he must trust his own intuition.

He continues to walk down the street, determined not to look back to see if the church's steeple has collapsed during the night. It is every clergyman's fear that his church will topple over while he is not looking. It is as much about a doubt of faith as it is a doubt of engineering. He sighs and looks back. Of course it is still standing. Across the street he can see the apostle birds flying around their tree. He likes these birds. He crosses over towards them, pulling the bread crusts from his pocket. The birds see him coming and begin to gather on the fence of number twelve.

He hears the steam engine climbing up towards Currawalli Street. The rails begin to sing, filling the air.

When the engine has passed, Thomas starts distributing the crusts, trying to make sure each bird receives an equal portion. He can never be certain that has happened; it is another one of the things that worry him.

An automobile turns into the street. He knows the colour, the same colour as a bishop's robe. The car is driven by Edward, the bishop's attaché; the bishop doesn't know how to drive an automobile. Thomas stops concentrating on the birds. They stop paying attention to his empty open hands.

Alfred is at his front fence, his hands in his pockets. He stops looking to the end of the street. He watches the automobile drive towards the church. Thomas watches too. It sails straight past where he is standing. Even though Thomas is sure he has seen him, the bishop makes no move to acknowledge Thomas. He thinks he is too important for such trivial people.

Thomas sighs again and walks back towards the church. Edward has already leaped out of the driver's seat and is standing by the rear door until Thomas nears, then he pulls it open. The bishop is sitting in the centre of the backseat and looks out as if he is a visiting member of a royal family.

'Hello, Your Eminence,' Thomas says, hoping he sounds sufficiently respectful.

'Good day to you, Thomas,' the bishop says in his small, shrill voice. 'I thought it was time I paid you a visit. Is your sister at home? I may need her to do some special work for me. Something of the highest order.'

The bishop tries to deepen his voice, but the moment he stops paying attention, it leaps back up to its usual high pitch. More than once Thomas has noticed Edward trying not to laugh as the bishop does battle with his vocal eccentricities.

'What sort of special work?' Thomas knows to keep the bishop away from his sister.

'Now, I don't really think it's any of your business, is it?' The bishop accepts Thomas's help as he climbs from the high leather bench seat, speaking all the time in an undertone. 'Really, Thomas, I find your curiosity quite vulgar. It may be of use to you with the people around here but I find it . . . unsanitary.'

The bishop needs the car seat high so that he doesn't look like the short man he is. But once he is standing on the ground there is no denying his small stature. Thomas towers over him. That makes the bishop angrier.

'There's no need to stand so close. No need at all. My highest apologies if I ever gave you the impression that you could stand next to me and pretend you're . . . my equal. Now don't fawn. Show some dignity.'

Thomas looks at Edward, who rolls his eyes, slightly enough that the bishop won't notice.

'S-sorry, Your Eminence,' Thomas stutters. 'My sister is not home at the moment. I believe she is . . . ah . . . out visiting.'

'Well, run along and fetch her, there's a good little fellow. I'm sure she would be wholly disappointed not to see me when I have come all this way.'

'I'm afraid I can't do that, Your Eminence. She is working on your behalf and the Lord's. Administering to a dying man.'

'Oh I see. The Lord's work. How well I know it. And how often it plagues me.'

Thomas doubts that the bishop even knows what the Lord's work is and is certain that he is never even touched let alone plagued by it. The bishop continues on, 'Well perhaps this man will die soon and she will return. I will look inside our church now.'

The orange cat comes out from behind a bush. It calls plaintively once and then watches as the bishop walks past. Although he pretends not to see it, the bishop doesn't walk any closer to the cat than he has to. At the door to the church he pauses and looks around at the small patch of lawn beside the building.

'Is this land ours?' he asks Thomas.

'Yes, Your Eminence. I maintain it and the congregation uses it as a meeting place.'

The bishop retreats from the church door and holds his hand lightly to his forehead. 'For a moment I pictured a statue in the middle of it. One of me in my robes would look very grand. Very grand indeed. Perhaps it could be the same as the one we have commissioned for that little country town . . . near . . . near . . .' he waves his hand delicately, '. . . out there somewhere. Of course the sculptor could make two. Why couldn't he?'

He turns to Thomas, who is not sure if he is supposed to supply an answer. Fortunately the bishop continues.

'I am standing with one hand extended, calling people into prayer. Very . . . very . . . what was the word that the sculptor used to describe my pose, Edward?'

'Serene,' Edward answers quickly.

The bishop turns back towards the grass. 'Yes. Serene. What a good description. We could have it unveiled by the archbishop—although . . .' he scratches his chin as if in thought, continuing to peer at the space, '. . . he might wonder why it isn't a statue of him. Perhaps we won't ask him to unveil either of them. But a statue of a religious figure in a humble pose would be an appropriate gift to give these people. Perhaps that is something you could look into, Edward.'

'Definitely,' Edward says with the conviction of one who will do no such thing.

The bishop walks back to the door of the church and waits for Thomas to open it, then raises his eyebrows. 'You don't keep this door locked?'

'Never,' Thomas replies. 'You can't tell when people might want to come in.'

'But you have valuable paintings and artefacts in here.'

'I would hardly call them artefacts. They are all new and replaceable.'

'But expensive none the less.'

'Yes, they are expensive, but—'

'Keep this door locked when you're not inside. Try to be a little smarter about these things. You're not out in the country any longer. People are different here in the city.'

Thomas breathes in deeply as the bishop sweeps past him and then waits at the inner door. Thomas lets Edward go forward and open it. The bishop strides down the aisle to the altar. He bows his head for a moment, holds his hand across his brow as if he has a sudden pain and then speaks to the two men behind him. 'I must go. I have business elsewhere.'

There is a strange set to the bishop's face as he walks back, as if he has just completed some physical exertion. Thomas feels Edward's hand grasp his arm as if warning him to stay still. Thomas looks into the bishop's eyes as he sails past. They are wide open and bright, yet

Thomas sees nothing in them that he can recognise. It is a look that he will think about many times in the future. Not the look of a man of the cloth in a church; it is the look of a man barely in control of a mind in turmoil. He looks over the bishop's head to his favourite stained-glass window: Saint Peter drawing water from a stream.

The bishop turns at the end of the pews and Thomas watches as the strangeness leaves his face as quickly as it came. 'Now, Thomas, we will leave you to lock up your church. And remember, it is only your church for a moment. Don't think you own it. It turns out that every man owns nothing—except his soul. And that really belongs to all of us. All of God's creatures own each other's souls. As for your gracious sister, I hope she is at home now.'

'I doubt it, Your Eminence. The dying man is on the other side of the city. She will be gone for all of the day and probably all of the night. I don't ask her to travel home after dark. It is too dangerous for a woman.'

'Is it? How dreadful,' the bishop murmurs.

They walk back out into the fading sunlight. By the time Thomas has shut the church door and pretended to lock it, the bishop is back inside the car. He doesn't look at Thomas again. Edward waves goodbye as the car moves off back down the street, the rays of the setting sun bouncing off the roof.

Standing in front of the church, Thomas watches the bishop's car turn into the little road. He feels as though he has just walked offstage from yet another of the tiny plays in which he has a supporting role. All these men masquerading. Always men.

Women are different, he knows that. He can tell that they see through the playlets that he performs when he puts on his collar, and he assumes that they also see through God. It is men who need religion, men like the bishop who needs religion more than it needs him.

He stands for a long time looking at the birds flying above and around the trees. He is stepping off the grass, onto the footpath when through the fading light he sees a wagon turn into the street. And a horseman. Johnny Oatley. He draws in a deep breath of the dusk air and walks down slowly towards them. The wagon driver, whose name Thomas recalls is Cedric, doesn't move from his travelling position when the wagon comes to a standstill in number nine's yard. Neither does Johnny; he stays seated on his horse next to it. The men don't talk or look around. Almost four minutes pass before Johnny gets down from the saddle and stretches gingerly. Cedric coughs and begins to climb from the wagon. He coughs again halfway down.

Alfred, Eric, Morrie and Lazarus come around the far corner of the street. Alfred speeds up when he sees the wagon and even though he is the one who's sick, the other two struggle to keep up with him. Johnny looks up from the saddle that he has dropped onto the ground, sees the procession coming and waves to Alfred. Cedric, who looks exhausted, watches Alfred blankly as he closes.

Thomas leans against number thirteen's front fence and watches the travelling men come to terms with reaching their destination. Home.

Thomas doesn't want to go any closer. His preference is for a distant wave, not a mumbled greeting.

❧ Chapter Seven ❧

At the same time that Cedric and Johnny were travelling along Choppingblock Road, beginning to look for the little road in the hazy distance, Alfred and Eric were halfway through their second mug of beer at the bar of the Choppingblock Hotel. If Alfred had been looking out the rear window of the hotel, he would have seen the wagon and the accompanying rider approaching in a swirl of dust.

As they drink, Alfred and Eric are waiting for Morrie. He hasn't been to the pub since his wife died and the two other men, following the orchestrated suggestions of Rose and Nancy, are preparing to usher him as gently as they can back into this particular bosom. A crowded bar is a good alternative to sitting on your own in a house full of undusted memories.

The truth is that Alfred and Eric have been somewhat slow in developing a friendship themselves. They talk when they meet on the street but still hardly know each other; most of what they do know comes from what other people—mainly their wives—have told them. So this outing to the pub is as much about advancing their relationship as it is about helping Morrie.

The first Alfred knows that Morrie has arrived is when Lazarus licks his hand. He looks down at the dog, reflecting that there is a contented depth in a dog's eyes when it feels at home in a public bar. Morrie is still standing at the door, looking for them among the sea of faces. Eric raises his arm until Morrie acknowledges him. As he walks over, the group near the door shouts in celebration at something one of them has announced. The tiniest triumphs are magnified in a bar. The three men wait until the yelling dies down before greeting each other. As Alfred turns to call the barman over, he pats Morrie on the arm. That tiny gesture is Alfred's way of a welcome. When the barman has served them, the three men touch mugs and take a mouthful of beer each. In a tiny ballet, they place their mugs on the bar at the same time. Eric and Morrie wait for Alfred to say the first words. He is the most senior of the three.

'Still bloody hot.'

'Bloody oath,' Eric agrees.

Morrie hesitates before he says, 'Bloody oath.'

Then there is silence.

'Bloody oath,' murmurs Alfred, thinking of something else to say. He remembers his wet hand. 'Lazarus looks like he knows his way around a bar.'

Morrie glances down at the dog. 'This is the first time I've been in here with him, but he does look as if he has been here before.' Lazarus lies down among the feet and tries to push his head under a stool.

Eric clears his throat. 'All bars are the same. Perhaps he's been in a pub somewhere else.'

The conversation is awkward but the environment helps. The three men are reassured by standing at the bar in between the stools. Having something to lean against makes them feel secure. The path that runs behind Currawalli Street is used as a short cut from the railway station by city workers who catch the train, and the pub is full of men stopping in on their way home from work. The hotel is far enough from the centre of the city to be able to stay secretly open past six o'clock, the designated closing time of pubs in Melbourne. Only the hotel's regulars are invited to stay on after closing time, and the other men drink faster as six o'clock approaches. Many who would prefer not to be drunk have to stagger home in that state.

At quarter to six, the three men wave goodnight to the barman and leave through the side door, Lazarus close behind them. Alfred is the first to see Cedric's wagon sitting in his yard. He looks back down the little road to see if the other is coming, then increases his pace to reach his gate. Alfred is puffing, yet Morrie and Eric struggle to keep up with him. Johnny waves and then returns to the saddle at his feet. Cedric stands silently by the wagon. The reverend is leaning against a fence further up the street.

'Where is she?' Alfred calls out when he comes close enough.

Johnny turns to him. 'They're fine. They just want to take their time, that's all—they'll be here tomorrow or the next day.'

Alfred looks at him and then at Cedric. 'They? Who's they?'

Cedric comes across to him and holds his arm. Alfred looks at Cedric's hand then up at his face.

'Fred. Everything went well. She went good.'

'What do you mean *they*?'

Cedric continues. 'All the measurements are exact, I made sure of that.'

'Ced, who's *they*?'

Cedric looks around at Johnny and Eric watching him. Morrie is looking up at the church. He turns back to Alfred. 'She went and got married, Fred. You must have met the boy when you were up there with her on the first trip. Nice sort of bloke. His name's . . .'

'Walter.' Alfred scratches his head. 'Walter. But he was already getting married. To a girl up there.'

Cedric shrugs. 'Yeah. Well you know how it is. Things change pretty quick when you're . . .'

'. . . a woman,' Rose says, as she comes around the corner. They hear the back screen door slam after she is with them so she must have moved quickly. She walks up to Cedric and kisses him on the cheek. 'Hello, Ced. Hello, Johnny. How did you go?'

'Pretty good. A couple of flooded creeks. A bushfire that we had to move out of the way of.'

'We've been smelling it for a few days.' She looks at Cedric seriously. 'So, she got married did she?'

'Yeah. At that little church in Darraweit.'

'To Walter? You were there?' Rose asks quietly, moving in front of Alfred.

'Yeah. Walter. I was best man,' says Cedric, smiling for the first time.

Rose turns to Alfred. 'She told you that she might do something like this. She told you. I told you.' Her words are curt, her voice is sharp.

Alfred's hands curl into tight fists. 'I heard both of you. But I thought he was coming in a few months?'

'No, Fred,' Rose says impatiently. 'That was the boy from Sydney. She didn't like him. I didn't like him. Only you liked him. She thought she did for a while and then she thought she should because you seemed to so much. You started to build a house for them next door.' Rose sees the confusion in Alfred's eyes so she softens her voice. 'She told you about Walter. I told you. But the whole world could have been telling you. You wouldn't hear.'

Rose nods at Eric and Morrie as their discomfort grows and they decide to leave. Johnny picks up his saddle and holds it strongly in one arm, as Cedric leads off one of the horses.

Rose steps closer to Alfred and touches his cheek. 'What did you think our daughter would do? When she thinks you are trying to take over her life? Picking a husband for her? You're lucky she is coming back at all.'

Alfred suddenly looks older. Johnny walks over and joins Cedric at the water trough where he is patting the horse's neck and muttering something under his breath. Johnny can't make out the words. He looks across at his own house. He wonders whether Kathleen is in there waiting and will soon pass by a window and see the wagon. He wonders whether she will see him walking across the street and rush out the front door to meet him. He feels exhausted by the journey now that he has stopped.

Johnny says a quiet goodbye to Cedric, wishes him 'all the luck', placing his hand on Cedric's shoulder for emphasis.

'Maybe I will have been to a war when next we meet.' Cedric's words are chilling even though Johnny knows it is just his way of saying that he expects they will meet again.

Johnny calls goodbye to Alfred and Rose as they continue their intense discussion, now on the porch. Alfred shakes his head in despair, then walks over to Johnny. He picks up an apricot stone from the ground and throws it high over the wagon towards the hotel. He has been talking so angrily to Rose that his thankyou to Johnny comes out as a croaky whisper.

He shakes his head, continues, 'Elizabeth thought I would get angry that she wants to marry a country boy instead of the Sydney city man I met in my shop. But I'm not. She's my daughter. I want her to be happy. I only picked him because I thought he was the type of fellow she would like. But apparently she doesn't like him anymore. Women! Will I never learn? I only get angry because Rose says that she tells me things but, in fact, I think she keeps them from me.'

Johnny lifts up his shoulders and holds his hands out, palms upward. He says goodbye and leads his horse across the street into his own yard.

Morrie and Eric shake hands and say goodnight. As Morrie and Lazarus stroll up the street, Morrie sees the reverend ahead of him, turning into the gate of number fifteen with the orange cat at his feet.

Morrie's thoughts are full of the pub: all those men of all ages, and with all sorts of lives. The regulars are easily identified: they have their names printed on the side of their mugs. Other drinkers are given anonymous mugs from under the bar. Alfred and Eric both have one of these personalised mugs and they told Morrie that he will be offered one the next time they all go for a drink. Morrie is the only man in Currawalli

Street who doesn't have his own mug. Even Cedric, the man who works for Alfred, has been given one. Morrie decides that he will instigate another session at the pub soon, and looks down at Lazarus. 'Even the reverend has his own mug.'

Lazarus doesn't show any interest in what he is saying; instead he is intent on finding the orange cat.

Kathleen and Maria have just stepped out onto the porch of number sixteen; they have been talking about onions, but they stop their conversation to watch Morrie open his front gate and wait for Lazarus to walk through. Maria quickly looks up to the heavens and offers a silent thanks to her saint who she asked to watch over Morrie as he steps out into the world more. Kathleen doesn't notice; she has seen the wagon sitting in the yard next to number nine.

Cedric is soon standing in the bar at the Choppingblock Hotel. The curtains have been drawn and the pub looks from the outside to be closed up for the night. But there are many men inside, talking in whispers. Cedric has said his goodbyes to Alfred and Rose; he declined Rose's invitation to stay the night, and as he left he saw Alfred—clearly unable to wait any longer—climb into the back of the wagon to look through the measurements.

Cedric quickly finishes his beer and puts his tin mug firmly on the bar. He nods to the barman, who comes over and shakes his hand. The other men wait in line to do the same. Cedric is to be the first drinker from the bar to join up. He doesn't say a word but nods his head continually at the words of each man as they stand in front of him. They all wish him well. The barman stands on the bench behind the bar so that he can reach up high enough to screw a hook into the wall. On it he hangs Cedric's mug, with his name showing.

'I'll take it down when you get back,' he says to Cedric. 'The first beer you drink from it will be on the house.'

The men clap. Not because of what he says but because it is a speech of sorts and men always applaud at the end of a speech. Also because there is the feeling that there is something in the air and Cedric might just be the first of many. Indeed, a man from a sheep farm further up Choppingblock Road calls out to the barman, 'I hope you've got a lot of them hooks!'

Everybody cheers. Under the cover of the yelling and clapping, Cedric disappears out the front door.

Kathleen opens the back door and finds Johnny sitting at the kitchen table, taking off his boots. He is happy to be home. The smell of smoke is still in his nostrils and it has taken him longer than normal to reassure his horse that all is safe and well.

When Kathleen first saw a herd of wallabies, she burst into tears. This was the first time Johnny had seen her cry and it confused him. He had just finished art school and had come home to the farm. She was just out from England, a nervous teacher for her mother's cousin's children on the biggest estate in the district.

It was their third meeting and they were getting to know each other more, perched on a fallen log at a district Women's Association picnic. He smiled nervously as he consoled her then.

He doesn't smile at her tears anymore; her sobs are too wrenching for him not to be torn apart in tiny ways. At the picnic he wasn't sure why she cried when she saw the wallabies, but he now knows there are many reasons why she does.

The moment she sees him at the kitchen table she bursts into tears. He rushes across the room and holds her in his arms.

She tells him she is pregnant.

Instantly he can feel the presence of another person in the room, and he is shocked.

After dinner and no longer tired, he walks into his studio and ponders the fact that it will be the baby's room one day and that he will have to do his painting somewhere else. He looks at the unfinished portrait of the bishop. Without a word, he picks up his palette and begins to mix together reds, whites and yellows to give him the skin colour that will be appropriate for the bishop standing in the shadow of a large golden crucifix.

Kathleen looks in on him and then walks back down the hallway, smiling. Johnny doesn't notice. The painting was almost complete when he went away and now, in a single session, he will finish it. By the morning it is done.

Kathleen wakes and sees that she has slept alone. As she slips down the hallway and peeks into the spare bedroom, the early morning sun is coming through the window above the front door. Johnny is staring at the painting; the brushes have been washed and are standing in an old jam jar on the shelf.

Kathleen continues on to the kitchen and stirs the coals in the stove until the flames come to life. She fills the kettle then places it on the hot plate, and sees on the kitchen table the teapot that Johnny has used in the middle of the night to replenish himself. She feels a momentary pang of guilt for not being awake to look after him, but that goes out the door with the tea-leaves. The kettle is boiling by the time she has the cups and milk ready and a piece of heavily buttered bread on a plate. She looks down at the plate. Out of a whole tea service it was the only piece of crockery that survived the trip from England. It wasn't the wild sea but the carriage trip from her mother's cousin's farm to Currawalli Street that did the damage.

She carries the painted tray of tea and bread back into the studio. Johnny has heard her in the kitchen and when she returns he is sitting facing the door. She looks from him to the portrait. She can tell that it is finished by the look in his eyes. He looks exhausted. The face in the painting looks fresh and young as if it has stolen all of Johnny's energy and life force. She puts the tray down on the shelf next to the jam jar of brushes; she and Johnny hold each other and she feels even more his exhaustion, so she pulls away quickly and pours him a cup of tea. He smiles the smile that first attracted her to him on a country Sunday morning and eats the bread then drinks his tea in four gulps. He is thinking about pouring himself another cup when she takes his hand and leads him out of the studio, along the hallway into the bedroom. He sits on the bed and pulls off his slippers as she closes the curtains to block out the sweet morning sunshine. He is asleep before she has finished drawing them. She finishes undressing him, pulls the blankets over him and then closes the door behind her.

She stops and looks at the light pouring through the window above the front door, illuminating the length of the hallway.

'A family lives here,' she says to herself.

❧ Chapter Eight ❧

The cooler evening air runs up Currawalli Street a little easier after the sun has gone down. The unscorched scents of the bush are more distinct; they mix with the cooking smells that float out of the houses. Maria likes this time when she and William sit alone on the veranda. She can hear the clatter of the dishes being washed by the children, the barking dog behind the pub, farm workers finished for the day calling out to each other in the distance, and William next to her, sipping his cup of tea.

She sometimes asks William what he is thinking about. William figures she only asks him because she expects him to have reasonably noble thoughts in his mind. He never has noble thoughts in his mind, so he never answers. He just smiles absently at her. Which makes it worse. She thinks he is deep into a line of philosophical thought that can't be shared with her.

But this evening when she asks him, he is inclined for a moment to tell her exactly what it is he is thinking about. Liquorice. But he thinks better of it and smiles absently again. She nods and puts a hand on his shoulder as she passes by to supervise the kitchen cleaning.

William is thinking about liquorice because he has been told that liquorice is one of the supplies you are given in the army if you are sent to war. It is said to have a calming effect. The sound of shells isn't as bad if you have a mouth full of liquorice.

He thinks about the army every time he reads about a coming war. War is one thing he has never experienced. Maybe his life will be incomplete without that experience. He used to feel this way about travel. That's what led him around the world.

But going to war is different. Or is it? Some days he thinks it is something best avoided and some days he thinks it is an experience that shouldn't be missed. He has two children and a good wife but they would be able to fend for themselves if he went away for a while. And this war will probably all be over quickly: if he doesn't go at the start, he will most likely miss it.

He is almost decided. He just has to find a way to tell Maria. He'll ask Morrie how to raise it. That will also give them something to talk about.

Two weeks have gone by and Morrie and Lazarus are at the pub again. Lazarus has a tin bowl of water on the veranda with his name on it. Morrie too is making good use of his mug. He has been here three nights in a row. He easily stays inside his limit of three mugs of stout for the whole evening and doesn't come close to getting drunk. To Morrie, what is addictive is the evolution of the conversations around him. Just as a family has a running dialogue, so do the drinkers at a hotel. Every sentence is connected to its predecessor, even sentences spoken the night before. A brother-in-law's name does not need to be inserted because it is known by everyone, and each listener has access to a library of knowledge about most of the subjects being discussed in the room of that pub.

Morrie now knows that the man standing over by the window is Joseph, who works for the farmer Edward from down Choppingblock Road and Edward stays up late and reads out loud. He also knows that Joseph's sister Edith is off to South Australia to chase a man who declared his love for her two years ago. To the annoyance of her family she didn't pursue the matter until now and Joseph suspects it may be too late. The South Australian man's name is Ronald and he is a friend of Joseph's and so whenever Joseph mentions Ron, Morrie is able to gather up all this information and locate Ron as one of the characters in the conversation.

Morrie believes, although he will never tell anyone, that this knowledge is what soaks into the walls and the woodwork of a place. Any place. He went once with his father to the house of an actor where a murder had been committed years earlier after long episodes of family violence. He could sense the cruelty straightaway and tell which room the murder had been committed in. He doesn't pride himself on being any more sensitive than the next fellow. He thinks any human being can sense things like that. Birds would not sing outside the window of the murder room, yet they were active everywhere else. They knew something bad had happened there; it makes sense that he would know it too.

Daniel, who always leans on the far windowsill, under the clock, works in the city for the police as a clerk and he lives near the

Choppingblock Hotel with his parents. Like Morrie, he drinks very little and stays out of most conversations. But when Daniel does speak Morrie always listens, and already he knows a fair bit about his work. There is a gangster, Bert Brady, who was recently living at this very hotel but left suddenly and whom, it is said, the police are trying to convict of a murder. Not a particular murder, it seems to Daniel, but any murder. And now, so he has heard, they have a murder at a race track that they have no killer for, and as Bert Brady is a gangster, he does some of his business at race tracks and he might have known the victim, then this looks as if it might be a suitable crime to aim at him. And who knows, he might have done it. So whenever Daniel mentions Bert, Morrie knows who he means.

As more men join up there are now six mugs hanging from hooks above the bar. He thinks about it as something he should do. Still, he would like to drink a few more stouts from his mug before it is hung up there.

Morrie looks over at the farmer Edward. Every night he drinks his two mugs of beer before heading home. Edward tries to be a friendly fellow but when he thinks he is demonstrating bonhomie he is actually displaying his nervousness. And so every man in the bar knows that the one thing Edward truly is, is nervous. On the farm, he stops breathing whenever he moves from one job to the next. And no matter how slow he tries to go, he always ends up rushing, as if the tasks are rafts and he has to swim frantically from one to the next.

At the pub he prattles on loudly as if he is talking over the top of a crowd, even if there are only one or two people involved in the conversation, and laughs like a drowning man thrashing about. He has a preselected store of subjects so he is never left having to perform off-the-cuff patter. He is unaware of the value of silence or that more things are explained in the pauses between sentences than in the words themselves. But at the end of the night when he does stop talking, a look of sadness crosses his face as if he has been defeated again. Morrie likes him. He sees a fellow struggler making a determined effort to be out in the world.

Morrie also likes Peter, another fellow that no one else talks to very much.

There is no doubt that Peter is a strange character. He asks a lot of questions and always listens carefully to the answers, as though conducting an interview. His hair, longer than the fashion, is tucked into his collar and he always wears the same brown coat. Because he never stops asking questions many of the men grow uncomfortable with him, but Morrie finds him invigorating. He tells Peter things about his life that he has never had to form into words before; he tells him about Gwen and how grief appears at odd times in his day. He talks about his childhood, about his family, and about being unpopular and misunderstood. He suspects that Peter knows something of these things as well.

For his part, Peter says that he comes from up north and that his parents have gone back there. He screws up his face when he answers a question; his words sometimes don't make sense, but sometimes they are as clear as a bell ringing.

Then quickly, he always finds another question to ask. Morrie assumes that he is hiding something.

Not that it matters in a bar. Everybody is hiding something.

*

It is now June and the weather has turned. The clouds are much denser and keep the sun's light off the currawalli trees. The rain now takes longer to soak into the dirt of the street and so there are many puddles to step around. Kathleen understands this type of weather more. She looks out the front window at the sun struggling against the grey sky.

William and Morrie are walking down the street. William's conversation is animated and high pitched. He laughs and touches Morrie on the back when a good point is made. It is the first time that William has been outside in his uniform. He took it off before he came home from enlisting but Maria has asked him to wear it so the children can see what he has become.

He and Morrie are just walking to the little road and then coming back again; William says he wants to wear in his new army boots but Morrie knows that he is embarrassed and nervous about wearing a uniform and so he wants someone to walk with. Morrie is pleased to accompany him because it is another indication that their friendship has reached a new level. Ever since William joined up, they have talked together more easily and openly. Men have always been like that. Put a finishing date to a friendship and suddenly they are good at being friends. Put a finishing date to a marriage and suddenly they are good at being husbands. Put a finishing date to their life and suddenly they are good at living.

The two men pause under the apostle birds' tree. William has some crusts in his pocket. Morrie is surprised because he has never seen William do this before. They watch the antics of the birds for a while, laughing out loud and calling to individual birds to come forward.

At the front gate of number sixteen, Maria watches the two men as they resume their walk down the street away from her. It is the saddest thing she has seen. She wipes a tear from her eye with her apron.

Kathleen, who has been writing to her sister, now comes outside to stretch her legs and catch the wind. Johnny is across the street helping Alfred and Walter erect the framework for the roof of the new house. She knows that he can't do much but he wants to be over there helping. As she stands on the front porch, touching her growing belly, she watches him hold the horses still while Alfred and Walter unload some timber from the wagon. He leads the horses away and notices her looking across at him. He waves just as William and Morrie appear. They have crossed the street directly from the apostle birds' tree to avoid the puddles and parade proudly past the men working. Just then, the sun goes behind some clouds and doesn't come out again. The light changes. Kathleen looks at William's uniform and then at her husband. His face looks momentarily stunned, his eyes still locked onto hers.

Rose sees the two men walk past her window and for a moment she drops her head to her chest. Then she rushes out the front door and looks up the street—not in the direction that William and Morrie have gone, but towards where they have come from. She is looking for Maria. Kathleen sees what she is doing and suddenly both women are hurrying up the street to number sixteen where Maria stands sobbing at the gate.

The true cold of winter has arrived and the colours of the street have changed. The greys of the currawalli tree have now changed to the khakis of the uniform. Cedric has already gone, and William has just left. The reverend's friend, Robert, is in uniform and just waiting for dispatch orders. Morrie is now talking abstractly about going too.

The sun has long gone and the rain has greedily replaced it, arriving in the morning and pouring relentlessly for most of the day.

Janet stands at the front window of the manse.

Her father said that rain always pours harder near a church. Of course Janet knows this can't be true, but sometimes it feels like it. The relentless drops hitting the glass affect her clarity after a while. She does not like to stay inside for too long. She never has.

And just as the rain is changing this street, her other world is changing too. There is a man, Charles, who wants more than she has grown used to offering. She is toying with the idea of inviting him to become involved in all of her life but she still feels uncomfortable with such an idea. She likes Charles. Enough to think about him when she is away from him; something she has never done before.

Her world, once still, is now spinning. She is waiting for it to stop raining because she is going over to have a cup of tea with Nancy, describe what she is feeling and see if Nancy knows what it all means. The solution that she normally employs is to run away. But that doesn't feel right this time.

She has talked to Nancy before on a number of occasions and Nancy said to watch out; there will be a man she touches who she doesn't want to let go of. Perhaps that man is Charles. But she has doubts about whether she is ready to not let go.

She first met Charles a year ago, both friends of somebody else. It may have been a dinner party. She thinks it was. He says it was at a stage show. He can even say what song they were singing when he looked across and saw her. But she now knows enough about him to not believe everything he says.

They met again two months ago at a restaurant where he was the friend of the guest of honour. Against her better judgement, Janet talked to him all night; people were leaving at the end of the evening before she turned to greet them.

What Charles is, he won't say. Janet laughs to herself at this. He knows he doesn't have to explain himself to her; he knows that she is already so interested in him that she can't extrude herself.

It is a situation that Janet always worked hard not to end up in; but now that it is here, she finds it quite exciting. Not that she would ever tell him, but she suspects that Charles holds her heart.

The sad truth is that Charles, a major in the British Army assisting the generals here, is returning to London in a few days.

That afternoon, Nancy and Janet are the last to join the other women around Rose's kitchen table; the coronation cake mix has already reached the stage where the beaten eggs are about to be added. The cake baking around Rose's table has become a weekly event. The women of the street keep every Wednesday afternoon free. That Nancy and Janet have been talking about something important is obvious to the others; both women have red eyes from crying.

And the truth is there is a lot of crying in this street now.

❧ Chapter Nine ❧

Sometimes the wind roars, sometimes it hums, but it is always running down Currawalli Street. Alfred leans on his front fence. There have been times when he has yelled into this breeze and times when he has whispered. Both have had the same effect. The wind doesn't listen. He looks at the line of houses across the street. His neighbours have sometimes heard his voice, sometimes they haven't. He has become a man with a lot to say, who talks to no one. His words are like dust: they come together; they drift apart. Sometimes he says what he means; sometimes he doesn't. Mostly his words are just blown down the street by the wind.

He throws an apricot stone over the roof of the new house. It is almost finished. He will be pleased when Elizabeth and Walter can move in. His house is too small to accommodate all of them. He looks at his apricot tree. The leaves have all fallen to the ground. He walks out of the front gate, leaving it swinging open, and begins to walk up to the manse. Everybody will be there by now. Rose has already gone up there with yet another coronation cake that the women baked yesterday.

Alfred has been loitering; the sky was clear for a moment and he wanted to watch it change. The clouds sitting heavily on the horizon seem to signify sad departures, the way they move steadily across from west to east.

He passes the currawalli trees, as silent as stones, their trunks grown white, grey leaves bowing to the ground; they are a little taller, the wind is a little stronger, the cockatoos are a little quieter, and the dust is a little more settled. As Alfred walks up Currawalli Street, the apostle birds sit still in their tree and make long squawking noises. The whole world changes but not for them.

Everybody is sitting around the long dining room in the manse: Johnny and Kathleen; Rose; Maria and her children; Morrie; Eric and Nancy; Elizabeth and Walter; Janet and Thomas. Lazarus is under the table. Only Robert stands—stiffly by the window, looking out as if his orders to depart might arrive by magic at any time.

As Alfred sits down beside Rose, Thomas rises to his feet. The sound of the chair scraped across the wooden floor draws everybody's attention. He touches his throat and then speaks. 'Neighbours, welcome to our table. I will say only a few words . . .'

'Hear, hear!' calls Alfred as he settles back in his chair. Everybody laughs.

Thomas continues, 'Winter is well and truly with us. The bushfires will leave us alone for another year. They have done their damage.

'We have gathered around this table to celebrate, be it belatedly—three years belatedly, in fact—the coronation of the king. The beautiful cake that sits on the table in front of us is the same as that made by people all over the Empire to celebrate this event. As you know, it was baked by the women sitting around this table and that will make it all the more exquisite to eat.'

For some reason unknown even to himself, Eric says, 'Bravo!' As if he is royalty at the opera. Nancy elbows him.

Thomas smiles. 'To take the place of the bushfire smoke we are now looking at heavy black thunderclouds in the distance. A war in Europe—God help us. We thought it would be just a small war, if there can be such a thing. But maybe it will encompass us. Maybe we are all going to be affected by it.' He looks at the cake and the cups around it. 'Acting as a neighbour, not as a member of the clergy, I asked you to meet here so that we can wish safe times for each other and hope that we are all left as untouched as one can be by what is coming.'

'Thank you, Thomas.' Johnny doesn't speak often in company, but impending fatherhood has forced him to make some changes in the way he acts around people.

Alfred stands. 'Down at the pub, there are now fifteen mugs hooked up on the wall. Plenty of men are joining up, leaving their wives and families behind. If the need arises I assume most of us will have to do the same.'

Thomas looks across at Robert, who is still gazing out of the window. Janet clasps her brother's hand.

'God keep us all safe,' Alfred finishes.

'God keep us all safe,' Thomas whispers.

'Now let's eat some of this cake!' says Eric.

Kathleen looks over at Rose. She is staring out the window at the little expanse of lawn next to the church.

Johnny looks across the table at Walter at the same time as Walter looks at him. Both men give tiny nods to acknowledge that they are in the same situation. Elizabeth is rubbing her belly. Kathleen smiles to herself as she touches her own stomach, knowing that in a moment Johnny will be listening to the distant train as it goes past.

But things are different now. It is the same engine, with the same pair of goods vans, the same passenger carriage and conductor's van, but it has a new driver who doesn't wave. The old driver has joined up.

Alfred eats his piece of cake, happy that his heart condition has improved enough to be nothing more than a minor inconvenience. He is pleased to be back in the shop, catching the train every morning to work in the city and leaving all the wagon driving to Elizabeth and Walter. He has yet to tell Rose about an offer that has been made to him by the army. It will be hard to refuse.

Nancy places a cup of tea in front of Eric as she regales Maria's children with tall tales of her childhood back in Scotland. Eric barely hears her; he is thinking about the sea. His old ship is one that will be adapted easily to wartime needs. It makes him sad to think of her sailing into danger. Vulnerable, without him to look after her.

Maria reaches down under the table and pats Lazarus's head. She looks over at Morrie and remembers William's words the night he explained why he was joining the army. They still don't make sense to her. The true taste of pasta. The taste of liquorice. What on earth pasta and liquorice has to do with his decision, she will never know.

Kathleen knows without a doubt that Johnny will go. He will be uncomfortable for the rest of his life if he takes no part. His sense of honour lies just below the surface of everything he does. She knows that. She knows him well enough to foresee that he will find a way to conceal his impairment.

Elizabeth is thinking about her baby and what it will need when it is born. Walter's love is one thing—and he may be away for some time. Living with her mother and father and a new husband hasn't been any-where near as difficult as she thought it would be. Her parents seem to get on better with each other now that her father has gone back to the shop. Her mother is still a misery of sorts though. But she knows Walter will go and fight if he has to protect his wife and child.

Nancy looks over at Kathleen and then at Elizabeth. It's not too late for her to have a baby. A little girl. That would be just fine. She smiles to herself. Eric is watching her as if he is thinking the same thing.

The orange cat has come inside and is rubbing against Thomas's legs. Thomas continues to look over at Robert. The sadness he feels at the thought of Robert's departure is in a place very close to the centre of his heart. He doesn't look forward to the day when Robert's marching orders are placed in that letterbox, and these days he dreads hearing the postman's whistle. He thinks that he and Robert are good together. Just as much as love is about a physical act, it is also about sitting quietly at a table, feeling content in each other's company and knowing exactly what the other needs to be happy at that moment.

In the end, a relationship is not measured by the grand gestures that might fill a day or the exquisite gifts that might fill a room but by the inconsequential moments that individually add up to hardly anything. If only I could fit that into a sermon, Thomas thinks. That is what we all need to hear.

Beyond Robert, out of the window, Thomas can see an aeroplane struggling in the wind as it comes in to land at the field where he is con-tinuing to take flying lessons; he watches as it is pushed around. He is pleased to be learning to fly. It strikes him suddenly that the aeroplane, so heavy and useless on the ground yet built to float effortlessly up in the air, is a good metaphor for the dilemma of a life of faith. This life that he has chosen, that his father chose too, pushes the boundaries of everything that is safe and comfortable. And logical. It makes no sense, yet nonetheless it exists right in front of him. Sometimes he thinks his faith is falling from the sky and other times he sees it sailing through billowing white clouds. Perhaps things aren't meant to make sense. Perhaps that's it.

He shifts his gaze from the window, to the photograph of his father on the wall above the sideboard. Maybe he doesn't have doubts anymore. Maybe he has been through his crisis of faith. Or maybe this sudden certainty is just a small plateau. He knows for sure that either this is or there will be a time soon when a man must hold onto something to be able to maintain a definition of himself. And the truth is, Thomas has nothing else to hang onto. Except his faith.

Rose looks down at her hand. She is holding something that Kathleen gave her two days ago, asking if Rose knew what it was: four bulrush heads stuck in a ball of yellow mud. At first Rose didn't know what it was, but now she does. Something or someone told her when she wasn't listening.

Kathleen gave it to Rose because she is the one it rightly belongs to. Rose first saw it when she was a little girl: it was lying next to her neighbour's fallen body. She saw it again as the floodwaters raced through the sheds at her parents' farm. It is the shadow of a spirit that still has work to do. She is going to bury it this afternoon in the centre of that little expanse of lawn.

She glances around the table and adds to what Thomas said. But quietly, so only Alfred can hear. 'We have arrived in this street, all of us, our backs laden with things that we can never throw off. Look at us; we have carried them into this room, just as we carry them everywhere.'

'What things?' Alfred whispers.

'The . . . heaviness of our memories, the emptiness of our past pains, the sudden glimpses of things unexplained, the strains from our sudden leaps of faith, the horizons of hills still to be climbed. We have to carry them, for none of us knows how to lay these burdens down.'

Alfred leans forward and touches her cheek gently. 'But what else can we do? Isn't this . . . life?'

She lifts her hand that had been cupping the small ball of mud, now sitting in her lap, and holds onto his at her cheek. 'Do you think that they will bury these things with us?'

'What do you mean?' Alfred's hand goes limp. Rose holds it for a moment then lets it fall.

'All those things I was just talking about. The memories, the disappointments, the hurts. Will they return to dust like us?'

He looks at her in a way that she hasn't seen him look for years. 'I don't know, Rose, I don't know. Maybe some of these things stay around . . . in the dirt. In the trees. In . . . whatever. So people know who we were. How else are they going to know? We won't be around to tell them, that's for sure.'

A willy-willy dances away from the church down the centre of the street, drawing in the dust that has been lying still as if untouched by the rain. A pair of green parakeets flies just above the ground, calling out loudly to the world.

1972

❧ Chapter Ten ❧

Jim closes the taxi door, feels the duffle bag fall hard against his leg, looks up the street to the church at the end. A willy-willy zigzags towards him. Although the street has long been asphalted, there is still enough dirt around in the gutters and the nature strips to give the willy-willy flesh. Of course he can remember lots of things that happened after the asphalting was done, but his best memories of this street are of when it was unpaved.

The willy-willy dances up to his feet and in a moment is past. It takes only a second for him to realise why it gives him a foreboding feeling. There is something missing; it comes to him like a snake of smoke. Where he's just come from, when the Iroquois landed, they would make willy-willies appear in the red dust. But over there the zigzag dance was sinister. And he has grown used to hearing the accompanying roar of the rotors. That is what is now missing. The willy-willies scamper up Currawalli Street in silence.

His dad once told him that they were the ghosts of Aborigines performing a welcome dance. Jim agrees that they are ghosts—though whose and what their purpose might be, he is not sure of anymore. It seems fitting that a ghost should come and greet him now, but he doesn't necessarily read it as a welcome.

For Jim, ghosts now live in everything. There isn't a tree, rock, piece of scrap metal or old pot that doesn't look as though it has a ghost residing close by. Vietnamese soldiers, he learned, don't like to sleep in the dark because of ghosts. And after Jim was over there for a few months, he became used to keeping a fluorescent light glaring fiercely every night. Now he doesn't know if he will ever be able to sleep in a darkened room again.

But the dark of the jungle is something else altogether. The ghosts generally don't venture that far from civilisation. The only ones you'll ever find out there are lost ghosts. And they are the worst kind: they're as scared as you are, as tense as you are and as ready to defend themselves as you are. He met one once. For a few seconds it got inside his head looking for something it knew. By the time it left him, he was two hundred yards from where he had first encountered it and his pack and rifle had gone. It took him most of the remaining night to find them.

This morning flying in over Melbourne, Jim peered out of the window at the houses and streets with the same methodical detachment with which he had looked at the jungle over there. Melbourne, he sees now, is just another type of jungle. There might be more cars than when he left—there seems to be one outside every house as well as one in every driveway—but he hadn't been looking properly before so he can't really say. He was surprised at the start of his tour of duty by how few specific memories he had of this street that weren't from when he was a child. It is as if he stopped registering any change in his landscape when he was about twelve.

Nineteen when he left. Twenty-two on his return; both parents dead. And not just dead but dead in a grand way that people are quick to talk about. They relish the flavour of each word as it leaves their mouth.

Jim didn't go to the funerals; he was still over there and at the time, deep in the jungle, uncontactable. His radio was the one that a sniper sometimes carries: small, with only enough power for one message to be transmitted out, they were not designed to ever receive anything. Besides cover, a sniper requires silence.

Jim had been waiting for an infamous North Vietnamese commander to reach a particular spot. Then he would use the radio. The cannons of a warship over the horizon were aimed at that place; the bullseye of a target.

There was rarely information of this kind about such a fluid enemy and it was seen by the command in Saigon to be an important opportunity in the conflict around this province. Jim also saw it as a potential trap in which he found himself at the centre.

After he made the call on the radio, he threw off his camouflage of leaves, climbed down the tree and ran from the area. The cannon shells started to fall within ten seconds. He remembers the goods-train roar of the shells over his head—a sound that you could never get used to—and how stiff his legs were after being up in the tree, not moving, for ten hours.

He walked out of the jungle into the Nui Pham township and was immediately sent back to Australia. He was on a 707 rolling down the runway at Saigon before he had wiped the tree sap from his hands. He arrived at Richmond airforce base still in his jungle camouflage outfit. It was only then, in the commander's office, that he learned what had been done in his house several weeks before. Jim didn't read the report until he returned home. The coroner said that Kim Oatley and his wife were murdered by a person or persons unknown. The report goes into the sort of great detail that newspapers are beginning to enjoy, but Jim didn't need to read any more.

And that's how he has ended up here, dropped off by a taxi at the end of Currawalli Street with a duffle bag at his feet and jungle mud still on his trouser cuffs, watching a willy-willy doing a sinister dance around him.

He begins to walk up the street, hesitates, turns back, heads left at Little Road and walks towards the Choppingblock Hotel. He can smell bushfire in the air. He is used to that, but he never grew used to the wafts of cordite that would blow into the camp on the wind.

The barman is staring at the door when Jim enters. Jim quickly looks around. A bar, just the same as it was, just the same as any he entered in Saigon. Or Nui Dat. Or anywhere. The towels on the counter are faded to the same colour as in any of those bars. Glasses make the same sound on the tabletops. The only difference here is cosmetic: a football club scarf is draped over the cash register and old tin cups are hooked to the wall above the bar. For a moment he assumes that the barman's gaze is welcoming but quickly he realises that his eyes don't move and that it is nothing more than a vacant stare of boredom. Jim puts down the duffle bag and is leaning on the bar before the barman can rouse himself enough to register that there is someone who requires his attention. Finally he strolls over, a stocky man in his late forties with Elvis Presley sideburns and lank hair down to his shoulders. Jim's own hair is shaved to his scalp, not as a fashion but to stop the tiny bright-red swamp leeches from boring unnoticed under his skin.

Jim was almost too young to drink when he left and now he feels he has returned after already having drunk his share. And that he has seen too much in too clear a light for any amount of alcohol to blur.

His dad always drank Victoria Bitter; he remembers this when he sees the advertisement on the wall. Jim only drinks whisky now. Beer is like water to him; it takes too long to have any effect. And time was something that nobody over there had enough of. Besides, it bloats the stomach, and a gurgling stomach is something you don't want when you are lying in an ambush position.

He finishes his drink before the barman can return to his original place, gazing this time at a spot on the wall. Jim walks away without saying thank you.

The barman waits till he is at the door and then says, 'Are you the boy from up Currawalli Street?'

'Yes, I suppose I am.'

'Bad business that.'

'What?'

The barman suddenly stands up straight. 'You don't know?'

'I know when to mind my own business.'

'But . . .'

'Do you?' Jim walks out the door, the taste of the whisky in his mouth. A cheaper brand than he is used to drinking but it still burns his stomach as the first one of the day should. He has promised himself that when the burning stops he will give up. But until then he will continue to drink.

He returns to Currawalli Street and continues the hard walk up to his family home. Number ten. A number that is always easy to remember. He reaches the house and immediately smells the honeysuckle growing along the front fence. His grandmother Kathleen originally lived here and he still remembers coming to visit her and smelling the honeysuckle as he ran up the backyard to watch the train coming. He was nine when his grandmother died and the house was passed on to his father and they came to live here. Soon Jim no longer ran to the fence to see if a train was coming. There was always a train coming. After a while, he didn't even notice the sound.

And that's what his adolescence consisted of: ignoring things he couldn't be bothered getting out of the beanbag for. At least, that is how he remembers it now as he opens the front gate. The honeysuckle still grows; it refuses to die. He has thought about that scent a lot. It is another smell that he now doesn't like much, perhaps because it represented the dread of going inside, the pain of being outside and alone, or maybe because it was the smell of boredom.

The front door might look the same or it might look different. There is a tall pot plant beside it that may have always been there; Jim doesn't remember. Things like that might be in his mind somewhere but he can't find where and he doesn't bother looking too hard. In fact, at the moment he finds it difficult to believe that he ever lived here.

The squeaking sound of the gate as he pushes it open is enough to draw his neighbour Val out of her front door. She looks at him, identifying him by his uniform even though she has known him for most of his life.

He nods at her. She looks older than he remembered. He hasn't thought about her at all for three years. He wonders if her life has changed. His mother told him that once she thought she was very popular. She was the sort of person who thought that people hung on her every word; she thought they found her satirical comments hilarious and needed to have a moment in her shining light. She thought it was her duty to give them that moment, and even if she was tired and had no more anecdotes to dispense that day, she always managed to find one.

The cold truth was, his mother told him, that no one liked her much and that the time they did give her was out of politeness and kindness; the sorts of things neighbours do for each other. Apparently Val's mother had been a bit superficial like that too. That's what his grandmother Kathleen told him.

Jim never knew Val in that way. He knows her only as the strange lady who lives on her own and doesn't go outside much.

Val clears her throat. 'Home from the war?'

'Hello, Val. Yes, I've come home.'

'My father didn't come home from his war. He was in the navy. His ship sank near Malta. My husband didn't come home from his war either. His tank blew up. He was near Malta too. Where was your war?'

'Vietnam.'

'That might be near Malta. I'm not sure. I'll find out for you.' She takes a step off her porch and comes to the side fence. 'You know about your mum and dad, don't you?' she asks, seriously.

'Yes, I do.'

'Because they're not in there anymore.'

'No, I know.'

'I heard the gunshots, you know,' she says, suddenly sounding like a child.

'Did you?'

'Yes, I did. I didn't know there was a murderer about in this street. It's not safe anymore. I saw the gun. It was big. I saw it being carried from the house by a policeman. I saw it.' She brings her hand to her chest and then matter-of-factly says, 'Oh, I'm sorry. Do you want a cup of tea?'

That's exactly what Jim wants. Anything to avoid going inside number ten. He looks up at the wooden silhouettes of the faces that join the roof to the walls of Val's house. He has stared at these all his life, it seems. Now the paint is beginning to fade.

'I would love a cup of tea. Can I come in?'

'Ooh . . . yes. Come in. The bathroom's not clean. It's not dirty. I don't keep a dirty bathroom. I don't like it. It makes the whole house feel dirty. But it's not clean.'

'I really don't mind.' Jim is actually a little disturbed that he has stepped back so easily into the role he always played with Val, of him being the adult in the conversation. As if nothing has happened in the last three years. He retreats out of the gate of number ten and enters number twelve. Val waits for him on the porch.

From the front window of number seven across the road, Mary watches Jim go inside Val's house. The phone rings. It is the station-master asking if she will come and collect her husband. She sighs. It is the afternoon. An agreement has been made that Patrick won't go to the station in the afternoons, only in the mornings. He has walked out without her noticing again. She gathers her bag, makes sure her purse is inside, picks up the half-composed shopping list from the table and heads for the front door.

✂ Chapter Eleven ✂

Later Jim sits in the living room of this house he grew up in, as uncomfortable as a stranger left suddenly alone in someone else's home. Uncomfortable because it is a room where there was always movement and now there is none. Uncomfortable because he has grown unaccustomed to the soft sagging cushions of the armchair. But mainly uncomfortable because it no longer feels like a room that has ever been lived in, but more like a museum display. The silence that has descended on this house paints the walls in a coat of grey semi-gloss muteness.

Outside the window, a branch from the black magnolia tree bends slightly in the afternoon wind. It scratches at the glass as if it is one of Jim's mates from a long-ago day calling him out to play. He stands, walks over to the window and looks out. The street is empty except for a dog sniffing patiently at something on the nature strip across the road.

Jim turns and glances back around the room. The silence has an echo. While looking out of the window, it felt as if his parents were still sitting around the TV behind him. He looks out the window again.

Where are all the people that had filled this street in his childhood? Do ghosts walk unnoticed up and down the street, going to work, where they are not noticed either, going to the shops to buy things no longer needed, coming home from work unannounced and unexpected? Do ghosts sleep at night-time? Or do they just stand still and watch?

These are jungle thoughts, Jim recognises, not appropriate here. The idle musings of a sniper strapped to a branch in a tree waiting for a target.

He was that sniper. And now he is finding it very hard to leave that role behind; yet all the time he was over there he could think of nothing else but doing just that. Only blood can be wiped away quickly, he supposes, everything else stays.

He looks around him at the walls. Perhaps a life is hardly more than enduring the inconsequential moments of a day, arranging neatly the many loose ends that make up the fabric of a person. And all that is left once they are gone is the colour of a head scarf lying on the grass, the slippers standing behind a door, a shirt still hanging on the clothesline, a single gardening glove on the bench in the tool shed. The TV shows that continue to go on unwatched. An alarm clock going off at the appointed time, unheard and unneeded. Letters that arrive in the letterbox, left unopened and unread. A ringing phone that no one will answer.

Perhaps life is nothing more than those moments that resonate in another person? Like an image reflected in a puddle in the jungle that disappears in a moment as if it was never there. And that is death. The sudden withdrawal of those resonances; the disappearance of that image. And perhaps a legacy is nothing much more than a good thought that doesn't deserve to die with the person who thought it.

Jungle thoughts.

Jim sees his own reflection in the glass as he looks out of the window; through that he watches the young woman from number nine checking her letterbox and then peering up and down the street. Can it be that a life is only real when it is reflected? And is that what a hermit is after, a life without mirrors?

He came across an old hermit early one morning out in the jungle of a disputed province. Jim gave him some food and left him. Perhaps that wiry old man didn't exist until he resonated in Jim, whose memory of him is still vivid. Of all the things he witnessed over there—the horrible things, the unbelievable things, the beautiful things, the dangerous things, the sweet things, the frightening things—it is the moment when the hermit's eyes locked onto his that stands out. When he thinks of that moment now, he identifies it as one of the precise times that his life changed course a little. Like a ship changing direction at sea. The old hermit looked into Jim's eyes and saw the unwritten fear of a young man, the uncertainty of what life was expecting, the confusion about how to walk through the world. The hermit saw it all and without speaking, said *None of it means anything.*

Now, right here in the spot where he stands, is an example, Jim realises, of a tiny moment of no real consequence that has become an enduring legacy. His father had never allowed this particular window to be opened, because, he said, 'your grandmother thought the wind was colder when it came through here'. Jim shakes his head. He knows when he needs a drink.

He throws open the window; strangely enough, the breeze actually does feel noticeably cold. Quickly he closes it again and walks out into the hallway. He opens the front door and looks down the path to the front gate. The black magnolia tree is in need of pruning. So is the honeysuckle.

Jim looks across the street to number seven and watches Patrick, his father's friend—a little bonier, a little greyer, a little more perplexed—pacing up and down on his front veranda. He regularly looks at his watch, as if waiting for a train to arrive. In fact, he is the stationmaster at the Choppingblock Road station around the corner. Patrick has always been stationmaster there, for as long as Jim can remember; although he doesn't recall seeing him walk up and down his veranda like this before. But perhaps he just hadn't noticed.

Jim closes the door and walks back down the hallway. He thinks about turning on his father's radio in the bedroom but decides not to. He doesn't trust that the radio won't still be broadcasting what it was before the killer came through the door and the gun was fired twice. Ghost radio.

He walks into the kitchen and looks at the pile of dust in the corner. From the cupboard under the sink he draws out the brush and shovel. He cleans up the dust without another thought, just like his mother would have.

Jim looks down at his open notebook on the kitchen table. There is one sentence written there. He reads it, then sits down and picks up the pen to add to it, but writes nothing.

Maybe it is the human lot never to resolve things. Jim doesn't seem to be able to. He always had something itching at him; he remembers Mai's words, one time in Saigon. From a sagging armchair in a not-so-cheap hotel facing a shoe factory she told him that he was a man with 'peppered thoughts'. He had looked out the window long enough to establish that he didn't know what a peppered thought was, and that he didn't think they should be in the hotel room any longer.

Two hours later a grenade was rolled along the floor into the café next to the hotel. If Jim's intuition told him to move, he moved, no matter how comfortable he was. If it told him to leave the food on the plate he left it, no matter how hungry he was. If it told him not to walk along a jungle track any further, he cut his way into the thick undergrowth.

His intuition helped keep him alive.

Standing in the kitchen with the brush in one hand and the shovel in the other he decides that he will pay for a cleaner to go through the house before he properly moves back in. The cleaner can deal with all the dust ghosts, shadow ghosts, fallen-moment ghosts, racing-form-guide ghosts, dirty-dish ghosts, half-used perfume-bottle ghosts, and all the quiet ghost noises that are calling to him and that probably only he can hear. Maybe he will go away to the beach until it is emptied and cleaned? Should he have each room repainted? He will call his friend Lukewarm to help him. Lukewarm is a painter—not a house painter, but he knows how to use paint to cover things.

He knows what Lukewarm will say to him. He knows the questions he will ask. Jim quietly clutches his forehead as if he has a sudden headache. In Vietnam he didn't make a move without listening for Lukewarm's soft advice. Sometimes it was hard to remember that Luke-warm wasn't lying in the mud with him, watching the sugar ants climb over his rifle. One day he will tell Lukewarm that his questions, advice and jokes were with Jim every day over there.

It was only the luck of the draw that Jim was conscripted and Luke-warm wasn't. It came down to the roll of some marbles. And as friends do who agree on something without saying anything, Jim took Luke-warm's heart with him over there, and Lukewarm kept Jim's here on Currawalli Street.

Jim thinks some more about his current situation. He knows that Lukewarm will advise him to stay here while the cleaner works in case they throw away things that should be kept. Jim can't think of anything that should stay at the moment. It all should go.

He looks at the closed cupboards.

Except for Grandfather's paintbrushes. Dad's tools. Mum's old swap cards. And, of course, Grandmother's silver box. No, he'd better be here to keep an eye on things.

Jim has taken off his dog tags and now they are rattling around uncom-fortably in the front pocket of his trousers. He knows where he should put them—in the place where all the important family documents were kept. It was only a small metal cash box but it was always known as the silver box. It originally came from the farm that Grandfather's parents owned and it always sat in the cupboard above the fridge, next to the unopened bottle of sherry, the maps that were pulled out only when planning for a holiday, and an old letter from a gangster to Grandfather.

He opens the cupboard. The silver box isn't there. He leaves the dog tags on the table, behind the salt and pepper shakers. He hurries down the hallway and out the front door to breathe in some fresh air, then stops at the gate and looks down the street.

Jim has seen Maddie walk up the street many times before. But never like this. Before it was the walk of a girl; now she has a woman's walk.

Maddie is Lukewarm's little sister. She is holding hands with a boy with hair as long as hers. He has grand sideburns that peek out occasionally when strands of hair bounce off his face. He looks at Jim then quickly his eyes dart away. Their hands stop swinging.

The boy carries a khaki canvas shoulder bag full of textbooks. It bounces off his hip as he walks. On the side of the bag is the yellow star of the Viet Cong. Jim looks at it again in case he is mistaken. But no, that's what it is.

Probably the last place he would expect to see such an emblem is outside his front gate in Currawalli Street. Wasn't that one of the reasons why he was sent to war—to stop this star appearing on his street? But it's here anyway. Carried by a local boy who doesn't know any better. A boy who most likely doesn't know what it means.

And Maddie. The little sister of his best friend. The girl who could be so easily teased is looking at Jim now as if daring him to say something.

'Hello, Maddie,' he says at last.

'Hi, Jim. You're home?'

'Yep. Cleaning out the house.'

'Luke said he is going to help you.'

'Really? I haven't seen him yet. He's alright?'

'Same as ever. Annoying and stupid. Just like Dad.' She tries to smile.

'But he's going to help me?'

'That's what he said. You know Luke, though—whether he turns up or not is another thing.'

'I hope he does. I could do with some assistance.' Jim glances at the boy who is continuing to avoid eye contact, looking away down the street.

Maddie says nervously, 'This is Oscar.'

'G'day Oscar.'

Oscar mumbles a hello and pulls his bag around to the front so that Jim can see the Viet Cong star more clearly. Jim stares at it. He remembers a wooden sign by the side of a track leading into the jungle. The track was once used by the Americans. The words, in Vietnamese, were faded, the wood beginning to rot, and the post was leaning heavily towards the creepers and vines. In deference to Maddie and to Lukewarm, Jim says nothing. In English.

But as the young couple begin to walk on, he leans over the gate, firmly takes hold of Oscar's arm and says quietly to him, '*Hay can than cua con rong ban danh thuc.*' A look of fear crosses Oscar's face and he pulls his arm away.

Maddie looks between them, confused. She slides her hand through Oscar's arm and hurries him down the street towards her house.

Jim walks back to the front door, looking down at the carpet in the hallway as he enters. He has always disliked its pattern and colour. It was a subject he and his parents could safely argue about without having to go near the topics that were the real source of disagreement. He didn't think it was old-fashioned enough to keep, even by his parents' standards. They emphatically stated that it was laid by his grandfather, and it was important to have something of his in the house still. After all, his grandfather had bought the house. He was an artist, Jim's dad always said. Not like Lukewarm; a real artist. As if being a good artist meant something that Jim could not be expected to understand.

He is itchy. He can't sit down. Something is scratching at his insides. He recalls a South Vietnamese soldier who started complaining of being constantly itchy on the inside. He couldn't sleep, eat, or sit still. Jim watched him walk into the jungle early one morning, not via the water buffalo tracks that had become well-used troop trails but through the lemongrass bulrushes next to the river. They never saw the man again. That sort of thing happened, he was told; local people disappear sometimes. They are not looked for. Their time on earth is up, they are expected somewhere else. If they don't listen to that command, if they choose to ignore it and continue to follow the demands of their twentieth-century life, then they begin to grow an itch on the inside. It will get worse until it becomes unbearable and they are forced to listen to the order and leave.

He can't think of anywhere else to be so rather than walk out the front door and leave this house behind forever, Jim decides then and there to rip up the carpet. Maybe that will start to change the dynamics of the house and make the itch go away. He knows where the tools are and, relieved to have a purpose, he strides through the house, flings open the screen door on his way to the shed, passing the clothesline with a tea towel flapping like a banner in the wind. Who took the time to peg that on the line? he wonders. A train rattles past at the end of the yard. He doesn't look at it. The shed door sticks a bit and he tells himself out loud that he will fix it soon. Then he stops. Dad had always said just that—he would fix the door soon. It was his dad's voice. He shivers in the wind, which is not cold.

Inside the darkened shed his hand goes straight to the hammer and a screwdriver, hanging in their usual place. The shed smells the same as it always has: dry cut grass and petrol.

Back in the house he begins to lift up the carpet closest to the kitchen. At first he tries to keep the noise down, as though his parents are around somewhere, maybe having a liedown. After a while, he comes to his senses and starts to rip and tear as loudly as he can. To drive out the demons and ghosts. With every inch of wooden floorboard that is exposed, Jim feels a new freshness coming into the house.

He works hard at the job, harder than if he was getting paid to do it. He rolls up the carpet as he goes; by the time he is at the front door, the roll is three feet in diameter. As he pulls away the last foot of carpet, he sees a piece of yellowed paper with old-fashioned handwriting and a thumbprint on it in a rich blue ink.

I laid this carpet in good faith, trusting that the people who walk across it will be worthy friends. I trust that they are. To you pulling up this carpet, I send you good cheer and wish you well.

Johnny Oatley

Lukewarm's dad found a note like this one when he pulled up their lounge room carpet. He said it was a practice that people used to do in the olden days, leave notes under carpets for people in the future to read. As he reads the note, Jim feels a rush of gratitude towards the grandfather he never met. It is a message that no one else in the family will ever read, as if it was written specifically for him.

'Thanks, Grandfather,' Jim says aloud. 'Everybody who crossed this carpet was a worthy friend. Except for one . . .'

He returns the tools to the shed. He decides to leave the carpet rolled up in the hallway for the night rather than put it out the front on the veranda.

Flying home on a crowded 707, it was easier to believe that his parents were no longer around. But here in this house, where the air is thick with their memory, where the scents of the rooms are the scents of both of them, and where the sounds of their voices are soaked into the walls, it isn't as easy.

He pulls the front door shut behind him and walks down the street towards the Choppingblock Hotel. It seems as though he hasn't been hungry for a long time but tonight he might actually have an appetite. He stands at the bar and drinks a glass of whisky while a waiter rushes past him to prepare the hotel dining room for the evening rush. The waiter starts to yell to someone in the kitchen but stops mid-sentence, evidently realising that his words will roll out into the main bar, drift into the ladies lounge and even echo to the bottle shop.

But Jim prefers it when people yell. He feels comfortable with noise and is unnerved by whispering. He tosses back the last of his drink, walks into the dining room and is escorted to a table. The sound system has been turned up to partially drown out the panicked voices in the kitchen. His table is next to a window and he watches as the sun disappears. Some workers are purposefully striding home; others are dragging their feet, truly beaten by the day. People are also beginning to appear in groups, walking at a more leisurely pace. Going out for the night. Three of the groups have entered the dining room by the time Jim has finished his chicken. He pays and walks out into the night.

The house has no place where he can sleep. His bedroom feels as if it belongs to someone else. The television screen glares blankly at him and he selects a book from the bookshelf behind the lounge-room door. When he opens it, though, he sees that someone has torn out the first page. That doesn't make sense to him. He lies down on the couch and looks at the ceiling. He listens to the ghosts in the next room reciting their prayers. Sometime after the informal drag races have stopped out on Choppingblock Road, he walks out into the hallway, lies down on the bare floorboards, calls out once to Mai, and falls asleep.

In the morning, Jim marches across the front yard to his parents' car, parked facing the garage, opens the door and sits in it without starting the engine. It is stuffy inside and smells of perspiration. Not the same as the inside of a troop carrier: that is more the scent of terror. But this is close. A shopping list is lying on the dashboard. He reaches for it but as his fingers touch the paper he withdraws his hand. He looks out of the car and watches a pigeon walking across the driveway towards him. It appears nervous even though there is nothing around. Jim is instantly a sniper again, watching and waiting for an ambush.

Something startles the bird and it flies off to another driveway, another world. Today, Jim wishes he could do that too. He has grown tired of encountering all these memories.

He leans over a little and looks out the rearview mirror. Lukewarm's green and yellow car drives slowly up the road towards number fourteen. It coughs as it stops, just like it always did. Jim looks out the driver's window and across Val's front fence as his lifelong friend climbs out of the car and hitches up his jeans. Like he always has. Jim watches as Lukewarm looks at the church spire rising above the currawalli trees as if he hasn't noticed it before.

Lukewarm is thin in a painful way. He looks threatened by the wind. He bends a little forward when he walks around the back of his car and down to number ten. He picks a piece of honeysuckle from the fence and tucks it into a buttonhole. It falls to the ground after he has taken two steps. His hair is dark and comes down to his eyebrows. He is tall but the thinness makes it unnoticeable until you are standing next to him. He smiles easily like a fool does, and the lines on his face show that he smiles a lot.

Jim opens the car door and climbs out.

'I thought you'd be back soon,' says Lukewarm. 'Trying your dad's car on for size?'

'Sort of, I suppose. I was sitting here getting a grip on things. Wondering how I should start. Whether I should just sell everything and move away.' Jim takes in the smiling face looking at him. 'It's good to see you, Lukewarm.'

'You too, mate. Let's go and have a cup of tea and see what needs to be done.'

'There's a lot, I'm afraid.' Jim leads Lukewarm back towards the house.

'Good. We're just the pair to do it.'

'You're going to help?'

'Yep. Nothing else to do. But I need a cup of tea first. I haven't had one yet. The pot was cold when I got out of the shower. Mum is having one of her days in town going to the pictures and so she wasn't there to make me a fresh one. Ah well . . . you got milk?'

'Yes, got it yesterday.'

Lukewarm tries to blow his fringe off his forehead. Jim smiles to himself. It is something Lukewarm has always done. He looks at Jim and says, 'I had to drive down to the shops to get something. But I got there and then forgot what it was that I had to get.' He smiles. 'That's because I didn't get a cup of tea first.'

The two friends walk into the house together. The only time they touch is when Jim holds the screen door open for Lukewarm and pats him on the back, ushering him through. Lukewarm's hands and shirt are smeared with oil paint, a yellowy red colour. He must have been working on a painting this morning or most of last night. Probably the latter.

'I'm sorry that I didn't write to you,' Jim says quietly.

'That's okay. I didn't expect you to. I guessed that a pen isn't the thing you've got in your pocket during a war.'

'Well, there's that. But really I was worried that I might send back a sense of some of the horrible things I was seeing and I didn't want to do that to you. You're not really the sort of bloke who should see what was happening over there.'

'I saw some of it on TV. Mainly American news. I looked for you but I never saw you.'

'No, I was a long way away from that sort of whizz-bang American stuff.'

'That's good. So . . . am I allowed to talk about your mum and dad being dead or do I have to be—what did my mum say—discreet?'

'No. For fuck's sake don't try to be discreet. I don't mind talking about what happened. If that's what you want to do?' Jim tries to keep his voice from sounding too serious.

'No. I don't want to talk about it at all. I just thought in the course of the day, little things might come up and I want to know whether it's okay to plough through them,' says Lukewarm quietly.

'Thanks for being here, Lukewarm. I appreciate it.'

'Good. You can thank me by coming to a family reunion with me.'

'Is there no other way I can pay you back?'

'Afraid not. You don't have to come this week but you have to promise to come to one with me in the next few months.'

'Okay. If I can't get out of it.'

These reunions aren't of Lukewarm's family, but of strangers. Every Sunday in the Fitzroy Gardens, far-flung families meet up; more often than not, they don't know each other and so Lukewarm jumps in and presents himself as a long-lost member of the family. One that no one can remember. According to him, the key is having the right colour-coded sticker on your lapel that says, 'Hello, I'm . . .' Lukewarm keeps a selection of different-coloured stickers in a case that he carries in the boot of his car.

Lukewarm likes being a stranger in a crowd of strangers who are all being nice to each other. He has always said that it is his vice and, compared to other vices, it is harmless. He started to attend these functions during his one year at art school with his new friends. He gave up art school, the friends, but not the family reunions. 'Hey Jim!' he calls out loudly as they both sit down at the kitchen table.

Jim recoils, and then laughs. 'What?'

'Welcome home. I was worried about you over there. With all those snakes and spiders and bullets.'

'Thanks, mate. It's still strange to be back. I suppose it's going to be weird for a while.'

'You must tell me one day what it was like. Did you meet any girls?'

'Lots.'

'Sleep with any of them?'

'Most of them.'

'Oh wow! I had sex with Lucy Ravenna.'

'From school?'

'Yep. In the back of my car.'

'How is she going?'

'Okay. I don't see her anymore. Once was enough for her, I guess.'

The kettle whistles.

Luke Warne is the son of an almost-famous football player known for shaking the ball above his head whenever he marked it. His trademark. A man suited to playing sport but not much else.

Lukewarm is so called for obvious reasons and because of his lack of passion or excitement about most things. Lukewarm and Jim have been friends all their lives. They went to school together, climbed trees together, caught measles together, fell in love with the same girls, ate at each other's houses, got to know each other's family secrets.

Thanks to Lukewarm's efficiency on the telephone, the cleaners are on the doorstep three hours later. Jim is glad Lukewarm is here to direct them because he is being paralysed by different levels of memories. He moves the tablecloth and sees the mark made by his dad's beer glass. The tea towel next to the sink is the one that his mother bought when they went to Lorne. The edge of it caught fire when Jim was attempting to make pancakes for the first time. There is a bookmark in the middle of a Georgette Heyer novel, as though his mother had just put it down. These sudden memories mean he has to stop every few moments and rearrange his thoughts.

But when he looks up from sorting through what was inside his grandmother's coronation mug, there is a pile out on the front lawn that rises to six feet in the middle and spreads from the black magnolia to the honeysuckle. It looks like garbage. He doesn't want to look at it long enough to begin to distinguish things. They can throw it all away.

There are three cleaners and they know their job. A good team: two men and a woman who is the advance. She walks into a room first and begins to make a pile near the door. The men then transport that pile outside and throw it on the big one. She is cool and calculated. She doesn't miss anything. Jim and Lukewarm have already put aside the things that they think Jim should keep. The wardrobes are untouched. 'We don't do clothes,' the woman had told Lukewarm over the phone. The rest is disposable. From the past. Not needed anymore.

Before long Jim finds himself getting tired. He looks over at Lukewarm to propose they stop but he has his work face on and doesn't notice. Jim decides to stick it out.

The cleaning takes two hours. At four thirty Jim walks down to the shops and returns with a Boston bun and they all stop for a cup of tea.

The cleaners leave as soon as their job is done. The tip truck out the front has been filled and the pile has disappeared from the lawn.

Lukewarm leaves as easily as he arrived.

The house is empty. The couch and armchairs are gone, the beds are gone, the rugs are gone, the lamps are gone, the glasses are gone, the cups and plates, the knives and forks, the pictures on the wall. The piano has stayed, all the wardrobes, the kitchen table and two chairs, the refrigerator. And everything in the shed.

Before the cleaners left, Lukewarm asked them to move each wardrobe into Jim's parents' bedroom. He then shut the door.

And now, the air inside the house is clean.

Jim feels as if something else other than the pile of rubbish has gone. Some shadowy part of his childhood that has been clinging to the furniture; and other, darker things that have been sitting like stale smoke in the back of the drawers.

Standing in the kitchen he hears a knock at the front door. He walks down the hallway, his footsteps ringing on the timber, and opens the door wide, his intuition sensing an odd difference in the air straightaway. On the veranda stands a long-haired young man with his cardigan buttoned crookedly and a t-shirt half tucked in. He looks like a fugitive from the previous decade. Jim has never seen him before. Thomas, the cat from next door, is circling his feet.

'Welcome home,' the man says, looking at Jim's hand on the door. 'I am a neighbour. I have brought you a magazine as a housewarming gift.'

Jim feels a cold wind. He accepts the gift—it looks like an electronics magazine—but doesn't stand aside to let the man enter.

'Thanks very much,' Jim says. 'I'm still getting settled. There's junk everywhere.' There isn't any junk. Jim hears the danger in the silence. The long-haired man is tapping his foot to some music that must be playing in his head.

Jim is wary. He rolls back onto the balls of his feet. Ready to react. 'Which house do you live in?' he asks.

'Number thirteen. Just across the street there. Next door to the priest.'

'Oh. Been here long?'

'Two years to the day. Two years goes pretty quick when you're busy. My parents normally live there with me but they have gone to Poland. That's where they come from.'

Jim looks closely at the face of the man but he can read nothing in his eyes. He says, 'My parents lived here. I grew up in this house. I've come back to clear things up after what happened.'

'What happened?'

'You don't know?' Jim drops his hands to his side, alert and ready.

'No. I keep strange hours. Often I am asleep or else I am somewhere else . . . if you know what I mean.' He smiles a disturbed smile. Jim doesn't know what he could mean.

'You didn't hear the gunshots or the police sirens?'

'No, nothing. I generally work with headphones on so I don't hear anything.'

'I thought the police might have knocked on your door.'

'If they did, I didn't hear. Why would they knock on my door?'

'Routine, I imagine. To see if you saw anything.'

'What a shame I didn't hear them knock. I see lots of things.'

'Oh well. They might come back. What's your name?'

'Peter Alexis. I am from number thirteen—'

'Yes, you told me . . .'

'You are more than welcome to come over anytime you like. I will be up. I only sleep four hours at a time. If I don't hear you knocking, it means I am either asleep, working with the headphones on or elsewhere.'

'Okay. I'll remember that.'

'And what's your name?'

'Jim.'

'Pleased to meet you, Jim. My name is Peter and I will walk home now,' he says in a monotone.

'Thanks again for the magazine.'

'That's okay. I am trying to be a more outgoing person. Left to me, I would stay inside for years and never talk to anybody. But the priest says I should be forcing myself to be a member of the community. I go to the pub.'

'Do you?' Jim says in a steady voice, still alert.

'Sometimes. Bye.' Peter turns and leaves. He fumbles with the front gate and is unable to close it. Jim tells him not to worry and shuts the front door. Suddenly, he runs at full speed down the hallway, through the back door and up to the back fence. He turns, and without stopping he runs back inside again. Then he sinks to the floor in the hallway and begins the breathing exercises that Brent, his sergeant, taught him.

After three-quarters of an hour, Jim is back in the kitchen thinking about dinner. There's nothing in the fridge, nothing in the cupboard except Boston bun. Still, he always liked a walk to the shop. He will think about what to buy on the way there. He turns right out of the front gate and begins to count his steps as he walks.

The Hendersons live at number eight. They are the perpetual new-comers to the street, even though they have been here for ten years. They have become known for a few things; noticed just as any new ripple in a pond is. At three o'clock one morning Mrs Henderson ran up the street in her nightie after a domestic screaming match. No one ever mentions it but everybody knows about it, even if they didn't see it happen. The Hendersons know that everybody knows about it and they think that they have to work to keep it unmentioned.

But the fact is, the Hendersons don't have to worry. No one will ever say anything. There are secrets that you keep inside your head, secrets that you keep inside your house and secrets that you keep inside your street. Mrs Henderson's nightie-fluttering run falls into the last category; that's why nothing will ever be said. Amid the Hendersons' insincere attempts to be cordial and everybody else's suspicion of the efforts they make, strange bonds and friendships are forged. Mr Henderson has become a person who can be relied upon to donate paper money to any child who knocks on his door with a charity can. Mrs Henderson has so little knowledge of how the women of the surrounding houses interact together and deal with the domestic business of the street that she is never included in anything important but always in something mundane or slight like a cake baking, or a group fitness walk, or cups of tea at the church.

Number six is the home of Norm Norman. He is the owner of Bruiser the dog, the unofficial guardian of the street. Norm appears to have always been old; he looks the same as he did when Jim was a toddler learning to walk. Jim can think of no other way to describe him; Norm is a nice man. As a word, nice has lost the effect it used to have; now it's another way of saying ineffectual, or neutral, or even dull. But Norm is nice in the traditional way, generous with what he has, trustworthy, and he doesn't ever take sides. Jim has always liked Norm. Everybody has always liked Norm. People are viewed with suspicion if they say they don't like him much.

But now the house looks faded, as if no one lives there anymore.

Number four belongs to the Alberto family. Old Joe Alberto died when Jim was thirteen. His daughter, Rosa, now lives in the house with her own husband and two children and Old Joe's widow Gina. Old Joe was such a strong presence. It still feels as if he is standing at the front gate.

Lower Lance lives alone at number two. He doesn't talk to many people. He is a quiet man. Not rude like his father was. When Edward ruled this house, people crossed the street rather than walk past it. When he eventually had a heart attack on his front lawn and died, people in the street were secretly relieved.

Jim, without conscious thought, speeds up as he walks past. Most people do.

As he rounds the corner, Jim can see the bustle of the shops up ahead. He walks into the grocery store still undecided and begins a circuit, looking for inspiration. It comes quickly: steak, egg and mashed potato. While he waits at the cash register, the young woman from number nine comes in, her head down, searching in her bag. She walks straight into an exiting woman who lives in Borneo Street. They both apologise and laugh. The sound fills up the front of the shop like little bells tinkling. For a moment it makes everybody smile.

The afternoon traffic is building up as Jim walks home. He has to wait to cross at Little Road. Halfway across the road, the shopping bag hits the back of his knee. It is only a tiny knock on an unprotected part of his body that he wasn't previously aware of. He shakes his head in resignation and turns into Currawalli Street; while he is walking towards the honeysuckle, he watches a funeral procession leave the church and drive towards him. The pain in the back of his knee from the grocery bag begins to resonate up his thigh. At the front gate of number ten, he looks at the house with new eyes. He imagines that he is seeing it the same way that his father had each day when he came home from work. I think I will paint it a different colour, he says to himself. Halfway up the front path, he suddenly remembers his father coming in the front door and calling to his wife: 'What about green?' or 'What about yellow?'

The house had never been painted. But now Jim can understand the reason for the sudden inspiration and why it didn't last for very long. Once his father closed the front door behind him, there was a house full of more important things to deal with. Besides, he had never liked the smell of paint. His childhood bedroom, the one that had become Jim's, always smelled of oil paint and turpentine no matter what his mother did to make it go away.

He walks down the hallway to the kitchen. He has seen a movement out of the corner of his right eye but there is nothing there. He touches the telephone while he is looking around. It rings. He jumps.

'You all settled?'

'Getting there.' He doesn't recognise the voice. A girl. He needs to hear more, so he asks, 'How are you?'

'Alright, I suppose. It's nice of you to ask.'

There is only one person this could be. Jim stiffens. 'You've got a cold, Jenny?'

'Yes I have. For two weeks. It won't go away.'

'What are you ringing me for?' Jim asks brusquely.

'I don't know. I know you've come home from the war and you're staying at your old house in Currawalli Street. I guess I want to let you know that I still think of you. Not in a girlfriend way. Just in a . . . connected way.'

'I thought you severed that connection before I left?'

'Sometimes it seems severed. Sometimes it seems pretty solid. I suppose this is one of those solid times.' Her voice begins to falter.

Jim notices that he is pulling his stomach muscles tight. He has a memory of this somewhere in his mind. He asks, 'How did you know I was back?'

'My mum was told by Lukewarm's mum. I thought I should ring.'

'Why?'

'I don't know. I suppose I wanted to hear your voice. I wanted to know if it still did anything to me.'

His stomach muscles remain tight. He remembers now what this reminds him of. Forcing himself back to the conversation, he asks, 'Oh. Does it?'

'I can't tell. I knew the phone number off by heart though.' She tries to say it lightly.

'That's something.'

'Did you think about me over there?'

'Not much.'

'But some?'

'A little. Jenny, is this all you rang me for?' Jim asks coldly.

'Yep. That's it. Doesn't seem like a good idea now. I wish I had rung someone else instead.'

Jim knows that she is about to burst into tears. That knowledge, and many other things, makes him say, 'I wish you had too.'

She hangs up. Jim scratches his chin as he thinks about the phone conversation and the memory that had come to him. In a tent one night by the light of a hurricane lamp, he listened to a classified operations soldier tell him and a few of his comrades that men expecting they are about to be tortured tighten their stomach muscles in such a pronounced way that before beginning any interrogation, torturers will amuse themselves by having the men take off their shirts. Jim was struck at the time by how the shadows climbing on the soldier's face made him look suddenly sinister, as did the delight he took in recounting the information.

Jenny once had a special place in his life. When he was someone else. She was his girlfriend. She left him because he had been conscripted into the army: being the girlfriend of a soldier was as uncool as you could possibly get. Jenny didn't want to be uncool. She dropped him. He put on his uniform with a broken heart. He eventually found out that he was not alone; many of the young men in his outfit had been dumped before they left Australia for Vietnam and some even after they arrived in that strange, dangerous, beautiful place. It was a cruel thing, being a soldier.

The truth is he forgot her pretty quickly over there and only thought seriously about her once, in Mai's room, when the afternoon sun ran across a torn newspaper on the floor, highlighting a photograph of a girl whose hair ran down onto her shoulders like Jenny's did.

By the time the steak is in the vertical grill that he found at the back of a cupboard, overlooked by the cleaners, Jim's equilibrium has returned. He is surprised to learn that Jenny's voice is still in his head;

surprised that, after the things he has seen, she can still have any effect on him at all.

He turns and sits down on a chair. His Saigon radio is sitting on the table. He turns it on, listens for a moment and then turns it off.

Advertisements are starting to hurt his head.

Just as he is finishing his meal there is a loud knock at the door. He walks down the hallway to open it.

Patrick is standing on the porch. 'Welcome home, Jim. Here's a present. It's a book.'

Jim looks down at the wrapped gift in Patrick's hand. He invites Patrick in. The book is thrust into his hands as Patrick crosses the threshold.

'The kitchen in the same place?'

'Yes. Of course.' Jim looks across the road and sees Mary standing inside her screen door, watching. The veranda light is on. Jim can see the moths circling it. She waves. Jim waves back and looks up at the sky as he closes the front door. It is dark but he has known darker. It looks like rain. He is about to say this to Patrick but by the time they reach the kitchen it has begun to fall. For a few moments, the drops are small and gentle but then, as the noise on the corrugated-tin roof grows louder, the rain becomes a summer torrent. Enough to stop conversation. Patrick and Jim sit contentedly together and watch the rain through the window. After about two minutes, Jim holds up the teapot and Patrick nods his head. They conduct their first over-the-kitchen-table conversation in silence. The rain thunders down for twenty-five minutes. It is so loud that neither of them would have heard the phone if it rang. When the rain stops it does so just as suddenly as it began. Jim's ears are distantly ringing in the sudden silence. Patrick puts both hands onto the table and hoists himself up. He is leaving.

'Do you think it will rain?' he asks dryly.

'No, I don't reckon,' Jim answers in a similar tone.

'Oh well. I'd better water the roses.'

It's an old joke that Patrick used to say to Jim's dad. It still works well as an end to a conversation. Together they walk down the hallway, then Patrick turns at the door.

'I have walked down this hall many times. And not once have I had cause to say goodbye. I was here the night before . . . just for a cup of tea. Like now. I should have said goodbye then, but I didn't know . . . what was going to happen. They were nice people. I liked them. I still do. Oh well . . . goodnight, Jim.'

Jim can only nod his head. He watches Patrick pick his way through the puddles on the path. The moon is reflected in the water.

This time Jim walks into the lounge room and sits cross-legged on the floor facing the window. Empty, this now feels to be more his space. The only items left to link it with the past are the old piano and the photo that has always sat on the music stand on the lid. In it, Grandmother is standing behind Grandfather as he sits looking at the camera.

Because the piano has always been in that spot, Jim looks on it as if it is a wall or a door, solid and neutral. He still feels connected to his grandmother and the photograph on the stand.

This house had been his grandparents'. His father had grown up in it. The residue left by years of laughter and yelling and talking and crying, of bitterness and anger, of affection and contentment, of confusion and coldness is always going to be in the corners and on the window-sills of this room. No amount of dusting would clean any room of that type of familial dust.

Jim looks up, sensing something watching him, surprised that his head had absently dropped to his chest. Thomas the cat is at the window. Neither of them is alarmed at the sudden eye contact. The orange cat mouths something and then withdraws into the night.

Jim leaves the curtains open. As the night becomes blacker, he settles in and waits for the ghosts. But they don't come. Maybe they know they no longer belong inside. He will keep the trees and flowers the same for them outside; they can walk around out there. They all can live in this place together.

He shakes himself. He is still too young to have so many dead people in his life.

Trust me.

Jim thinks at first that he has heard the words spoken aloud. But there are no ripples in the silence around him. It is unbroken; nothing has been said. Those words were scratched into the footpath outside the supermarket this afternoon and, like the echo of a bell, they must have resonated in his head. And then he remembers Mai said them to him once when he hesitated before going with her down a crowded alley behind her parents' house.

He dismisses the memory sadly and decides to go to bed. Bed is on the floor in the lounge room. He is not ready for anywhere else yet. Before he falls asleep, he hears a long freight train go by beyond the back fence. It rocks him to sleep, as it has always done.

❧ Chapter Twelve ❧

When all is said and done, Patrick knows what his job is. He knows what is needed. He has done it all his adult life. And even though he can do it without thinking, he prefers to put a lot of thought into it.

Being a stationmaster is a science. A stationmaster needs to know the exact timetables; what unexpected delays may occur to his trains (a good stationmaster calls any train that passes through the station 'his'); which driver to approach to ask for a child to be given a birthday treat of a drive in the front cabin; how many carriages each train will have; which carriage of any approaching train is the emptiest; and to be alert for any mother struggling to alight with a pram, or any elderly veteran or widow trying to measure the drop of the step. He also likes to know how the weather is panning out. (He keeps a dozen umbrellas in his office to lend: they are always returned.) He tries to remember everybody's name. A brisk 'Good morning, Mr Chard' can put a sudden spring in the step of someone reluctantly heading into a new day.

And he likes the platform to be kept clean; the first sweep in the morning he always does himself. People smile more easily on a clean platform: that's what he tells the station assistants, and isn't that what their real job is? Isn't that what everybody's job is? To make each other smile? The response from his assistants has always been blank stares.

There was only ever going to be one problem with the job. He knew it was coming. But it still surprised him when it did. Patrick was retired from the railways one year ago.

There is a new stationmaster, a former senior assistant from Flinders Street Station in the city. Patrick has known Brian McGuinness since he started work there, young and keen, a stationmaster in the making.

But Patrick wasn't ready to give Brian his station.

As he always has, Patrick still goes to his station every morning to sweep the platform, between the 6.08 and the 6.18 (stopping all stations except North Melbourne). The customers expect to see him, the new stationmaster expects to see him, the train drivers wave to him as they always have. But then, at around ten o'clock, his wife or one of the neighbours comes to get him. He is resigned to leaving the station in Brian's hands; although he is an inexperienced young man, all in all he has the makings of a good stationmaster. But if only Brian McGuinness was somewhere else. This is Patrick's station. Everybody knows that.

Brian McGuinness knows it. He allows Patrick to sweep the platform every morning and stand at the gate and greet the peak-hour passengers. He is happy for Patrick to keep on wearing his stationmaster's uniform. Brian realises that it makes his own job easier.

But it doesn't make Mary's job any easier. She sends Patrick off every morning, cut lunch in hand. At ten am, after dropping in to the shops, she walks up to the station. She always says hello to Brian, watching his face for a hint of displeasure at Patrick's morning routine, but never finds one. On the days she can't walk up to the station herself, she asks a neighbour to collect her husband; sometimes, if they happen to be going up to the shops, one of them will ask her whether she would like them to get him. Patrick then eats his cut lunch on the front veranda, and she watches as his mind evaporates with each cheese sandwich.

Patrick studies the current timetables at night while Mary watches the television. Mary sometimes looks across at him during the advertisements. He doesn't generally notice but when he does, he smiles at her quietly as he has always done. That is what makes Mary continue to support his habits. She doesn't know why the rest of the street offers support but she suspects that Patrick is well liked.

The afternoon sun is hot. Jim is standing in front of the statue of the soldier, looking absently at the names. Suddenly he can sense someone coming towards him. The birds have stopped singing. They know there is danger about. The jungle is still.

He doesn't try to stop the tension as it runs down his neck muscles into his spine, rushing through his arms until it reaches his fingernails, then racing down the tendons of his legs to the soles of his feet. His hearing becomes acute. His eyes no longer see the statue. He concentrates on the movement of the wind on his body and the sounds of the person approaching, trying to register any change that might signify an attack. Inwardly he tightens everything, ready to spring in whatever direction his intuition tells him. His hands are clenched, his jaw is tight.

'Hi, Jim.'

Breathe out. Wind everything down. Blood rushing through body. Wait for a moment. Smile at statue. Use the face muscles. Lift the toes. Use the calf muscles. Pretend to be chewing gum. Find a release. Think about Mozart.

Come back. You are safe.

'Hi, Maddie. What's happening?'

'Nothing much. I was coming home from uni . . . saw you standing here . . . came over to say hello properly.'

'You going to uni? That's great. Doing what?'

'Arts. Everybody is doing arts.'

'Are they?'

'Seems like it. I don't know what to say, Jim,' Maddie says, her voice suddenly quiet.

'About what?'

'About you going over there. About your mum and dad. About . . . anything, I suppose.'

'Don't worry. There's not really anything to say. Life is going to go on, whether we like it or not.'

'I don't have any words . . .'

'Is that bloke your boyfriend?' Jim tries to sound light.

'Oscar? Yes, I think he is. You know, Jim. Once I used to . . . think you were . . . pretty cool. I had a crush . . .'

'Did you? I thought I was imagining it.'

'So you knew? It was that obvious?'

'No, it wasn't obvious at all. I didn't really notice until your brother brought it up.'

'You mean, Luke knew? Oh my God. That's dreadful.' She turns away from Jim, looks down the street and waits for her embarrassment to disappear. Jim smiles and stares up at the statue when he speaks.

'It's not too bad. He didn't let on to you that he knew. Some little sisters get tortured by their brothers for things like that.'

'I suppose so. Jim, I was sad when you went away. You looked as if someone had . . . dressed you up in that uniform.'

'It felt like it for a long time.'

'I was so mad at Jenny. For what she did . . . I put dog shit in her handbag.'

Jim laughs. 'Did you? Good!'

'Don't tell her, will you. No one knows that I did it. It was a big drama in the neighbourhood for a long time.'

Jim nods. They look at each other. He stays quiet but wants to tell her to be careful about what she and Oscar do to people like him. To warn her that people who have been over there can't help how they react; Oscar might say the wrong thing or show that star on his bag to the wrong person and Maddie might get hurt too. That these are truly dangerous people who are finding it hard to come back and be the same as before they left. But Jim doesn't want to scare her and so he says nothing.

'It was horrible?'

He shrugs. 'It wasn't too bad.'

What he wants to do is take her by the shoulders and look into her eyes and tell her the truth. That it was beyond horrible. Horrible is having to lie motionless and let a poisonous snake slide over your leg because you are in a ditch that is its home and you are hiding from a man with a gun who will blow your arm off your shoulder. Beyond horrible is holding someone you have never met before as your friends try to press his intestines back into the hole in his stomach and your trousers are drenched with his blood while you look at him, trying to think of something to say. He knows he is about to die just as you do and the memory of the look in his eye and the way the grip of his hand goes from strong and desperate to soft and flaccid is something that doesn't fade. That's what is beyond horrible. That's what he thinks about at night sometimes and what he feels he has a responsibility to keep to himself.

But Maddie must have seen something of his thoughts written across his face. She has gone white. Jim reaches for her and holds her as her whole body shakes with sobs. He holds her for a couple of minutes. Then she pulls back from him.

'I'm so sorry, Jim. I'm so sorry. I'm so sorry . . .'

She turns and runs home. Just as she used to do when he and Luke-warm teased her. Jim watches her, unable to call out.

Hay can than cua con rong ban danh thuc.

Beware of which sleeping dragons you awaken.

The reverend from the church at the end of Currawalli Street is a big man. He is comfortable with his size and that confidence makes him somewhat disarming, rather than imposing. He used to think people were drawn to him because of his character, his eloquence, his courage, even his sense of humour, but eventually he realised that they liked to stand close to him because of the power that lies just behind his gentle

manner. Men tell him things that they probably don't tell their friends.
Women tell him things that they don't tell their husbands.

His name is Jan Domak. His wife is Sally. They live in the manse
next to the church. They have been there for five years; the bishop has
no interest in moving his reverends around. Jan doesn't mind; he likes
it here. The double murder was a little bit confronting but he was able
to draw on the things he knew of violence and its consequences and he
found some appropriate passages from the Bible to assist those in his
congregation who were suffering.

It is a striking thing, he thinks as he walks down Currawalli Street
towards Little Road, that the art of living can be shrouded in so much
unimportant incidental dust that it is easily forgotten just how frag-
ile life is and what a thin knife edge each human being walks along
between life and death. And when someone falls as hard as the Oatleys
did, how devastating it is, to people who should know better—himself
included.

This afternoon he has forsaken his collar for a turtle-neck jumper.
The Choppingblock Hotel is where he is headed.

That strange thing has happened again.

Three weeks ago, in the pub, a woman made a wordless erotic suggestion to him with her eyes and her lips. Since then, as is his custom,
he has stood in the public bar of the Choppingblock Hotel at four
o'clock in the afternoon every Tuesday and Thursday and she has been
there in the ladies lounge opposite him and made the same suggestions
in the same unmistakable way. So he is striding confidently towards the
hotel today to see if he can gently move the adventure forward. The
first time something like this happened, he expected to feel guilt and

remorse—for his wife, Sally, who has never done him any ill, and for the church and his calling, which have also never done him harm. But, truth be told, all of these episodes have given him a deeper understanding of his married life, his religious devotion, and even himself. He knows that if anything beyond a physical attraction ever develops then it will have devastating effects on those things. But he is not planning to let this happen. It is this realisation and decision that puts the spring in his step and makes the coins in his pocket jingle.

He knows that this woman lives in Currawalli Street and that she is aware of what line of work he is in, because he has seen her and her family in the Sunday congregation and she has also seen him with Sally. So she knows too that he is married. But desire is an untameable beast that must, on occasions, be given its head. And so on he walks, to feed the beast. They are the words he uses in his head. And he laughs aloud because it sometimes sounds as if a destructive monster is about to be released, when in fact he is doing nothing more than seeing if an arrangement can be made between two consenting adults. There is nothing to feel guilt or remorse about; it is just playful subterfuge.

He walks in the front door of the hotel, looks briefly up at the tin mugs on the wall and, as he always does, greets the barman, who sets a coaster in the spot where Jan always stands and then turns to pour his drink. Jan walks up to the bar, touches the coaster once and looks up. Through the bottles and glasses, he looks into the ladies lounge. She is there, and she returns his look. He glances meaningfully down at his hand and, after the barman has placed his drink on the coaster, he turns his hand over and opens it, palm up. In fact, he fully extends it, and as he does he looks at her. It is a strange movement for somebody to make and he sees a ripple go through her as she tries not to show any excitement. His gesture is an open hand accepting her invitation. No one else looking on would know that, but she does. He watches her take a deep breath and feels the need to do so as well. They breathe out at the same time.

Her friend, sitting with her at the table, says something and quickly she turns to answer. The moment is slow to be swallowed up by the lunatic orchestra of voices and the cigarette smoke, but it gradually disappears and he attends to his drink. He watches her as she draws heavily on a cigarette and listens to her companion's comments. Only once does she look up at him again; it is only for a very tiny moment and there is no readable expression in her eyes but that look is branded like a flash in his mind. This situation is one that will drive him crazy if he does not do something about it. He knows that about himself.

Suddenly she and her companion are standing and picking up their bags. They walk through the public bar to the door. She is looking the other way as she brushes up against him but he feels the warm touch of her hand as she passes a small piece of paper into his. The same hand that he opened. He looks elsewhere. He hears the front door close and feels the blood running up his neck behind his ears. He holds the note, if that's what it is, tightly in his hand and finishes his drink. He quickly orders another and makes a show of looking through his wallet for the money. When the drink is delivered, he feels that he can unfold and read the note as if it is something he has come across in his wallet.

483 5202 Between 6.15 and 6.20.

He puts the note into his jacket pocket and finishes his drink much more quickly than he normally does. He says goodnight to the man standing at the bar next to him; it happens to be his neighbour in Currawalli Street, an odd but friendly man with lively eyes and long scraggly hair who claims to be Polish. He is opening his mouth trying to say something as Jan walks away.

Jan leaves the hotel by the front door and is at his desk in the church office by five thirty, looking over some receipts but paying no attention to the figures. He sits at his desk for a while then stands up and walks around the room. At sixteen minutes past six he rings the number on the note. It rings once before she picks it up.

'Yes?'

'I am at the office, working. I'll be here till late. Do you know where it is?'

'Yes, out the back of the church.'

'Come through the main doors. They are the only ones that are open.'

'I might just do that.' She hangs up while Jan is waiting for her next word.

And so begins an affair that happily exists only in the twilight gloom of a church office. Never will it be acknowledged elsewhere.

❧ Chapter Thirteen ❧

Sally Domak has always walked fast. Her steps are small but her legs move quickly. She is used to having to stop and wait for walking companions to catch up to her. It is something she has been doing all her life. That's one of the reasons she prefers to walk alone. She walks up and down Currawalli Street as often as anybody else but is so intent on walking that she doesn't see in the front yards or on the verandas the people waiting for her to address them.

She generally leaves for university early in the morning, intent on catching the express train. It is earlier than she needs to leave but this is the train she wants to catch. The man who was the stationmaster told her about it on the platform one morning. She had seen him at church but didn't realise that he lived in Currawalli Street. He is no longer the Choppingblock stationmaster but, like all decent occupations, his job will not leave him alone even though he has finished with it. She used to talk to him at the station often, but then she began to catch this earlier train. He doesn't look up from his broom so early in the morning.

She likes Currawalli Street at this time. The night has picked up her skirts and left and the day has just stretched the sleep out of her bones and is easing into the business at hand. Willy-willies are a different colour; they carry the pink of the early morning sun and rise higher in the lighter air. The statue of the soldier glistens with dew, delicate lines of spider webs drift into her face, the sound of her quick steps echoes in the quiet street. Sometimes she can still hear Jan snoring as she closes the front gate. Not because he is a loud snorer but because she is attuned to it.

At first, Sally went to university to study European painting but midway through she switched to social studies. In some ways she feels like she is waking up for the first time. That's why she didn't tell Jan about changing courses. She suspects now that he has happily kept her in a state of slumber ever since they have been married. She has realised that keeping secrets is as much a part of a marriage as confessions and disclosures.

The university is on the outskirts of the city proper and Sally spends her whole day discussing with other women what they are happy about, what they are angry about, and what they can do to change what they think must be changed. The course is called social studies but most of her classmates have crossed out the word 'social' on their notebooks and replaced it with 'women's'.

And today they are marching on the city in the first of a series of strategic demonstrations.

Sally steps off the train and begins to work out what she needs to organise in what order. She is in the university grounds before anybody else and by the time that her classmates arrive, most of the preparation is done.

The protest chants are carefully orchestrated; Sally organises choir practices after class that appear at first to be quite innocent and unremarkable. But this is where the most powerful chants are chosen and arranged. Lessons have been learned from rallies around the world. Women have returned from Lebanon, Thailand, Burma, Guatemala, China and Ireland, places where the power of voices chanting in unison is recognised. Sometimes the windows seem to rattle, even when there is no chanting.

The anecdote that galvanises all of Sally's classmates and what binds them to their concerns is one that she innocently told one morning over a cup of tea. How Jan likes to ask her questions about her study but never listens to the replies. Yet he considers himself to be an enlightened man. And every woman had a similar story.

And as far as she is concerned, therein lies the real issue. Probably most men need only to be woken up rather than beaten over the head. The enemy doesn't lie in men; it lies elsewhere. Men and women, in different ways, have both been suppressed by discrimination and chauvinism. That's the opinion she currently holds, especially when she sits across the table from Jan and sees in his eyes the delight that he has always shown when he is with her.

The rally begins as a decent downhill walk to the centre of the skyscrapers, far enough away that the most passionate and strident of chants begins to sound tired and unconvincing by the time any protest reaches the parliament building that signifies the centre of the city. And so it was Sally's suggestion to stay silent until the marchers turn the corner into the main street.

And as they walk the silence becomes powerfully dramatic. Anybody who sees the line of silent marching women, their heads bowed, thinks they are witnessing a religious ceremony of great richness and intense dread. The silence held along the line makes the energy of the marching women grow. And so the strong ranks are among the shoppers and businessmen before anybody has time to comprehend the meaning of their presence, and when they begin their chant, it is like an explosion: the resonating calls like weapons, slashing and stabbing at the occupants and representatives of the Establishment.

Peter Alexis, the young Polish man with the wild eyes and long scraggly hair who lives at number thirteen, is resigned to living alone. At this very moment, two o'clock precisely in the afternoon, he is seeing a young woman out the front door. It is for the first and last time. He doesn't know it for sure yet, although he suspects it.

Most people think Peter is strange. Sometimes, strange in the simplest of ways. In quaint, gentle ways. Sometimes not; some people think that his apparent simplicity hides a tangled and dangerous complexity just under the surface. He is not disliked; he is just best left alone.

On some days, strange is too strong a word for Peter. Odd is better.

Merryn is turning the screen door handle as she listens to Peter continue his story about a casual evening he once had in Geelong. The tightness of her grip belies the pleasant expression on her face. She feels that it is okay to turn and look at Peter now that the door is swinging open.

'So remember,' he says, 'Friday night is my Electronic Music Night. Once a month without fail. I stay home and listen to some music. I get Chinese food. It's a real buzz. Can you be here at seven thirty this Friday?'

'I don't think I want to. Look, Peter, I'm not sure that we're suited. We should let this settle down and see what is there before . . . before.'

'But this is only the first time you have come around.' The smile leaves Peter's face as he realises what Merryn is saying. 'Oh I see . . . I understand . . . Well, thanks very much. It was really good getting to know you.'

'I'm sorry, Peter. I wish it could be different.'

'Don't worry about it. At least you came around. That's the main thing. Are you going to be okay to get home?'

'Of course. I'll just walk down to the station. I'm glad there are no hard feelings.'

Peter looks confused. 'So am I. See you later.'

Merryn walks to the front gate. It's a sunny afternoon. The door is already closed when she looks back. She won't visit him again. She had liked the look of Peter when she met him at her sister's boyfriend's party. She thought he was shy because he didn't say very much. She was pleased to come to his home and see his cat paintings when he asked. She likes artists. But she soon realised he was not what she thought he was. Which is more her fault than his. She has always misjudged people, especially men; she often assumes there is more to them than there actually is.

To her right is another house, a little grander than Peter's, then the little park with the statue of the soldier with the bowed head and, beside that, the church. She stops and looks at the church again. The letter 'T' has fallen off the sign on the wall and so it reads THE CHURCH OF CHRIS. She laughs. She turns and begins to walk down the street. Across the road a young man is trimming a long-established honeysuckle growing along a fence. She likes honeysuckle. He stops pruning to look at her. She looks back at him, unafraid of meeting his eye. There is something about this man gardening that gives her an unusual courage. He is thin and muscled like a circus worker. His cropped hair is black and his shirt looks too small for him. Perhaps he hasn't worn it for a long time, she thinks.

'What made me think that?' She speaks aloud but quietly to herself. The young man is still looking at her. He has seen her lips move.

'I love honeysuckle!' she calls out.

'Good for you!' he calls back.

She smiles and walks on. Then she hears footsteps behind her. When she turns he is standing there. He has green combat boots on. They look well worn. She looks up at his face. The shadow of the jungle is there. Not that she recognises it for what it is.

He hands her a spray of honeysuckle. 'There you are,' he says. He is halfway back across the street before she can call out thanks. He either doesn't hear or ignores her. She resumes walking. At the end of the street she turns and looks back again. He has disappeared.

She walks along Little Road to the station. Two streets run off to the left: the first, closest to Currawalli Street, is Borneo Street and the next is Battlefield Street. It has a few shops perched awkwardly near the corner. She can't see what they are. Her grandparents used to live in Borneo Street. Not this one, but in a suburb on the other side of town.

By the time she is standing on the platform, the train is pulling into the station. She is quickly gone, transported away, thinking about the honeysuckle man rather than Peter.

*

Jim watches the young woman leave number thirteen. She walks quickly to the gate. He sees her notice the sign on the church and thinks for an instant of the letter T now on his mantelpiece. She is dressed like a hippie girl going out for the day. Her hair is brown and long. She looks like she is wearing combat boots, but they are probably not. They don't have the right heels for the jungle. He looks down at his own. They are the only shoes that fit him at the moment. His feet grew so used to being wet and swollen that they are now a half size bigger than before he left.

He has been struggling with the honeysuckle growing across the front fence. It is old, grows bark like dried-out leather. But it is the smell of his childhood and represents his life in this street. The strongest memory he got of home while in Vietnam was when his unit walked through a deserted village and he caught the fragrance of honeysuckle on the wind. That was the day before Brent stepped on the mine.

Over there he was surprised how often he thought about this honeysuckle. Going away, he had discovered, is all about thinking of where you have come from. It wasn't number ten Currawalli Street that he remembered specifically, but rather the smell of gum trees and bushfire smoke, the big empty sky, the sound of his feet on the footpath, the magpies calling out to each other, someone laughing in the distance, radio sounds rolling across a front lawn, the knowledge that the heat would go away at the end of the day. And the sweet smell of this honeysuckle.

The young woman is wearing a pair of jeans that look new. He sees her lips move but he doesn't hear what she says. He concentrates on her face and forces the echoes of Brent's scream to go away.

'I love honeysuckle!'

So that's what she said. What do you say to that? Brent's one scream is like sonic glue on the back wall of his mind as he tries to find an adequate response.

She is abreast of him now on the other side of the street. If he doesn't say something then she will think he is mute or, even worse, uninterested.

'Good for you!' That's it? That's the best you can come up with? What's wrong with you? No wonder she's still walking.

Quickly he picks up a few trimmed stems of the honeysuckle and as he walks across the street, ties them together into a spray. He knows that she hears him coming up behind her; he is making enough noise so that she won't mistake him for a sandshoed assassin.

As she turns he holds out the honeysuckle. 'There you are.'

All of a sudden he realises that he doesn't need this. He wants to be inside. He doesn't need to be handing out flowers to strange girls like he is a pimpled teenager. He turns and walks back across the street to number ten and goes inside.

But for the next hour, he struggles to remove from his thoughts the picture of that girl's brown hair moving towards him as she accepted the honeysuckle. It is a long time since anything good has stuck in his head. It brushes away the thought of the strange look on Brent's face when he put his foot down and heard the mine click.

Lance Barron lives at number sixteen. He has lived here for ten years. He likes his house. He likes the colour of it, he likes the trees that shelter it, he likes the creaking sound the corrugated-tin roof makes when the sun heats it up, he likes the ruined chook sheds that have grown over with geraniums, he likes having to cut the grass in the backyard, he likes the train line at the back, he likes the house two doors down with its face silhouettes supporting the eaves, he likes living next door to an almost-famous footballer, but most of all he likes Debra, inside his house.

He is known in the street as Lance From Up The Street or Upper Lance. He doesn't mind: they are better nicknames than some. The reason for the nicknames is so that Lance From Up The Street or Upper Lance is not confused with Lance From Down The Street, also known as Lower Lance. The two men are of roughly the same age, but of vastly different temperaments. Lance From Up The Street is calm, and happy to talk to people. Lance From Down The Street is reclusive and tense. They share the name and the street and the neighbours but that is all.

Upper Lance walks to his front gate and checks the letterbox. It is empty. He sees Jim from number ten run across the road and give some-thing to a girl who is walking on the other side of the street, then turn and walk quickly home.

Jim must be a tortured young man, Lance assumes. He was a nice boy before he went to the war. He might still be a nice boy; Lance has not spoken to him since he was brought home from Vietnam. He remembers him as a kid who rode his bike a lot and sometimes sat out on the footpath and looked at Lance's house. He was good to talk to, kept Lance informed about things that he didn't know he was interested in. Football. Rock and roll music. The World Surfing Championship.

Lance also assumes that Jim is suffering because he has not come home like a returning soldier should. Not that any of these soldiers will.

According to Debra. The war in Vietnam has made everybody uncomfortable; rather than being grateful, the community hopes that if they ignore the soldiers they will disappear back into the streets and lanes where they came from. And the war can be forgotten.

Lance is forty-two years old. Debra is thirty-eight. They have one child, Pam, who is twelve. At the moment Pam is on holiday in New South Wales with her grandparents.

Debra comes to the front door. She calls to Lance, 'Has he been?'

Lance shakes his head without turning. Debra doesn't move away from the screen door. She keeps looking at Lance. 'He's late some days. He'll be here. Why don't you come inside and get ready for work?'

Lance turns to see her framed by the door like a painting. 'I'll come in a second. I just want to look at something first.'

'What?'

'The apostle bird tree. They should be back by now.'

'They are. I saw them yesterday when I went to see Val. Come in.' She smiles at him gently. That is enough to bring him up the path to the door. She holds it open then closes it behind him. Into her arms he slips and sinks away to another place. She knows this is what happens to him sometimes and she understands. She holds him until he takes a deep breath and sighs.

'The day continues. Thank you.'

'For what?'

'For everything.'

Just then they hear the postman's whistle down the street. They look at each other. They don't have to say anything but what they both think is as loud as a shout. They step back outside and walk to the gate just as the postman reaches their letterbox. He hands them a duck-egg-blue envelope. He lets the whistle fall from his mouth.

'G'day. Sorry I'm late. We're short three men down at the post office. Nice weather. They probably went to the beach. Looks like it'll stay like this for a while.'

'It does. Although this is Melbourne—it might start to rain in a moment,' says Lance.

'That's true. I'd better push on. Off to work soon?'

'Yeah, soon. Just got time to read this letter. From my daughter. She's on holidays.'

'Still? It's been six weeks now, hasn't it?' he asks. Debra smiles because the postman remembers.

'Six weeks, four days.'

'Miss her?' It is the postman's turn to smile.

'A little. We're both used to there being three people in the house. Two makes it feel . . .'

'Empty,' Debra finishes.

'I understand,' the postman says. 'My boy has gone to New Guinea with the church. My wife and I have trouble finding things to talk about. Just the two of us.'

'New Guinea is a long way away. Our daughter has just gone to Sydney.'

'Coming home soon?' he asks as he looks into the sack on his handlebars.

'This letter will tell us. Your boy?'

'Next week.'

'How long has he been gone for?' Debra asks.

'Six weeks. The same as your daughter. Have you got relations up there?'

'My parents,' Lance says.

'Are you a Sydney boy, then?'

'No. I come from Albury, about halfway between both cities. I went one way, they went the other.'

'Right. I must keep on. Cheers.' The postman cycles towards the church.

'He didn't seem very interested in where I came from,' Lance says, scratching his chin.

Debra has torn open the blue envelope and is reading quickly. She looks up. 'Two days' time. She's coming on the train. She wants to see the house as she goes past. No, he wasn't interested at all in where you come from. He was just being polite.' They walk back inside.

'Two days. Better see if I can get some time off work. Speaking of which, I'd better go.'

Debra turns to him and smiles. Her mind is miles away. Lance doesn't notice. He kisses her on the cheek and walks quickly into the kitchen to pick up his bag and the dinner that he has made himself: cold lamb sandwiches. He looks at the clock on the wall. Five past six. He had better go or he will be late for night shift. He'd rather go to bed early with Debra. Tomorrow night will be their last night apart for this month, he decides. He will tell the foreman not to expect him for the next three nights after that. The thought makes him feel better.

As he walks out the front door, he imagines he can see the smoke from the factory's chimney in the distance. He walks out the front gate, down Currawalli Street and waves to Rodney up in the apricot tree. 'Hello, Rod. Anything been happening?'

'Two fire trucks went up Choppingblock Road at three twenty-five. They both returned at four oh nine.'

'Trains on time?'

'Yes. You catching the six eighteen?'

'Yep. Have I got time?'

'You'll have to hurry. But you should make it. Bye bye, Mr Barron.'

'Bye, Rod. Say hello to your mum for me.'

'Okay.' Rodney settles back down on the branch.

Lance thinks about Rodney and his mother Eve all the way to the station. Rodney is three years younger than Pam. Eve is the same age as Debra. Rodney spends most of the time he is not at school up in that apricot tree keeping a record of everything that happens in Currawalli Street and its surrounds. Lance feels for the boy but can't find any way to connect with him other than by discussing train running times. Some days that makes him feel sad. Rodney's dad was killed in a car crash five years ago. If Lance died, he would not like Pam to be so isolated, so unapproachable. Up in a fruit tree all day.

Eve is nice when she has the time to smile but more often than not she is being harried by tiny demons demanding her time, making her eyes sting, her nose runny, her breathing fast. But when she is allowed to stop and look at you, it is as if you are giving her a gift. Lance would like to hold her in his arms for a while. His intuition says that that is what she would want; not for any other reason than to feel the warmth of another body. But he is not capable of explaining that to Debra or of dealing with whatever after effects there might be. No one believes a man can be an innocent when it comes to anything intimate.

As he walks onto the platform he sees the train coming. It is red and dirty at the front. It looks as if it has been going all day, which of course it has. As it stops, he pulls open the closest carriage door. Before he can step aboard, a woman steps out. It is Eve. Speak of the devil. Lance looks at her. There is something different about her. Lance notices that but cannot think what it might be.

She looks at him. 'Hello, Lance, off to work?' She touches him on the arm. Her hand is warm.

'Yes, I am. I just spoke to Rod. Asked him to say hello to you.'

'I just waved to him from the train. Have a good night, Lance.'

Lance closes the door and the train moves out of the station. He sees Eve smiling to herself as she walks to the gate. She looks suddenly happy, Lance thinks. That's good. Something nice must have happened.

Rodney turns around in his apricot tree and looks up the street. He can see the pub and the path that runs behind his house. A lot goes on. He keeps a journal, a logbook of what planes fly overhead, who walks along the path, when trains go past, who goes into which houses. Eve has talked to a few different medical people about Rodney's obsession with statistics and his reluctance to engage with children his own age. He is liked by adults but ignored by other children. He is happy to keep his records and prefers not to be disturbed.

His record keeping is well known in the street. It is now common-place to see him sitting high in his apricot tree, checking his watch and writing something down in his logbook. These days, whenever some-one in the street does something or stops to chat with a neighbour they habitually glance over at the apricot tree to see if the boy is up there. It is a harmless thing for a boy to do. But like any type of observation it is only as harmless as the event being observed.

Rodney knows at what time each family in the street has dinner; he knows that the Hendersons always close the front curtain on the left and then the one on the right at six thirty every night whether the sun is still shining or not. He also knows that Mr Oatley used to have visits from a lady in a green car when his wife was away on holidays. And that the five police cars arrived at Mr Oatley's within a space of twelve minutes and that he had heard the first gunshot at sixteen past ten, the second at twenty-one past.

His records show that three days ago he saw Val's orange cat, whose name he thinks is Thomas (he put a question mark after the name), leaving her yard and walking up the footpath, going past the church, past the bowing soldier statue, past the reverend's house and into Peter Alexis's front yard. It is not the first time that Thomas has gone in there. He does so most days. Rodney watched until Thomas's tail disappeared behind the Chinese lantern bush.

Once Rodney saw Thomas arrive just as Peter was standing at the front gate. They showed such affection for each other that you might think that Peter was the owner of Thomas. That time they immediately went inside together.

But Thomas the cat is now missing. He hasn't been seen for three days.

Sally Domak, feet sore from the marching, throat sore from the chanting, stands at the back fence of the manse. She is not a keen gardener.

She feels no affinity whatsoever with the soil. Her husband seems to walk more easily on this ground than she does, even though he is from the other side of the world and she was born here. Jan is in his office doing his records, as he does every night at this time. She picks up the spade and laughs. Her husband. Only once has she broached his . . . office work. Two hours a night on church records? He is not running an insurance business. There surely isn't that much written work to do. When she did say something, he replied by pushing a Bible across the table at her. Bibles! She hadn't realised that being married to a man of the cloth would involve so many Bibles. Sure, she expected some, but one in every room? One in the car? The garage?

If she was a jealous or a highly strung woman, she would march right over there and burst into his office. But she already knows what she would find, she just doesn't know who. And it would be harder to smile on Sundays as she is forced to if she had a face to recognise.

She will never tell her classmates about Jan's affairs. She will never tell them about his genuine need to conduct them. Not only does she not want them to think less of her for putting up with it, she doesn't want anybody to see her husband as another example of chauvinism run rampant. He isn't that. She is not sure what he is, but it isn't that.

She looks down at the crepe myrtle bush that has been blown over in a recent storm. Its roots have come out of the ground. She looks closer, between the roots. A small box lies newly exposed in the soil. She bends down and picks it up. It is covered in red embroidery that must once have been of great beauty but dirt and water have faded it. There are initials sewn across the top in pale gold thread. *JT*. It opens easily.

Chapter Fourteen

Although Currawalli Street is generally a peaceful place, Lower Lance is in the middle of a strange little war with Upper Lance: each of them tries to put out his rubbish bin ahead of the other. And the two men are the indicators for everyone else of when garbage day is; both Lances know that no one else in the street puts their bins out until either of them does.

Even though they have never discussed the war they are engaged in, both men know the rules. Bins must only be put out on the afternoon of the day before. Anytime after noon on the day preceding garbage day is allowable. In the morning is not permitted, and leaving them out on the nature strip all week is strictly prohibited. Touching the other's rubbish bin is not allowed either. The conflict is waged like a cavalry war of the seventeenth century, with a time and a field agreed on and battle only starting when each army is ready.

On one occasion, both Lances were carrying their bins out at the same time when they noticed that Craig Henderson, who had just moved into number eight, had already placed his bin on the nature strip. Both men stopped in mid stride to look over at the Henderson bin. At that instant they both had the same thought: 'New player in town.' That was the closest they have ever come to acknowledging that they are in a war on opposing sides.

Henderson was new in the street and eager not to miss out on bin day. The next week he was more relaxed; he put out his bin when he noticed Upper Lance's sitting out the front of number sixteen.

Most people in Currawalli Street know about the war and they look upon it as one of the foibles of their community, along with, say, the apostle birds, or the 'T' that has recently fallen from the wall of the church, or Patrick's recitation of train timetables. It is something that just happens. There's no need to pay it much attention. Upper Lance doesn't talk to Debra about it but she knows. She shakes her head in mock despair when he takes out the bin.

And that's how it is in Currawalli Street. Strangers drive up the street only to visit the church; dogs that don't live in the area turn up sometimes and bark; casual strollers and people walking home from work in the next suburb use the path behind the houses. Sometimes people use the street to walk home from the pub, but only if they know the way around the back of the church that leads onto the next street to the east. It is a backwater of sorts.

Gail Henderson from number eight climbs up onto the bottom rung of the side fence and peers into the house next door, as she does every morning. She remembers hearing the first gunshot; by the time she had turned down the TV and eliminated in her mind every possible cause for such a sound except a gunshot, the next one followed.

The first thing she did was climb up on the fence and look over to the back of number ten. She saw Mrs Oatley's legs poking through the bamboo string curtains at the back door. She blinked for a while before she realised that she might be in danger. She climbed off the fence and ran inside, slamming the door shut, then ran through the house locking all the windows. She thought about ringing Craig before she rang the police, but he would only tell her to hang up and dial emergency, and so she sat on the kitchen floor out of sight of the windows and dragged the phone down to her.

The police arrived quickly and eventually there was a knock at the door. She looked out the lounge-room window to make sure it was a detective knocking and not a murderer. She realised then that she couldn't tell the difference; the man knocking was wearing jeans and a black t-shirt, had a gun on his hip and most likely hadn't shaved that morning. He looked like he might be a murderer. But there were enough police cars out on the street for her to assume that her life was not about to be put in danger.

She opened the door and told her story.

And that is why every day now she stands on the bottom rung of the side fence and looks at the back door. She can't get over the fact that she saw a fresh murder victim's legs sticking out over the door mat. The blood was still running fast but she was no longer Mrs Oatley, she was a dead body: a real murder victim.

Ever since they came to Currawalli Street, Gail and Craig Henderson have always been known as a pair. They are always known as 'the Hendersons' or, if discussed individually, 'one of the Hendersons'. They have been lumped, packaged, boxed together. That is because they do everything together and one doesn't answer a question without a silent referral to the other. Even the smallest of societies needs a scapegoat and for the residents of Currawalli Street the Hendersons are it. They don't help themselves much. Gail tried to have all the peppercorn trees along the rail line removed. She has suggested to Mary to keep Patrick at home. To keep the 'poor man' safe.

Craig is not much better. To illustrate this, the neighbours tell the story of the broom.

One day there was a broom leaning on the front fence of number seven. No one knew where it came from. Patrick swept his front path and veranda with it and then on an impulse leaned it on the front fence of number five, in case it belonged there. A few days later, old Mr Travers swept his path with the broom and placed it in front of number three. Bill Casey swept his path and the gutter with it and leaned it against the fence of number one. Rodney came down from his tree and swept the yard and then Eve took it across the street to number two. And so it made its way around the street. By the time it was worn out, it had been around seven times and Kim Oatley replaced the head without thinking about it too much. And so on it went.

Until the Hendersons came. Craig Henderson discovered it leaning on his front fence as he was leaving for work one morning and he snapped it in half and threw it beside his rubbish bin, planning to throw it out when the garbage truck was next around. The handle snapping was heard metaphorically around the street and the snap marked the Hendersons as outsiders who didn't really want to belong and most likely didn't deserve to.

Gail Henderson steps down from the fence just as a train passes her yard, straining up the rise. A boy is leaning out the window, and the train is moving slowly enough for the boy to make eye contact with Gail. He waves. She doesn't. It's not that she doesn't want to, it's just that she is too busy with her day. And besides, the boy shouldn't be leaning that far out the window. What is his mother thinking to let him behave so dangerously?

The postman is running on time today, and he delivers two letters to number seven, both addressed to Mary. One is from her sister in London; she will read this later and savour every copperplate word. The other is in an official envelope marked VICTORIAN RAILWAYS. With a sudden twinge of dread, she opens it.

> *Dear Mrs Cummings,*
>
> *It has come to my attention that your husband Patrick Cummings has been harassing our customers regularly at Choppingblock Station.*
> *I must therefore ask you to ensure that he henceforth refrains from doing so. He is permitted on railway property only as a paying customer.*
> *I notify you in this way as a courtesy due to his forty years of service.*
> *I have no wish to notify the authorities, but should Mr Cummings's behaviour continue I will have no choice.*
>
> *I trust that this letter has found you well.*
> *Yours sincerely,*
> *Bernard Sweeney*
> *Victorian Railways Manager, Western Lines*

Still standing at the front fence, Mary can hear Patrick inside the house singing to himself. She scratches her head and looks along the footpath. Perhaps she is looking for someone to help her. Perhaps she is just trying to get her mind around this. That it is an insult, she is certain. It also has the potential to break Patrick's spirit and maybe his will to go on living. That she will not have. A curse on Mr Bernard Sweeney, Victorian Railways Manager, Western Lines. He would not even have a job if Patrick had not done his own so well. The father cuts down the trees, digs up the roots, puts up the fences, sleeps in the cold. The son grows up and looks down from his tower on all the green pastures and the warm farmhouse as if they have always been there. So it is with the railways. Mary shakes her head.

She notices Jim standing across the road in his front yard also holding a letter. She smiles at him. On an impulse she calls him over. He slowly walks towards her.

'I have yet to welcome you home,' Mary says contritely.

'Thanks very much. It feels . . . sort of strange to be back.'

'I'm sure it does. I wish you had returned in better circumstances. Are you coping alright in there on your own?'

'Well, to be honest, I have grown used to a faster pace of living. This slowness is beginning to unsettle me.'

'Ah . . . good. I don't mean it like that. I mean . . .' She thinks for a while. Mary was once a weak woman who has had to grow strong. Jim can sense that. She stands like a well-established tree that was staked crookedly when it was first planted.

She suddenly changes tack. 'Jim, would you like a job? A temporary one?'

'Doing what?'

'Turning our front veranda into a railway station platform.' Seeing Jim's surprised expression, she shows him the letter and then tells him about Patrick and his routine. 'It never bothered anybody before. The new stationmaster keeps saying that Patrick is an asset. The passengers are all friendly. No one seems to mind. Except . . .' She looks over at number eight. The Hendersons' place.

'Ah,' Jim says. He has no wish to involve himself in any neighbourhood disputes. But a bit of hard physical work might be just what he needs. The army taught him to build, and he wouldn't mind putting those skills to use. 'Have you any idea how you want it done?'

'Well, the notion has only just come to me. For a start, the steps should be at the end of the veranda and not at the front. Can you do that?'

'I think so. There's not much to it. When do you want me to start?'

'Whenever you can. The sooner the better. It will break Patrick's heart if he realises what the railways have done to him.'

'I can start right now. I'm not doing anything except trying to find the courage to start clearing my mum's clothes out of her wardrobe.'

'I can do that for you. Let me. I would like to be able to do something to help.'

'In that case I can start straightaway. Thank you, Mary.'

'Patrick has some tools in his shed . . .'

'And I still have Dad's tools.'

'Come and have a look then.' She opens the gate for him but he holds up a finger and takes a step backward.

'I had better lock the front door first. I'll just be a second.' He hurries back over the road. Mary wonders why he needs to lock his door when he will only be across the street. The younger generation. Perhaps it is something they do.

Jim returns and they walk to the steps, centrally located at the front of the veranda. A path leads from them to the front gate.

'We can lay a path from the new steps. I'll dig up the old one after I have finished the new one. The first thing is to shift the step.' He bends down for a closer look. 'I would be inclined to use new timber rather than try to salvage the timber from this step.'

'Of course. This step is as old as the house. It was built in 1914, so it is probably due to be replaced.'

'Is the hardware shop still in Battlefield Street?'

'Yes, it is. Still the same people running it.'

'Old Mr Berbain?'

'Yes, Mr Birdbrain. Still there. Still grumpy.'

Jim nods. 'I'll work out what we need and walk around there now.'

'Thanks Jim, I really appreciate this. If Patrick asks what you're doing, you can tell him you are replacing some rotten wood.'

About to turn away, Mary stops. 'Jim, what about payment?'

'A cup of tea, some of that coronation cake you used to make and the odd sandwich. That'll do. The army is still paying me.'

'That doesn't seem fair . . .'

'It's fair. We're neighbours. It all balances out in the end. I'll be happy to have a project to do. You still make the coronation cake?'

'I do. I'll bring you out a piece with a cup of tea when you get back from Birdbrain's.' Mary watches him leave through the gate. When she went out to collect the post this morning, she wasn't even contemplating turning the veranda into a railway platform. Now, fifteen minutes later, it is all happening. She turns towards the house. Patrick is still singing to himself.

I like his voice, she thinks to herself. I always have.

Lower Lance is sitting in his car, parked in the driveway of number two. He doesn't drive it much nowadays. He has nowhere really to go. His sister moved to Norway a year ago and she was the only person he ever used the car to visit. So now he sits in the driveway. When he hears people walking past his front fence, he pretends to be looking at something under the dashboard but the rest of the time he just sits there. It is really comfortable and the windscreen being so close means that everything looks filtered and a little bit distorted. And nowadays he prefers that to the real world. He knows that he is acting like a really old person and that he isn't even close to being that old. In fact he is only forty-seven, but life has just got too difficult for him.

He works at Coveys, a map and atlas shop in the city, and his days are spent surrounded by maps of the world. The only people who come into the shop are those who are about to travel and are excited. He is tired of their excitement. He wants to be the one buying the maps. One day it will be him—if he doesn't get too old first. That's what he fears.

Meanwhile he sits in his car.

Suddenly there is a knock on the passengers' side window. He jerks in fright, recovers and looks across. A woman with long brown hair looks in at him. It takes him a moment to realise who it is. Eve, the widow from number one. He leans across and winds down the window.

'Eve, hello.'

'Are you going somewhere?' Eve asks as she opens the door and slides in beside him.

'No, not really. I was just looking at the . . . ah . . . indicator wires. They're playing up.'

'My dad used to love sitting in his car and not going anywhere. When I asked him what he was doing, he always said just that. The indicator wires,' Eve says conspiratorially.

'Oh.'

'You shouldn't feel ashamed. Really, most people would love to sit in their cars if they had the chance.'

'Really?'

Eve looks at him with amusement in her eyes. 'I don't really know. I made that up. But it sounded good.'

'It did. It did sound good.'

'I came over to ask if I could borrow a spade for the afternoon. The handle just broke on mine and I have some bulbs that I have to put in the ground. They're spread out on the lawn.'

'Of course. I'll go and get it. It's around the back. Shall I bring it over?'

'Okay, if you don't mind. Say, do you know what the Vietnam soldier boy is doing at Patrick and Mary's place? He's torn out their front steps.'

'Let me see.' Lance climbs out of the car and walks to the front fence. He looks up the road to number seven. 'It looks like he's building new steps at the side. Want a cup of tea?'

'Yeah. Why don't we have one at my place? I just baked some biscuits,' she says, as if delighted by something else.

221

'Okay. I don't really have anything at the moment. Hang on, I'll get the spade.'

Eve waits until he returns and then they cross the road together. Lance speaks as they reach the other side. 'If you don't mind me asking, how come you're being nice all of a sudden? Normally you just say hello and even that looked hard.' He is quietly spoken but this is softer still and so Eve has to lean forward to hear him. His question and her leaning forward makes him feel awkward.

'Did it? I just didn't feel like talking to anybody. I didn't feel like getting to know anybody. Did you know that everybody says you're grumpy and hard to get on with?' They both laugh.

'Do they? I thought they didn't want to talk to me. Oh well, I don't have much to say anyway, so it's probably for the best. But you feel like talking to people now?'

'Yep. At least the neighbours.'

'So you can put faces to the names that appear in your son's logbook.'

'*Logbooks*. Plural. He's on his ninth, I think.'

'It's harmless stuff.'

'I hope he'll grow out of it. Come around the back way.'

They walk down the side of the house and turn into the backyard. Lower Lance has never been in here before. 'I didn't know you had so many apricot trees!' There must be at least twenty. It is like an orchard. The biggest is next to the fence; it is in that tree that Rodney does all his surveillance work.

'Yeah, I've made plenty of apricot jam if you ever want any.'

'As a matter of fact I love apricot jam.'

'Good. It's coming out our ears. Come in.' Eve holds open the back door. Lance walks through into a kitchen straight from the 1940s. 'I know.' Eve grimaces. 'One day I'll do it up.'

'No, I like it like this. It reminds me of my nan's.' He sits at the table. 'You'd better tell me about yourself. Just so I know whose house I'm in and who I'm drinking tea with.'

Eve fills the kettle and puts it on the stove. 'And then you tell me about your life. Although I already know that you work at that big map shop in town. Why aren't you working today?'

'Sick day, I didn't feel up to it. I'm not really sick. Who told you where I worked?'

'Mary from up the road. She knows everything. Did you know that Alfred Covey used to live in this street?'

Lance nods. 'Number nine. He built it.'

'And Mary's house. Patrick is his grandson.'

Over four biscuits and two pots of tea, Eve and Lance share their stories. For a while, they have no choice but to listen to Bill Casey next door as he curses his lawnmower.

'He goes mad at it a lot,' says Eve apologetically. 'We hear him all the time.'

'He's always been like that.'

'Has he? Apparently his wife left him some time ago. Ran off with someone, they say.'

'Who's they?'

'Mary up the street. She knows everything.'

Lance turns his cup around in its saucer and then says, 'I knew her— Mrs Casey. He was alright to her, but it . . . wasn't enough. I remember the day she left. I . . . helped her go actually.' Lower Lance smiles. He looks at the window as he continues. 'Bill's not too bad. That's not why she left. She just happened to fall in love with someone else, that's all. I miss her. We were good friends.'

'Well, I'm sorry to hear that. He loves apricot jam, that's for sure.'

Lower Lance nods. He is suddenly sad again. Eve sees that.

When Rodney comes home from Choppingblock Primary School, he looks at Lance with a certain amount of suspicion, goes outside and climbs the apricot tree. Surveillance has begun.

When Lance comes out of the front gate two hours later, crosses the street, and goes inside his own house, the first thing he does is pull down from the cupboard the map outlining his own proposed trip overseas. He looks at it, feeling that somewhere there is something different. Somewhere on the map. Somewhere in his head. Maybe it's finally time to go.

Rodney notes that Lance checked his letterbox for mail and didn't notice that Upper Lance has put his garbage bin out.

❧ Chapter Fifteen ❧

At number nine, Megan hears the work going on next door. She heard it yesterday as well. It is not like Patrick or Mary to be hammering so solidly. It sounds like the type of noise that a stranger makes. She looks out her front window but can't see anything. She decides to check the letterbox, even though it is far too early for the postman. She looks up at the painting above the fireplace and shakes her head, as she always does when she looks at it.

Derry insists it has to be prominently displayed here in the lounge room, above the fireplace where everybody can't help but notice it. She wanted their wedding photo, the one taken outside Luna Park, to be on the mantelpiece. But Derry didn't agree. He says the painting is a talking point. He's right too. But no one talks about it when they are in the lounge room; she imagines they talk about it in the car, driving home.

'Did you see that painting?'

'It's obscene.'

'It looks horrible.'

'Imagine getting up in the morning and having to look at that.'

'Who would paint such a thing? And why would you hang it where everybody can see it?'

Derry imagines that they say other things.

Megan hates the painting. It casts a shadow over her life in this house.

She walks out the front door. The son from number ten is working on the side of Patrick and Mary's veranda. He looks as if he knows what he's doing. It's the hammering of a professional. He was over there in Vietnam fighting those communists. But then his mum and dad were murdered. Who would do a thing like that? This isn't America. Most likely communists heard that the son was over there killing them and so they sneaked in and did away with the parents. That's a hard price to pay for protecting us from the Soviets and Chinese. She watches him wielding the hammer, his cloth hat bouncing back off his forehead with each blow, the muscles in his arm so defined and tight. She blinks and concentrates on opening the letterbox. The hammering continues a little longer. When it stops she looks back over at him. He is looking at her. He nods. She nods back and smiles, half closing her eyes. She lets her head tilt to one side. Then she tosses her hair and walks back into the house. She leans against the kitchen sink for a moment, pulling on either end of a tea towel.

This is a good feeling, she decides. The hammering continues in her head so she is unaware that Jim has not recommenced but is still nursing his throbbing thumb.

Through the door to the lounge room, she can see in the reflection of the TV screen the painting and, on top of the sideboard, a photograph of her and Derry at his sister's wedding anniversary. He is holding his stomach in for the photograph.

Megan's mother, who is an observant woman, had warned her against marrying an older man. 'You will be on your own even when he is with you,' she said. 'He only thinks he is like you at the moment. The time will come when he has to satisfy the demands of his age and he will recede into that world. A world that won't include you. And he will most likely die before you, and you will be alone again.'

Her mother did give her one helpful piece of advice. 'The older he is feeling, the more he will try to hold his stomach in. When he holds his stomach in tight, try to be nice to him. When he lets it out, you can relax.'

Megan laughed gaily at the time but now she sees that it is a blank truth and that her mother didn't say it for her amusement.

At first Megan didn't believe she was reading the signs correctly. But as time went on and Derry's dalliances became like something she had to step around in the bathroom, she came to assume that this was part of being married and that every wife experienced it and put it with the other things that were never talked about to anybody. These days she can tell from the way Derry acts and talks and from the quality of the gifts that he brings home to her what stage in an affair he is up to. From meeting a potential partner to organising a meeting, the first time they have sex and when they call it all off, Megan can read every sign.

Before she was married, Megan assumed that when she experienced sex herself then she would finally understand the allure of it. But even after three years of marriage she doesn't understand it at all. Such a fuss is made about it by everybody, yet it seems to be hardly anything.

Derry is plagued by guilt, Megan can tell that too. She thinks that if she was ever to give him a gift that is something he really needs and wants, it would be to say to him that it is okay; he doesn't have to feel guilty. But she is not ready to give him that gift.

It is still fairly early in the morning. The flattening business of the day hasn't taken hold yet and the light outside is fresh and young and it is easy to picture what the day might become rather than what you expect it to be. The sun hasn't yet warmed anything too much and it is the sort of morning when you say, 'This is why I love being here' if you are happy where you are, or 'This place isn't too bad' if you are not.

Derry has already left for work because of a managers meeting, he said. He walked out of the house leaving behind a vapour trail of his special aftershave, something he doesn't douse himself with for a managers meeting. It is more the aftershave he would wear if he was headed to the wetlands car park by the side of the freeway to meet someone for frantic sex before work.

Their marriage is still at the stage where Megan thinks that she and Derry are an indomitable team. And that is something she is very happy about. When his dad had the heart attack which ended up killing him, she cancelled her regular visit with her friends to the café on Choppingblock Road and drove straight to the hospital to sit with Derry. And if anything happened to her or her family, she knows Derry would also be there for her.

Derry has been gone for half an hour but the cloud of his aftershave hangs about in the still air of the kitchen and so she opens the side door to let the breeze in. The door opens onto the driveway and, beyond that, Patrick and Mary's fence. Just as she opens it wide and takes one step forward to look over the fence, two things happen. First, the wind gusts suddenly and blows her Japanese half dressing gown open over her thigh up to her hip. Second, Jim pops his head up over the side fence as he carries a long piece of timber to the front of the house.

For both of them it is an unexpected confrontation. They are only twelve feet from each other. Jim tries to smile. Megan recognises his attempt and responds accordingly. She tries to cover up her leg with the dressing gown but she can't find the fabric, so her hand ends up resting on her thigh. 'Do you want a cup of tea?' she asks in a voice still croaky from disuse.

'If you're having one.' His voice is similarly rough.

'I'm about to pour it.'

'I'll come in.'

She is just taking a cup down from the cupboard above her head when he steps inside. She notices that his footfall is gentle as if he is walking on paper. She looks down at his feet and comments, 'You walk so quietly.'

He looks down at his feet too. 'Habit, I guess. I learned to step very lightly and quietly over there.' He dips his head to indicate a place to the north of where they are standing.

She is at first unsure of what he means. Is he pointing towards his home? Perhaps his father made him walk softly. But then she realises that he means Vietnam. She gasps. 'Oh God.'

She leans back against the bench and then realises that her arm is still stretched up, holding the handle of the cupboard door. Both pairs of eyes, his and hers, follow her arm up past the elbow where the deep-green dressing-gown sleeve has slid down to, then along her forearm, past her wrist to her hand. She opens her fingers but her arm remains raised. She looks at Jim and can't find the place in her mind that will command it to return to her side. He has taken in the hand quickly and is now looking at her face. She doesn't know what to read in his expression but for a moment she thinks it is somehow aligned to the softness of his footsteps. She thinks she is seeing a jungle in his eyes.

Jim moves forward to pick up the teapot and pours the fragrant liquid into his cup.

'It's green tea,' she says.

'I know.'

He is close enough to her now that she can smell the tobacco on his breath. He stands in front of her and lifts the cup to his lips. She thinks she can hear the clock ticking on the fridge, which is funny because it hasn't been working for two months. He gently blows some of the steam rising from his cup onto her face. Later on she can't convince herself that she felt anything at all, but at that moment it is like being soaked completely by a hot tropical shower.

As he lifts the cup to his lips again and drinks, she feels his other hand dispense in one unhesitant movement with the obe keeping her dressing gown closed. There is no tug or frantic pull. That hand is now sliding slowly down her belly, gradually through her pubic hair, and then, tentatively, one finger touches her while the finger on either side keeps her exposed to its touch.

She shudders and softly gasps, which is something she has never done before. Not seriously, anyway. Only for effect. She shudders because she sees a look in his eyes that she can't recognise—perhaps because his face is expressing nothing, as if it has no connection to the finger that is circling her so slowly that her mouth fills with air because she has closed her lips to stop any further gasps. Indeed, he holds the cup up to his lips and drinks slowly. But his eyes have not left hers. He gently blows some more steam over her face and instinctively she closes her eyes, grateful to have a moment to step inside herself so she can assess what is happening. When she looks at him again, he is still holding the cup to his lips but suddenly his finger stops moving. The energy between them changes. His expression, or lack of it, doesn't. Nor does hers: she is still holding her mouth tightly closed.

His finger doesn't move. She feels his hand press up against her and she imagines that she can feel his pulse through it. Her mouth is beginning to open. She cannot internally voice the command to prevent it.

She sighs with a depth that she has never heard from herself before. The warm still hand is now a beautiful ache and she silently pleads with him to resume his movement. Her eyes do not betray her pleading, but he knows and drinks once more from the cup. Her right arm is still lifted above her head and she raises her left hand to hold onto another handle. Now she feels totally exposed to him. But they seem to have crossed a certain point a long time ago, and exposure of that kind doesn't matter anymore. She stands with her arms up and open and suddenly her head is filled with his voice, even though his lips don't move.

Shall I continue? Shall I?

Yes. Yes. And then I will . . . I don't know.

His finger begins to circle again, now faster and now slower. Just when the rhythm settles he changes the rotation or the speed. He never takes his eyes off hers. Her chin lifts as she lengthens her neck but still her eyes are fixed on his.

What begins as a slow out-breath that she sees rising to the ceiling as a stream of evaporating mist becomes a tiny shudder that grows larger until it is a convulsion of great and sudden beauty. She arches her back and knows that she is perfect and that she is in a perfect world.

Yes, you are perfect.

Her cry comes from somewhere much deeper than her throat and goes on unbroken for almost a minute. She slams her hips backwards to close the arch of her back. His hand is there and takes the brunt of the impact. She hasn't noticed that he put his cup down on the bench and slid his hand behind her. And that is how they stay for a few minutes.

Her hands come away from the handles and her arms fall to her sides. Only for a moment does she drop her head down. When she straightens her neck again, his eyes are still on her.

Okay?

She nods and breathes in strongly so that her shoulders are pushed back. His hands have not moved from her and now with a strength that she already suspected was there they move her hips away from the bench towards the kitchen table. Only two steps but her legs have grown weak as if she has just woken up.

Firmly, steadily he pushes her down across the table and for a moment she looks at Derry's cereal bowl close up. Then she feels the back of her dressing gown pulled up to the small of her back. She knows from watching him hammering this morning that he keeps the nails in his back pocket and it is a ringing sound that she hears as his trousers fall to the tiled floor.

She thinks she should reach her hand back to guide him but instead she finds that she is reaching forward to grasp the far edge of the table. Just as she finds it and her fingers begin to explore the underside, she feels him touch her once, twice, and then enter her slowly. She feels the hairs of his belly against her buttocks and his hands are holding her hips. She can feel his fingers pressing into her skin as he pulls her body back to hit his and then slides her away. She can actually feel the webbing between his fingers. She is still holding the edge of the table but relinquishes her grip slightly when he pulls her back to him. When he can pull her back no further, when her buttocks are squeezed up against his belly, they exhale at the same time.

The dance begins, the rhythm unknown to those not dancing. For a moment she sees a wild pig trail in a dark jungle, steaming with a sudden rain and crowded in by large dark green leaves that swallow up the path ahead.

He has stopped pulling her towards him and his hands are now on her shoulders. He is thrusting and thrusting. The rhythm has gone from his movements and an animal urge has taken over. The thrusts are faster and not as deep and he now talks under his breath in another language. The syllables are far apart and the sound is guttural.

Suddenly his hands let go of her shoulders and grab her hips again as he pulls her back to him. Then he is deep inside her and he calls out a name which is neither hers nor one that she has heard before. But she knows it is a name. She lifts her chest up off the table and once more arches her back as he shudders and grips her hips tightly.

He falls onto her, exhausted, and she drops back onto the table. They lie like this until he rises from her and she hears the nails again as he pulls his trousers up. She thinks they must have been around his ankles.

Thanks for the tea, she hears in her mind as the door opens and then gently closes. She decides she will go back to bed and start her day a bit later on.

After lunch, Mary comes out to see Jim's work. Already it is starting to look like what they discussed.

Yesterday she visited the railway station and the new stationmaster gave her a box of expired tickets, an old sign with the name of the station that had once sat over the ticket window and, most touchingly of all, Patrick's old office chair. The chair and the tickets now sit under a tarpaulin on the veranda. Jim thinks he has one more day until the job is done. Then he will spend another day helping Mary dress up the platform so that it looks authentic.

The name of the real station is Choppingblock. Mary has decided to name the new platform Currawalli Street. The new signs are being painted up by Peter Alexis who apparently has an eye for that sort of thing. His father is a signwriter, he says. Mary took the old station sign up to Peter yesterday so that he could make three new signs in the same style. He said he would start on them straightaway. She is a little concerned that he won't achieve a convincing result.

And now, as Mary is standing on the veranda looking at Jim's work, Peter comes walking down the street with the four signs under his arm. He sees Mary when he is still out the front of number nine and he stops and holds up one of the new signs. It looks just as it should. The words

CURRAWALLI STREET are clear at that distance and, best of all, they look authentic. Mary feels a touch of relief.

She claps her hands silently in approval as Peter walks in the front gate. He pauses as he looks for the veranda steps, which have been moved from the front to the left-hand side.

'The signs look really good, Peter. Will you come in for a cup of tea?'

'No, I can't. I'm working on something at the moment and I have just this morning had a breakthrough, so I must get back to it while it's fresh in my head,' he says seriously.

'What are you working on?' Mary didn't know that Peter works.

He steps up close to her. 'I paint cats,' he whispers.

'Oh.' Mary doesn't know what else to say. But Peter is already stepping down from the veranda and heading through the gate. He certainly is an intense man, Mary thinks to herself as she watches him retreat up the street. She places the signs down next to the tarpaulin and walks to the screen door. She hears Jim call her as he comes in the gate. He doesn't bother walking around to the step, just jumps up onto the veranda in front of her.

'I was thinking last night, Mary, that I could change the configuration of that window there'—he points to the small one that looks out from the dining room—'to make it a sash window that you can open and, I don't know, sell tickets, or make cups of tea or something.'

Mary looks at the window and then at Jim. 'Can you do it?'

'Easy.'

'That's a really good idea, Jim. Are you sure you have the time?'

'I'm sure. I'm really enjoying all of this. It's a good way for me to get used to being back. I try to do a bit at home every day—weeding the garden, washing tea towels—but my heart isn't in it . . . I suspect that my head isn't ready yet.'

'I don't see how it could be,' Mary says gently.

'I suppose not. Every time I go into the house I can hear my father telling me to get a move on, but I'm not having much luck. Luke helped me get a few things done—the general stuff—but there are things that I think I should do myself. Mum wouldn't like too many people going through her clothes and things.'

'If I were you, I wouldn't even try to do that at the moment. Focus on what you need to do—what you want to do. No offence to your parents, but they're dead; they're in no rush. What's the hurry? As I said before, help me get Patrick's platform done and then I will help you at your place. We'll make it a brand-new home for you with only as many reminders of your mum and dad as you want, no more. If you don't do that, you'll always have your parents looking over your shoulder at whatever you do. They are very hard to get rid of once they have established themselves.'

Jim looks momentarily puzzled, so Mary explains. 'The ghosts of parents. They never want to leave. You have to force them. Don't worry, I know how.'

'How do you know?' Jim asks, suddenly serious.

'This is Patrick's parents' house. His grandmother lived next door, at number nine. After Patrick's mother died, I pushed all of the ghosts out onto the street: his grandmother and grandfather, his father, his father's friends, and his mother. That's all it took. They never came back, so I can only assume they weren't angry enough with me to kick up a stink. The thing is, I knew what needed to be done because it was Patrick's grandmother, Rose, who told me. I don't know who she learned it from. Apparently she was some sort of psychic. I was just married to her grandson, but she took the time to show me how to do it. She said that I might have to use it one day to get rid of her ghost.'

'Was it easy?'

'Yes and no. She said the secret is knowing where the essence of each ghost lies.'

'Where do ghosts lie?' he asks, the image of that old hermit suddenly appearing in his mind.

'In the most surprising places. The bottoms of drawers, in old paper-work, the backs of cupboards, even in the garden, entwined in the roots of plants . . . Don't worry, we'll move your parents on.'

Jim looks at his elderly neighbour, seeing her in a new way.

Mary looks at him narrowly. 'You're shaking your head. Don't you believe me?'

'Oh no, I believe you. I was just thinking that I don't know very much about people at all. I look at all the external things to show me who they are—what sort of person they are. It doesn't work, but I make do with it each time. I must take everybody the wrong way.'

Mary smiles. 'I think that's what we all do. But you must remember that most people are pretty good at hiding themselves in among what they present to you. Most people don't want you to know who they are. So don't be too hard on yourself. We all have secret lives. And we are all pretty good at keeping them secret.' Mary stops and laughs. 'Listen to me! I never used to be this philosophical. I think it is only since Patrick has gone that I have thought about such things. So there you are. That is another secret you know about me.'

'What do you mean, since Patrick has gone? I saw him this morning.'

'I mean since some of his mind has gone. He hasn't the ability to talk to me much anymore. The reality, which he is sometimes actively engaged in and talks to me about, is, sadly, not the same as mine. And the difference is getting bigger each day. Unfortunately, it has arrived at a time when we were both becoming more reflective and starting to look back on the past more than looking towards the future. That's what I mean.'

'He seemed alright when he came over to my place the other night,' Jim says, frowning and trying to remember if Patrick did anything strange.

'Yes, he comes and goes. I can never predict when he is going to be with me or when he is not even going to recognise me.'

It has been a remarkable day; something has changed. Certainly, Megan has never felt this way before. Her head is in Derry's lap as he talks. With closed eyes she pictures what he looks like as he speaks, for the first time ever finding it satisfying and calming. They are on the couch in the lounge room; he is sitting upright nursing a glass of rum with one hand and she is lying on her side with her feet curled up under her. Her own glass is empty, abandoned on the coffee table. She opens her eyes to ask him a question and then closes them straightaway to hear the answer.

'Why do you like the painting?' There is no need to identify which painting she means. There can be only one worthy of comment. It is hanging in front of them.

'Besides the colours and the candlelight, I like the subject,' says Derry. 'It is strange enough to be remarkable. The man is curled up on the mother's lap as if he is a naked baby but he looks unnatural and tense. He isn't really showing any expression, when you think in that position he would. After all he is just about to be, or he has just been, breastfed. But his face, although it has been competently executed by the artist, shows an odd detachment. Which makes the whole thing very strange.' Derry takes a sip of his drink before continuing. 'But the things that really attract me to the painting are the religious images. The stained-glass windows, the gold candlesticks, the rich brocades, the mother looking up to heaven. That religious tone must make the painting offensive to some people; people who we let through our door even though perhaps neither of us likes them very much.'

Megan raises herself up on one shoulder. 'Like who?'

'Geoffrey and Alison.'

'I thought you liked them. I put up with them for your sake.'

'No—I thought *you* liked them.'

'Not at all. She is so neurotic and he is . . . weird.' They both laugh.

'Well, that's good to hear,' says Derry. 'We don't have to have them over here again.'

'And we won't have to go to their dinner parties anymore.'

'Hooray!'

Megan sinks back down onto Derry's lap. He brings his drink to his lips. 'Now continue about the painting,' she instructs.

'Well . . . I found out who the man is. We've never really talked about the painting before, only to disagree about it, so I haven't told you. I was looking through a book on the history of this area and there was a photograph of a priest taken outside our church in 1914. He is standing with a small man, the bishop of the district. And that man in the painting is that bishop. Can you believe it?'

'Are you sure?' Megan asks, a little shocked.

'Positive.'

'But that woman is breastfeeding him. Bishops don't . . .'

'Who do you think that woman is supposed to be?'

'I don't know.'

'Who do you know in the Bible who's a mother?'

'No!'

'That's who I think it is. Look at the way she's looking up to the heavens and the way he's gazing at her face—just like the Baby Jesus.'

'And you're sure he's the bishop?'

'Yep, it's him alright. After I found that photo I looked up histories of the diocese and his picture appeared again. He was bishop from 1910 to 1923.'

'And then?'

'He died in a car crash. The car he was a passenger in went over that cliff up Choppingblock Road a bit. You know the one? The driver managed to jump out before it went over.'

Megan sits up again and looks at the painting. She shudders. 'Where did you get it from?'

'Across the road—number ten. The bloke who got shot found it under his house, of all places, wrapped in oilskins and tarpaulins, a few days before he gave it to me. He must have wanted to get rid of it before his wife saw it. I was just getting out of the car at the time and he called me over. I hadn't talked to him before.'

'I thought you bought it from an antique shop.'

'No—I might have told you that at the start so that you would let me keep it.'

'Oh. Do you know who painted it?'

'I think the bloke across the road knew but he didn't want to say. And there's no signature.'

'The artist didn't want to be held responsible, I suppose.'

'I suppose.'

'Bed?' asks Megan.

'I'm not really tired.'

'Me neither. Bed?'

Chapter Sixteen

The Choppingblock Hotel stands on the corner of Choppingblock Road and Little Road. It is the oldest building in the district, mistakenly built in an empty paddock miles from anywhere by a drunken builder who misread the address on his directions. The streets came later to cluster around it like village houses around a Norman castle.

The Choppingblock Hotel is mainly frequented by men. It is a fact that men generally don't like women to overhear them when they are talking to other men and so the manager frowns on women leaving the ladies lounge. Whenever there is an occasion for mixed company it generally takes place in the hotel dining room over a plate of ham steak with pineapple or nasi goreng and a bottle of Porphyry Pearl. There are topics of conversation for these occasions that are masculine without being revealing. But they are not really satisfying. That's why the men in these groups are always ready to leave.

But they don't have to be anxious to leave a public bar. A shallow glance would lead you to think that perhaps it is alcohol that keeps men from all walks of life at the bar, but it is not that particular vice at all; it is the demon spirit of conversation. Here they can say and hear what they know to be true and do not have to argue any difference of opinion that uses words or emotions they don't understand. That's why many sober men stay until closing time and have to be ushered from the premises.

It is the type of late afternoon when the bushfire smoke has been blown away by a southerly breeze. Jim leans against his front fence looking across the street to the block of land next to Megan's house that is number eleven. As a child, he often found himself looking at that land without having noticed that it had drawn his attention. He didn't like it then and he still doesn't like it. But now he knows land like this. He saw it in Vietnam. Nothing ever grows there. It is barren as if from a drier part of the country. Most likely something bad happened there. There was a spot like this near the camp where he was last stationed. The local people wouldn't walk across it, they wouldn't eat anything that grew near it; they wouldn't drink water from the stream that ran near there. It was a place where something evil had happened. Number eleven feels like that.

Jan Domak walks in front of the block of land and crosses the street to Jim. 'Fancy drinking a beer with me?'

Jim nods. 'Yes, I was planning on going down to the pub. I may as well go now. I don't drink beer though.'

The reverend holds the front gate open for him and they walk down the street side by side. At Little Road they wait for a break in the traffic and then step across to the pub car park together. Inside, the public bar is surprisingly quiet for this time of day, and they lean on the bar together underneath the thirty-eight tin mugs.

'Do you know why they're up there?' Jan asks.

'Well, I've heard stories about men nailing up their mugs on pub walls before going away to the Great War but I don't know whether that is what these are. Maybe the barman knows.'

He doesn't. Jim isn't surprised. It's the same barman as when he first walked in here on his return. Jim turns his drink around before raising it to his lips.

'So, you come from around here?' Jan asks.

'Lived in Currawalli Street all my life. Where are you from?'

'Czechoslovakia. I was brought out here by my parents. That was when I was a baby and so I have very few memories of there.'

'What do you remember?'

'Snow on my father's shoes when he came inside and the smell of breath.'

'What does that mean?' Jim lifts up his empty whisky glass and shows it to the barman who doesn't register what Jim means by this action.

Jan considers. 'I think there was a lot of sausage eaten, a lot of garlic, butter, chicory coffee, and over the top of it all was cigarette smoke. It added up to a certain smell of breath.'

'I see.'

'I was only a baby, so it could have been just my family's breath that smelled like that, but the truth is, whenever I smell garlic and tobacco I think of Czechoslovakia. And snow on my father's shoes.'

Jim finally resorts to words to get the barman's attention. Thus prompted, the man flies into action and a new drink is in front of Jim in seconds.

'Do you ever want to talk about your parents?' asks Jan.

Jim has his glass halfway to his lips. He puts it back down gently on the bar. 'No, I don't. Something happened, but I don't know what, other than what the police and the coroner said. I suppose that one day I will find out. And I don't know if finding out will be a good thing or a bad thing.'

'Did he have secrets?'

'My dad?'

'Did he?'

'I would think he had secrets. Only they wouldn't be secrets if I knew about them, would they? I'm not interested in talking about this. If it's why you invited me for a drink I'll go home and wash the floors.' Jim has met one or two men like the reverend before. Always asking questions at the wrong times. Women know when to ask these same questions, and when to talk about something else.

'Every man has a secret world that he goes to sometimes, a shadow life. I just wanted to know what your father's was, that's all. I'm sorry. I just . . . if you ever want to talk . . . I'm always available,' Jan says quietly.

'Do you have a shadow life, Reverend?'

'Of course. All men do. You know what yours is, I know what mine is.'

'Good for you.' Jim pushes his glass away unfinished. He turns to leave.

Jan draws in a deep breath. Remembering the note that was thrust into his hand at this very spot, he says, 'I must go too. I have important work waiting in my office. No one else can do it.'

The barman doesn't notice their departure.

Jim waves to Rodney in the apricot tree as they walk by. He waves back and writes something down in his logbook.

As the two men walk up Currawalli Street, Jan says, 'I'm sorry, Jim. It wasn't my intention to be insensitive . . .'

'What was your intention?'

Jan stops walking and turns to him. 'To offer you my . . . services if you ever need them. That's all.'

Jim is looking up the street at the church spire. 'Thanks, Reverend. I'll keep it in mind. I don't know what will happen or how I will feel. I may want to knock on your door. You know, I knew a man like you once. Over there. He got bitten by a snake. He was too big to move out of its way.' Jim's voice is cold and on the edge there is a touch of anger.

'I always watch out for snakes. Goodnight, Jim.'

'Goodnight.' Jim crosses the street and leaves Jan to continue on alone.

The cool air eases Jim through his front door, which he leaves ajar. He walks through the house to the back door and pushes it wide open. The screen door is being assaulted by a Hercules moth. Jim sits on the grass, looks up at the stars starting to come out, and thinks about the reverend's statement that every man has a shadow life. It's not strictly true, he thinks; in Vietnam there was never any need to keep a shadow life: men did what they wanted, out in the open, because all around was darkness and everyone was living in the shadows.

Jim looks into the darkness now, tired of needing to know what is out there. Suddenly, though, his body jerks into alertness.

Before he hears them in the sky he can feel the shells coming closer. The earth begins to vibrate in very quick, small movements. Without pausing to process the information he falls flat to the ground. That is what you have to do: men who stop to think before they take action are the men who die.

Now the sound overtakes the vibrations. It is a screaming machine that roars in from over the horizon. It pushes Jim into the ground so hard that it seems to force the air out of his lungs. He buries an ear into the dirt and slams his hand over the exposed one, but that is good only for a moment. Before long he has to turn his head and bury his face in the dirt with his arms thrown out ahead of him.

The sound gets even louder. He lets his mouth fall open, needing to rid his body of some of the screaming noise that has entered through his ears, eyes, nose and skin and whips along his veins to his brain, which feels as if it is swelling dangerously. His throat has begun to hurt and he may even be yelling or screaming himself but he can't hear it over the noise of the machine, which keeps getting louder.

He knows that he is sobbing though because he can feel tears on his cheeks and his shoulders are jerking up and down.

It is too much. He gives up, lies out flat and doesn't attempt to protect himself anymore. Makes his peace with God and the moment.

The sound very quickly dies away. The shells will not land here, he sees. They are meant for somewhere else. Now he can hear the *crump crump* as they hit the ground a few miles further on.

Jim often finds himself thinking about bravery. Specifically, what makes a man take a positive action when it is acceptable and understandable that he take no action at all? Does that compulsion come from a conscious thought or an unconscious thought? Jim has no idea where the impetus comes from.

He remembers Brent bending over him, yelling for him to move as he lay spreadeagled in the middle of a track, paralysed by the noise of shells. It was the first time he had heard such a salvo roaring in close overhead, and it wasn't until the following evening that he realised his fingertips were causing him great pain. He looked down and saw that there was dirt packed under his nails right down to the quick, he had grabbed the earth so hard. As he discovered, it wasn't unusual to see men with no fingernails remaining; nor was it strange to see soldiers with trails of tears on their cheeks as they returned from patrols.

The sound has now completely left his mind and roared over the horizon. It is then that Jim sees he is lying close to the lemon tree in the backyard and in the air is the smell of the diesel fumes of a goods train locomotive. He looks up at the railway line over the back fence.

All is quiet.

At number four the Alberto family is drinking wine. Rosa finishes hers quickly and walks over to a pot boiling on the stove. Her husband, Gerald, sips from his glass and looks across the table at his mother-in-law, who is shelling peas. Her glass, almost empty, sits on the table beside the basket of peas that she has brought in from the garden.

Gina has a flourishing vegetable garden. She only ever goes to the fruit and vegetable shop to buy potatoes and look at the prices. She doesn't grow potatoes because they take up too much room. Gerald doesn't mind, even though he likes potatoes. He is smart enough to comprehend the role that Gina plays in all facets of their life, from cooking to house painting, from joking to child minding, from good company to silent presence.

The only contentious issue in the house is who has control of the stove, Gina or Rosa. The problem would be easily resolved if Rosa could say to her mother, 'You are a guest in our home and therefore I want you to stay out of the kitchen unless I invite you.' But it is actually Gina's house. Rosa grew up here; her dad Joe died one night in this very kitchen. Rather than live in an empty house like a widow, Gina invited Rosa and her family to move in. So she still retains a little authority. The lines are grey and blurred. She has moved into the bungalow out the back, right next to the train line.

Gerald doesn't mind who claims domain over the kitchen. He simply likes to eat good food.

Rosa and Gerald have two children. Kathy is twelve years old and listens to the radio all the time. Bradley is eight and spends a lot of time digging holes. He likes to look over the fence at the trains.

Across the road is where the strange boy Rodney lives. Kathy often sees him up in his tree and her intuition tells her to be wary of him. She doesn't have to worry. Rodney has no interest in talking to her.

Next door is Norm Norman's house. He comes over for dinner every Thursday night. His dog, Bruiser, always comes in about half an hour later. The dog generally stays out of Gina's garden other than to scare the birds away with a bark, for which Gina rewards him with a polpetta that she makes specially for him. And for Gerald. Mainly Bruiser sniffs around the windows and empty paint cans to see if there have been any cats about other than Thomas.

The Albertos' backyard is Thomas's hunting area. There are always mice in the garden and sometimes sleepy birds. Thomas and Bruiser have an understanding. Bruiser will only chase Thomas if he is out of his designated hunting areas. But he is nowhere to be seen at the moment.

As she shells the peas, Gina suggests that Gerald build a chook shed. Rosa agrees. Both women look at Gerald, who only looks up from the paper when he feels the heat of their stares.

'What?'

'Mum is suggesting you build a chook shed,' Rosa says brightly.

'Me?' Gerald is nonplussed.

'You could do it. It won't be difficult.'

'Time is the issue. There is a busy time coming up at work right now and I don't know when I will be free. Why do we need chooks, anyway?' He lowers the paper to his lap.

'The eggs, of course. Why else do people have chooks?'

'Their good looks? Their beautiful singing? Why all of a sudden do we need more eggs?' Gerald is the only one who laughs at his joke.

'The pub wants Mum to supply their kitchen with pasta. Norm told the manager how good her pasta is and so he came around yesterday. She wants to do it.'

'What about using that young bloke who's been working on the Cummings' veranda? He might be cheap. Anyway, I'll pay for it.'

'Okay, we'll do that then,' Rosa says, happily.

Immediately a plate of Romano cheese is placed in front of Gerald and Gina brings over the wine bottle to refill his glass. The women begin to talk happily about the suspected assignations of a woman they know in the street. Before Gerald can catch her name, he realises that his offer of payment for the chook shed was probably the result required. This has happened before. He looks across the table. Rosa smiles sweetly at him. So, unusually, does Gina. And then Kathy follows suit. So his daughter is in on it too! He looks down at Bradley, playing on the floor with a fallen bread crust, pretending it is an aircraft carrier, unaware of the scene that has just played out. Gerald recognises him as his only future ally.

He sighs and returns to his paper.

Mary looks down at the old newspaper clipping on the table in front of her: 'A coronation cake to celebrate the Coronation of George the Fifth, 22 June 1911, created by Sir Stephen Bolton, Master Chef to our Royal Family.' Mary loves this newspaper clipping. It was inside a recipe book given to her by Patrick's grandmother when Mary first moved in. The recipes were mainly of English cakes and Mary made a few. One day when she picked the book up, the clipping fell out from the back. Mary took it in next door on her visit for a cup of tea the following day. By then Rose was crippled with arthritis and she drifted away a lot but she smiled when she saw the clipping.

'Make it and bring me a piece,' she said to Mary. 'Will you do that?'

Mary went home, grabbed her bag and walked straight down to the store. They had all the ingredients the recipe required. She made the cake that afternoon and took over a piece that night. Rose was too tired to eat it but she asked Mary to hold it under her nose so that she could smell it.

Rose closed her eyes as she spoke. 'The first time we made that cake was right here at this table. Most of the women of the street were here and we took turns to beat the mixture and tell stories. What a good day it was. I know the year—1914. This clipping came from London and was sent to Kathleen Oatley—the mother of Kim across the road in number ten—by her mother living in London. She was a lovely girl, Kathleen. They all were.'

'Yes, I remember her,' Mary says patiently.

'My own daughter, Elizabeth, who of course you know, was away at the time meeting her husband, Patrick's father. I remember because Alfred and I were worried about her. But she brought the wagons home and a husband to boot. The house you're living in was being built then and they moved in a few months later. Then Elizabeth was with child and Alfred and Walter went away together to the war.' She fell silent.

'So Patrick's father wasn't there when Patrick was born?' asked Mary.

Rose looked at her for a long time. 'No.'

And now the clipping is even more yellowed. Mary doesn't need to look at it to make the coronation cake; she just likes to do so for some reason that she can't really fathom. Perhaps it is because she is starting to see that her own life is only relevant when she looks at it as history. Just as the clipping is fading, maybe she is too.

Mary puts the clipping back in the tin on top of the fridge and turns to the window. She sees Patrick pulling at weeds outside in the garden. He picks up an old rusted horseshoe and throws it behind him to be placed with all the other rusted horseshoes they have always found in their yard.

❧ Chapter Seventeen ❧

Almost symbolically Jim hits a nail into the veranda floor that doesn't really need to be hit again. That should be the final blow. Just then, Mary steps out the front door carrying a tray with a cup of tea and a piece of coronation cake on it. She puts the tray on the wooden bench just under the new ticket window.

'Finished,' Jim tells her. 'I think I've done everything we said. Can you see anything that I've forgotten?'

Mary looks around. 'Other than the signs, that looks like it to me.'

'We can put them up now.'

Mary walks along the veranda to where the signs are leaning against the wall. She pulls away the canvas that has kept them dry overnight and, with two hands, carries them back.

She puts two of them on the ground below where they are going to be attached to the wall. Jim picks up his drill and plugs it into the extension cord that is snaking out of the front door. The first sign is going to be hung next to the ticket window, and Mary holds it in place while Jim drills the holes. They work together well, Jim thinks as he puts the drill down at his feet and pulls a screwdriver from his top pocket.

'It's level, isn't it?' he checks.

'Yes. Good enough for me.'

Jim begins tightening the screws. It is harder than he thought it would be. Even though the timber is soft, it is biting hard on the screw and squeezing it tight.

Jim finishes the second screw and they both stand back and look. 'Peter did a pretty good job,' he observes. 'Maybe he should be a signwriter?'

Mary looks at the sign, then at Jim. 'I think he is better off doing what he does.'

'Probably. What does he do exactly?'

'I don't really know. He's harmless though.'

'He did paint these signs well. You've got to hand that to him,' Jim says, as he uses the screwdriver as a back scratcher, at the same time tilting his head to see the sign.

'His father was a signwriter. Now, he was a strange potato. There are lots of stories about him. He's back in Poland now.'

'Mary, did the police ever talk to Peter?' Jim asks quietly.

'They did more than that. They took him away for a few days. Locked him up. They thought he was the one who . . .'

'He didn't tell me that. He pretended that he didn't know anything about the shootings.' Jim looks at her for a moment then out towards the street. 'But he wasn't, was he?'

'No, they had to let him go. I don't think they could get much sense out of him.' Mary's hand goes out towards the sign on the wall. 'I don't know whether he would have been pretending not to know anything about it; it's probably more likely that it just left his mind. He's a troubled boy. What must go on in his head, I don't know.'

'He had an alibi?'

'I don't know exactly. I wonder . . . Have they been around to talk to you yet?'

'They rang. They're coming tomorrow.'

She rubs her forehead as she says, 'Life goes on, even when we don't want it to. If you don't mind, when we have finished with these signs here, I will start going through your mother's wardrobe, throwing things out. Is there anything you particularly want me to keep?'

'Nothing. Nothing at all.'

'Are you sure?'

'Positive. Nothing.'

'Good. It will make it easier to . . . clear out her ghost.' Jim flinches. Mary thinks she has spoken too coldly. 'Sorry. I don't . . .'

Jim straightens up, standing taller than usual, and gives the tiniest of coughs. He says, 'That's alright. They are only words and it is what has to be done. Sometimes though it is hard to keep her in the place where I keep dead people.' He looks at her quickly and tries to explain. 'I mean, in my . . . head. I don't keep real dead people.'

'I know what you're trying to say. Words seem to get themselves in the way of your meaning sometimes.' She places her hand on his back and rubs it twice. 'Let's finish here and then I'll go over.'

The last sign goes up easily and Mary disappears inside for a moment while Jim puts his tools together and rolls up the extension cord. He is standing in the hallway when Patrick walks out of the kitchen, followed by Mary. She ushers him out through the screen door. Jim stays in the hallway and listens.

'We've finished, Pat. Your very own platform. I don't want you to have to walk up to the station anymore. This way we can be together like we always wanted. Remember how you used to say you wished we lived in the station as that way we would always be together? Well, this is pretty close.'

Patrick walks over and fingers the lettering of one of the signs. 'But there are no trains.'

'That's true. I can't do anything about that. But there will be plenty of people who will come onto the platform to sit and talk to you,' Mary says softly.

'Will there? Oh well. Trains aren't everything when it comes to a station. I was getting a bit tired of walking up there. The other day, a man spat on the concrete in front of me.'

He walks along to the end of the platform. 'I like the look of this. I could make up my own timetables.' He looks around. 'I'll need a good broom.'

Mary smiles sadly at him. 'We'll buy one.'

Patrick goes to the screen door and looks in. 'Jim, I didn't really know what you were doing. I see it now. Thank you.'

'It's my pleasure, Patrick.'

'Did you learn to do this in the army? Over there in Vietnam?'

'This is some of what they taught me.'

'In its own way that makes it worthwhile. For me anyway.' Patrick looks up and down the platform before he says, 'Did you enjoy doing it?'

'Yes, I think I did. It was good work.'

They hear voices. Upper Lance and Debra are coming in the front gate, responding to Mary's open invitation. Megan is just closing the front door of number nine to join them too.

'You'd better get some cake ready, Mary,' says Patrick.

By the time Jan returns from his office work that evening, Sally is at the front window waiting for a friend to pick her up. All the classmates are going out to celebrate something, nothing important. But a night out together is what is needed and so no one declines.

Sally knows that it has been a long time since Jan has seen her dressed up like this. He has probably forgotten that she could look like this. She notices him trying not to stare too hard.

Since her life at university started, Sally has noticed that many things are, if not changing, at least altering. She has never been so aware of her mind before. She has never been so aware of her body before. She attributes this to spending so much time with other women and the rhythms they create together which resonate strongly through her. She didn't comprehend the meaning of the word 'sensual' until she heard it come from another woman's lips. It has less to do with desire and more to do with an awareness of what her classmates call her spirit.

Jan would never understand that, no matter how much he pretended to. Sally is confident from seeing his face that she looks good and he knows from the way she is looking at him that she is aware of what he is thinking.

Jan sighs, knowing that he is transparent to her. As she turns back to the window, he notices the earrings.

He is about to ask her where she got them from but by the time his mind has run through the possible answers, he has decided to stay quiet and pretend not to notice them. They are not the gift of a relative or even a close friend. They are the gift of a lover. The blue light that they reflect sears straight into his mind and without another word he walks from the room, accidentally knocking a Bible from the sideboard as he does so.

As her friend's car pulls up on the street outside the manse, Sally smiles.

❧ Chapter Eighteen ❧

The apostle birds won't settle in the branches this morning. Their fluttering and arguments draw Val from her house to look up into the tree. The colony has been in that tree longer than Val has been in the house. The silly old railway man across the road said that they were already there when he was a little boy. Mr Oatley, from number ten, told her that apostle birds select a tree and the flock will stay there for generations. She believed him, though, in hindsight, she thinks he probably lied to her. People who get murdered aren't the sort to have any regard for telling the truth to next-door neighbours.

Val decides to look up apostle birds next time she is at the Choppingblock Library. She actually came outside to see if it was Thomas disturbing the birds. He has been gone now for a week and she has stopped pretending that she isn't worried. It is unlike Thomas to be away for so long. Something has happened, of that she is now sure.

That dog from down the street—the one that fouls the nature strip and treats each lamppost as if it is his very own urinal—now comes to the front gate and looks in. His look may not be of dejection but Val reads it as such. She watches the birds for a few minutes and then goes back inside. The house seems cavernous without Thomas.

Val thinks back to how she coped with her husband's death. He was only forty and she was thirty-two. She dealt with his death as any robust thinking person would: she replaced him with physical, tiring duties and worked at them hard until she felt brave enough to stop. It took three years. But her expression of grief was minimal. Now, though, with Thomas, she doesn't think she can begin a new round of frenetic activity; she feels too tired.

She walks over to the mirror and when she looks at her reflection the tears begin. They are hot and stinging. She has an uncontrollable need to call out to someone. She can't say Thomas's name but she can say her husband's. The tears are full and run easily down her cheeks. She leaves the mirror and walks into the lounge room. There is a picture of Thomas on the mantelpiece, next to a picture of Keith that she took when they were on their honeymoon in Sydney.

When the tears begin to dry up and the aching begins in her chest, she picks up the picture of Thomas to bring back the tears in force. At least they keep the aching at bay. She cries like this for the next twenty minutes. But the next time she looks down at the photograph she is clutching, she realises that it is the one of Keith wearing his uniform. She starts to cry again.

Keith was a good man. He would never have let her answer the door on her own when the postman delivered the telegram. He would have stood by her side with a hand on her shoulder as she read it. He would have known how sad the news would make her and he would have held her tightly in his arms. He was a good man.

And he would be out there now looking for Thomas.

The tears dry up, her breathing becomes steady and she feels as if something has been pushed a little further from her mind.

She turns to the window as she dries her cheeks. In front of her house, looking up at the apostle birds, is the priest, Jan. Without too much thought, she walks to the front door and opens it, just as he has begun to walk on down the street. He is jingling some coins in his pocket. He turns his head and looks at her, lifting an imaginary cap. She notices that he is not wearing his collar.

Keith would not have liked such an exciting man.

Jim listens to the apostle birds in the tree next door as he finishes his ham sandwich. He feels comforted by the sound. It is the silence in nature that he has grown to be wary of. Birds won't sing when there is impending violence in the air; when men are sneaking up on each other or shells are about to fall from the sky they know to fly to another place.

That was one of the first things that Jim was taught when he arrived in Vietnam. Out on a jungle track, he was answering a question from one of the other men about his life at home when he noticed that no one was listening anymore. They had stopped walking and opened their eyes wide. It made him so scared that he fell silent, the word about to leave his lips forgotten.

The birds had stopped singing.

Brent moved quickly to his side and pushed him into the cover of the large leaves surrounding the trail. As one, the other men followed. Brent put his fingers to his lips but no one needed that reminder.

Twenty feet away, six soldiers from the North walked down the trail towards them; they must have been just as aware of the silence of the birds, but had evidently decided to keep moving and trust that they would be safe. And they were. Happy not to engage them, Jim's platoon let them walk on. The men didn't set off again until the sound of birds returned, and they didn't talk until they reached the relative safety of the main camp, where their voices had to be raised to be heard over the sound of the helicopters.

So the restlessness of the apostle birds now tells Jim that it is safe for him to continue on with his day. To celebrate finishing Patrick's platform, Jim is wearing his favourite shirt that Mai picked out for him in Saigon. Mary ironed it for him. He found it hanging on the lounge-room doorknob. It is a deep red, too light to be crimson, too dark to be pink. He steps out the back screen door and pulls the hammer out of the holster of the nail bag as he walks over to the side fence. Yesterday he noticed that the rusted nails had loosened, and some of the wooden palings are listing. He is going to pull out the original nails and replace them with new ones that will keep the palings in place for another sixty years. He puts some nails head first between his lips and then pulls the first of the palings away.

A sulphur-crested cockatoo sits in the tree above the fence, head turned sideways, looking down at him. He is shocked to see a grey-haired man leaning on Val's wall, carving out what looks to be one of the decorative roof supports around her house. The man's face looks lined and wind beaten, and he retreats quickly back around the corner of Val's house. He shows no emotion and Jim doesn't feel at all compelled to engage him. It is a strange vision.

And it is enough to make him put off fixing the fence today. Just as he is stepping into the kitchen he hears a knock at the front door.

Mary is standing on the porch, looking back out towards the street. At her feet are some small calico sacks, a big paper bag with a department store name across it, and an empty cane basket. When she hears the door open she turns to face Jim. 'I thought now might be a good time to finish cleaning out your mother's wardrobe. Is that alright with you?'

'Now is as good a time as any—come in. Shall I help you?'

'Of course not. Why don't you go down to the pub for a while? Or there is a seat free on Patrick's platform if you prefer to go there.'

'I might do both. Shall I leave you the key?'

'What for? No, you go. And don't rush back. This will take a while. That shirt looks good on you.'

'Thanks for ironing it.' Jim grabs his wallet from the windowsill where he left it last night, and finds himself stepping out the front door without any firm idea of where he is heading. At first it is an uncomfortable thought and he realises he hasn't enjoyed this type of spontaneity in the three years since he was conscripted. It gives him a strange sense of freedom and, without giving the decision too much consideration, he heads across the street to number seven where Patrick is overseeing a small number of neighbours who have answered Mary's request and come over to see the new platform. Patrick engages him as he comes through the gate and climbs the steps.

'Good afternoon, Jim. Trains are running late today, I'm afraid. But Mary has made some tea and there is some of her coronation cake. And there is room for you to sit along here.' He points to a spot on the bench between Megan and Debra. On the next bench, Eve, Rodney's mother, and Bill Casey from number three sit watching the street. Each person has a cup of tea and a piece of cake. Jim leans into the ticket window and pours himself a cup and grabs a slice of cake. Everyone stays silent while he is doing this but as he lifts the cake to his mouth to try a little bit straight away, they resume talking. As he sits down he knocks Megan's hand, which is holding her teacup.

'Oh, I'm sorry,' he says, politely.

'Don't worry. It's empty. How are you?' she responds, just as formally.

'I've no complaints. Something strange, though—I think I've just seen a ghost in my backyard.' He rests the piece of cake on his knee and scratches his head.

'You mean one of your . . . ?' Megan begins nervously.

'Oh no. This was one from next door. You know, Val's place. I've never seen him before.'

'I'm glad I've never seen a ghost. I don't know what I'd do.'

'No? You strike me as the sort of person who would be pretty good if something unexpected happened.'

'Really?' She looks at him. '. . . Was I?'

Jim nods. 'Yes.' But it is Mai's question he is answering. *Am I good for you?*

Debra has been talking to Eve, but now she turns to greet Jim. 'This is wonderful cake,' she says. 'Has Mary told you where she got the rec-ipe from?'

'No, where?' Megan asks, speaking past Jim.

'It came from the old woman who used to live in your house, Megan. She was Patrick's grandmother and she had been making this cake since before the Great War.'

'Really?' says Megan, looking suddenly uncomfortable. Being this close to Jim made her think of the surprising event in her kitchen, and what with his talk of ghosts and now the old woman's cake originally coming from that kitchen, she feels decidedly uneasy.

'It is good cake,' Jim adds, noticing Megan's sudden discomfort.

'Oh, hello!' Debra and Eve say together as Jan Domak comes through the front gate.

'Hello, ladies. Has anybody seen Peter, my neighbour?' he asks, to no one in particular.

'Not since he brought down the station signs,' Jim says, with a mouthful of cake. He was trying to remember what he wanted to ask the reverend.

Jan puffs out his chest and turns to look at the street for a moment. Debra and Eve are looking at each other, suddenly aware that each has used the same tone of voice to greet the reverend, and beginning to suspect that the other may be feeling the same sort of tingle in their stomach. At the same time, they both look towards Jan who still has his back to them and continues to speak, this time as if he is addressing the street.

'Mary says he has done this before. Apparently he wanders off some-times. Well if you see him, come up to the church and let me know, the door is always open. Well, nearly always.'

He sweeps around to face the others.

Jim notices that Debra moves suddenly in her seat, making the bench squeak, and that Eve has leaned forward and is quite still, not breathing. She reminds him of a sniper about to fire a shot. Instinctively, he freezes too. He steals a look at Megan, smiling quietly at the reverend, her mind evidently elsewhere.

Patrick walks to the end of the platform, consulting his watch. He returns it to his pocket, looks into the far distance, clasps his hands behind his back, and begins to bounce on his toes.

Jim stands too and places his empty cup on the tray by the door. When he turns around, he finds that the reverend has taken his seat between Megan and Debra. He suddenly remembers what he wanted to ask him. Are secrets the same as things never spoken? The three women and the large priest are now engrossed in conversation, all four leaning forward. Bill Casey has wandered off down the platform to ask Patrick something. Jim's farewell is answered only by Megan and he walks to the front gate. Patrick turns from Bill and watches him leave. A willy-willy runs down the road; on a whim Jim follows it till it blows itself out at the end of the street. He continues on to the pub where he stands alone and looks at the reflection in the glass of whisky.

A South Vietnamese soldier told him a legend as they waited for a retrieval helicopter to find them. If the spirit of the person who stole your heart is around you then you will sometimes see their reflection in still water. A bath. A sink. A pond. A glass of whisky.

Jim looks for a while and then swallows the liquid in one mouthful.

He walks back to number ten, goes inside and instantly notices that the house feels different. First he is struck by the smell. His mother's smell was always easy to identify. Lavender rose, she called it. Lately, it has been the strongest he has ever smelled it, as if she has just walked through the hallway on her way out shopping. But now there is no real sense of her presence anymore. Instead there is a new scent, one he recognises but can't identify.

Mary peers out of the bedroom. 'Feels better, doesn't it?'

'Sure does. What did you do?'

'Just cleaned out her wardrobe and cupboard. There is nothing of hers left there anymore. And I lit some Chinese incense to keep her spirit from returning.'

Jim realises now why the scent is familiar—he remembers it from the town temples he walked past in Vietnam. 'How do you know about incense?' he asks Mary.

'Patrick's grandmother told me about it.'

'Hello!' another voice calls from the bedroom. Lukewarm. 'I'm cleaning out your dad's wardrobe. There's nothing that you want to keep, is there?'

'All I want is that tie that he never wore, the one with the hula girl on it.'

Lukewarm appears around the door, the tie draped around his neck. 'I thought that you might want to keep it.'

'Good on you.'

Lukewarm disappears back into the bedroom, and Jim takes in the new feeling of the house.

Mary steps out into the hallway. 'Jim, are you going to be okay?'

He shrugs. For a moment he can't find the words he wants to use. 'In general? I've thought about it and I just don't know. I can't work it out. I figure I will be if I keep busy for a while.'

Mary takes a deep breath. It is the sort of breath taken when a tender subject is about to be broached and the other person's reaction is unknown. She looks at him closely and says, 'You know, hindsight is a dreadful thing sometimes. Looking back, I think your dad had become thinner and that he had rings under his eyes. He mustn't have been getting much sleep. He had stopped talking to me and the other women in the street. He still talked to Patrick, though. Your mum said she was worried about him. The police asked all of us if we had noticed anything. At that stage we must have been in shock; I said I hadn't.'

Jim says nothing. Mary's eyes had shifted to his shoulder, but as she finishes, she looks back into his eyes. 'The truth is, the only person around here who really notices anything is that boy up the apricot tree.'

Of course. 'Rodney?'

Mary nods. 'He sees everything and makes a note of it.'

The potential of this statement springs Jim's mind to attention. 'What did he tell the police?'

Mary is quick to answer because she has recognised something in Jim's voice: the same still coldness that she heard when he asked about Peter. 'Nothing. He was at school when they interviewed everybody.'

There is now a method in the way Jim speaks. He has become someone who knows how to get information quickly and efficiently. His emotions have sunk deep inside him. 'So he must have been at school when it happened.'

'Oh no. He had the day off. I remember seeing him sitting up there when I heard the gunshots.'

'Well, maybe I should talk to him.'

'Only if you want to find out.'

Jim looks at her. 'What do you mean? Why wouldn't I want to find out?'

'He might just tell you something . . .'

'Something I don't want to hear? Like what?'

'Like why a woman kept coming around when your dad was home alone.'

Jim takes a small step back. He blinks. 'What do you mean?'

'A woman was a regular guest in your house when your mother was away. That's all. I don't know who she was. I don't know what they got up to. It was none of my business. I sometimes wanted to say some-thing to your mother but I never did. I figured she must have known. She wasn't stupid.' Mary pauses, and adds gently, 'She went away a lot.'

Jim is now looking beyond Mary's shoulder, out the door. The apos-tle birds are still unsettled in their tree. 'Yeah, she has a sister in Sydney.'

'That's right. I met her at the . . . funeral. She seemed to be a pleas-ant woman.'

'Yes, she is. I suppose.'

Mary holds out her hands and lifts her shoulders. 'Well, I don't know. Maybe the boy in the tree holds the key to it.'

'Maybe.'

'You could ask him. Eve is his mother's name.'

'Yes, I just met her. She seems nice.'

'She is.'

Jim is now looking around the hall as if searching for a chair to sit down on. As though unaware that he is speaking aloud, he continues, 'I don't want to scare him. A boy who sits in a tree all the time is prob-ably a bit sensitive.'

Mary reaches out and clasps his hand. 'I'd say so. But why don't you talk to Eve and see what she says?'

Jim's smile is pained. He looks down at her hand and says, 'I'll do that.'

❧ Chapter Nineteen ❧

Jim bides his time. He sees Rodney up in the apricot tree on two separate occasions before he decides to pay a visit. It is dinnertime at Eve's house and Jim's knocking disturbs them halfway through their chops and peas.

Eve looks a little concerned when Jim tells her he wants to speak to Rodney, but she leads him into the kitchen to where Rodney is sitting at the wooden table, his fork poised.

'Rodney, this is Jim from up the road,' Eve tells him.

'I know who Jim is. He was the one who turned Patrick's house into a railway station.'

'That's right, I did . . .'

'And he was the one who crossed the street and gave that girl a piece of honeysuckle, then quickly walked back home and went inside.'

'Yes. And I haven't seen her since.'

'She turned to talk to you when you were walking away and she has been in the street once more—not to see the strange man Peter but to look at the soldier statue in the park. She kept looking back at your house.'

'Really? When was this?' Jim says, amused but interested.

'Hold on, I'll get my books.' Rodney pushes back the chair and jumps up.

'What about your dinner, mister?' Eve calls.

'I'll be straight back.'

'His logbooks are in his room,' Eve explains to Jim. 'Do you want a cup of tea?'

'Only if there is one.'

'There is. The pot makes two cups; it's too hard only making one cup.'

Jim looks at her, unsure if she is making an opening comment about something deeper than tea. Jim knows that she is a widow.

She is immediately aware of his uncertainty and hastens to remedy it. 'Rodney doesn't drink tea.'

Jim smiles at her in gratitude. 'Doesn't he? I'd like to have one.'

'Milk?'

'Yes please, and no sugar.'

As Eve gets up, Rodney returns with five pocket-sized exercise books.

'Are these your logbooks?' asks Jim.

'Some of them. They are this size because they are easiest to climb a tree with.'

Jim is struck by this. He spent a lot of his time in Vietnam up trees, and everything he carried had to pass exactly that test: whether it could be taken up a tree. Water bottles, pens, sunglasses, food. He is slowly discovering that the strange dark world he lived in over there has a lot more in common with the normal everyday world over here than he'd previously realised.

'How long do you spend in the tree?' he asks Rodney.

'One hour in the morning. Two hours after school, until tea. Then another hour until it is dark.'

'Comfortable?'

'Very. There is a spot to rest my book and another branch to keep my pens on.'

Over there, Jim could never be so relaxed about the things he carried into position with him. If he dropped something from one of his perches, he would have to climb down immediately and recover it. If he couldn't find it, he would have to move to another tree, sometimes as much as a valley away. Men searching for snipers look for clues on the ground more than in branches.

'Have you worn away the bark where you sit?'

'Yes I have. It is very smooth.'

'And slippery, I bet. If you have a piece of coarse sandpaper in your pocket you can easily rough up the surface again, and that will stop you from slipping. Not altogether, but a little bit. And a little bit helps.'

'That's right.' Rodney nods, impressed at Jim's knowledge.

'Look, I've got some in my pocket. You can have it. This will do the job.'

'Thanks, Jim,' Rodney says, taking the sandpaper.

'You know a lot about this subject,' Eve says.

Jim looks at her. 'I used to have a job that involved sitting in trees.'

'Wow! What sort of a job was that?' Rodney asks.

'I was in the army. I would have to sit still for a long time. It wasn't a very nice job.'

'No, I wouldn't like to have to sit still. I'd prefer to drive a tank across creeks and logs.'

Eve recognises what sort of job in the army requires tree sitting and so she changes the subject. 'What are you planning to do now that you're home? You are home, aren't you? Or are you going back?'

'Oh no. I never want to go back there again. I'm not sure what I will do now. I enjoyed the building I did for Mary and Patrick and I may just keep doing that sort of work. As of now, the army is still paying me.'

'Exactly three weeks ago today,' Rodney says.

'Excuse me?' Jim is momentarily puzzled.

'When that girl you gave the honeysuckle to came and looked at the soldier statue.'

'Oh, right. Well, she might come back again.'

'And then you can kiss her.'

'Rodney!' Eve says.

Jim laughs. 'Maybe. Maybe not. I think I'd like to get to know her first. Find out what her name is, that sort of thing.' Jim sits back in his chair and pushes his teacup to one side. 'Rodney, can you tell me what was happening in the street the day all the police cars turned up to my house?'

Rodney looks at him without answering and then selects a logbook from the stack and begins to flick deliberately through the pages. 'You mean the day your dad and your mum got fired by the gun?' he says at last.

'Yes, that day.'

'Well, that morning, your mum went down to the shops. Patrick went to the train station. Val's cat went straight into the strange man's house when Val let it out the front door. Your dad walked down to Choppingblock Road and stood there for a while.'

'Doing what?'

'He watched a funeral drive past. You know, when the cars all have their headlights on and they drive in a line slowly.'

'Oh yes. Did he come back after that?'

Rodney consulted his logbook. 'Yes, straightaway. The time was nine thirty am.'

'Ah.' Jim looks at Eve to see if she appears worried by his questioning of her son. She doesn't. If anything, she looks more concerned about Jim. 'Rodney, do you remember a woman who used to come visiting my house when my mum wasn't home?' Jim senses Eve flinch.

'You mean in the green car?'

'Yes, that's who I mean.'

'Well, she used to come all the time when your mum was away. I figured that your dad couldn't wash the dishes on his own and she liked to come by and help him. My mum can't do the dishes on her own. I have to help her.'

'Yes, I imagine that's why she was coming by.'

'She didn't come anymore after her car got smashed by the truck. You should have heard the noise. It made all the cockatoos go quiet.'

'Where was that smash? Here in the street?'

'No,' Eve says.

'In Choppingblock Road,' Rodney explains. 'Just down from the corner. The police and an ambulance came. The truck driver cried.'

'Was the lady in the green car hurt?'

'No, she wasn't hurt. She was dead.'

'Oh, Rodney,' Eve says.

'She was. I saw an ambulance man put a sheet over her face. That's what you do with dead people. So they can't look out and see what's happened.'

'That's right. When was the smash?' asks Jim.

Rodney consults his book again, turning back seven pages. 'One week before the gun was fired and made the apostle birds fly out of the tree. They had just settled back down when the gun went off again. They didn't come back for a while after that.'

'I think that's enough,' Eve says.

'Yes. That's enough. Thanks, Rodney. Can I just ask one more thing?' Jim looks at Eve. The question is for her.

'Sure,' Rodney says. Eve nods slowly.

'Did you see anybody knock on my front door before the shots were fired?'

Rodney keeps his head down, staring at a page in his logbook. 'Yes, I did,' he says finally.

'That's *enough*,' Eve says as she stands.

Jim sits back from the table and tries to take a deep breath without gasping. He fails. Rodney looks up at him. Jim tries to smile at him and says, 'Okay, let's forget about it. There's no need to talk about it anymore.'

'And your dad buried the silver box in the front yard the night before the guns fired off. That was great. I reckon it must be real treasure. Are you going to dig it up?'

Jim leans forward again. 'Where did he bury it?'

'He dug the hole near the big tree.'

'I think I'll go home now and dig it up. I'll come and tell you if it's treasure. Tell me, do you ever get tired of sitting in the tree?'

'Sometimes. But . . . I don't really know what else to do.'

Jim opens his two hands, palms upwards, on the table. Rodney and Eve look down at them as if Jim is about to perform a magic trick. He says, 'You could come up and help me sometimes, if you want. I'm going to build a chook shed for the people across the road. The Albertos in number four.'

'What would I do?'

'Do you know how to hammer?'

'No.'

'Do you know how to saw?'

'No.'

'Great. Then that's what you can do first. Learn to hammer and learn to saw. I'll teach you.'

'Would you?' asks Eve. Rodney and Jim look at her.

'Yes. I'm a good teacher. I'd like to do it, if you don't mind?'

'I'd love you to,' Eve says.

'Rodney, can you whistle?'

'Yes, Mum says I'm a good whistler.'

Jim smiles at Eve. 'Then in return you can teach me to whistle. I can't and I would like to.'

'Can we start on the chook shed now?' Rodney asks.

'Sort of. Rosa has told me what she wants and how big. You and I will have to draw up plans so we know how much timber and wire to buy.'

'And nails,' Rodney adds. 'When can we do these plans?'

'I want to talk to your mum about homework and what other commitments you have.'

'What's a commitment?'

'A promise that you have made to yourself or someone else.'

'I don't make promises in case I can't keep them.'

'Good for you.' Jim turns again to Eve and lifts his eyebrows in a question.

Eve has already thought about it and has an answer ready. 'Tomorrow night we have to go shopping for a new pair of shoes for school. The next night is free. How's that for you, Jim?'

'That's good.'

'Come for dinner,' she presses.

'Okay. But Rodney and I will have a lot of work to do. We won't be able to sit around after dinner and talk.'

'You might have to wash the dishes on your own that night, Mum. Will you be alright?' Rodney asks.

'Yes, I'll manage.'

Jim gets up and heads to the door. 'I'm so pleased I have an assistant to help me do this job. Oh, by the way, I'll pay you.'

'You don't have to,' Eve whispers, behind him.

Jim stops at the door. 'No, fair's fair. The Albertos are paying me. And if you like this sort of work there's more to come. The Hendersons want me to build an arch for their roses.'

'We'll need to draw plans,' Rodney says.

'We will. I don't know how to build an arch.'

'The pub has an old one in the backyard. You can see it from my lookout tree.'

Jim laughs. 'Alright. When the time comes, I'll climb up and have a look. Now, I'd better go. Thanks for the cup of tea.'

'You're welcome,' says Eve and then out of Rodney's earshot she asks, 'The police will want to talk to him, won't they?'

Jim opens the door and looks at the new night. He turns back to face Eve. 'No. I'm not going to say anything to them.'

She flinches as if she is trying not to cry. She mouths a thank-you to him. He nods and walks out into the night air.

Eve closes the door. 'Wow,' she says.

'Wow,' Rodney echoes.

Jim walks straight home, throws open the side gate and grabs the shovel, which is leaning against the side fence. Just before he thrusts the blade into the soil, he pauses, his body poised to dig. He knows that thoughts are quick and that unless he stops and attends to them as they come into his head, they will fly away with the wind.

Overseas Jim witnessed many injustices that have been left ignored and unremedied. He has seen that these injustices pass into history in the same way as the ones resolved. And so he decides that the information about his parents' murder in Rodney's logbook should be left there. And that the boy in the apricot tree should not be disturbed again.

Only once did Jim try to fix an injustice, and all it did was create another one. The knife he pulled from Mai's belly he returned to the GI who owned it, by plunging it into his chest. The money that he ripped from Mai's fist, he stuffed into the mouth of the GI. And the ghosts of both people have been with him ever since.

*

Jim feels a sudden connection to his father as he digs out the same soil that his father filled in. His intuition tells him when he is about to hit the silver box before there is any physical indication. He uses his hands to scoop out the last of the soil and soon the silver box shines at the bottom of the hole in the new moonlight. Jim looks down at it, feeling a quiet heartache as if he has just discovered something from his childhood. He reaches down to it. There are letters in the silver box. He unfolds the first one, reads two paragraphs and then refolds it. Jim doesn't know the handwriting, but it is clearly a woman's. He takes another letter from near the bottom of the pile, reads a little and then folds it back up too. He empties all the letters from the box into the hole and puts the empty silver tin down on the path beside him. Then he fills in the hole, pats down the dirt and covers it with leaves. The ground looks undisturbed. He picks up the box and carries it and the spade around the back.

Inside he wipes out the box, finds his dog tags on the table, places them inside and returns it to its former place in the cupboard over the fridge. He sits for a moment at the kitchen table. Where his father always sat, although it doesn't feel like it's his father's seat anymore. He remembers what a forgotten soldier said to him while they were standing out on a street in Saigon, watching as the two sad girls with smiling faces whom they had picked up easily and would most likely never see again walked into a department store to spend the money the two Australian soldiers had just given them. The soldier was married and talked constantly about fidelity. He said that secrets are, in fact, living things. They expand, contract, stay silent, cry out. And like any other living thing, they eventually emerge into the sun.

Jim smiled because he understood now. He may have sweated in his hurry to rebury those letters, but it didn't matter; his father's secret is now stretching itself in the light of day.

He picks up the photo of Kathleen and Johnny, posing by the side of the house, and tries to decipher some more of the words written on the back.

All day, the clouds have allowed the sun to pass by undisturbed. The wind blew the smell of a bushfire down the street in the morning but now in the late afternoon it has drifted away and been replaced by the currawalli tree scents. The only real noises during the day were the trains and the cockatoos and now there is the last of the birds and the first of the crickets.

Upper Lance stops at the First World War monument, the statue of the silent soldier. He looks idly at the list of names. The fallen, from the streets around here. He reads each name aloud and notices there is only one woman. He doesn't know what that means.

What do men normally do on their evenings off? he wonders.

Go to the pub.

He begins to walk slowly down the street. Although he doesn't normally think twice about going to work, now that he doesn't have to go for a few days it feels as if a weight has been lifted from his mind and body. He must dread it more than he realises. He tries to put a spring in his step. He has time to look down driveways and paths. When he is walking to work he keeps his head down and tries to think over the things he has been meaning to do that day because he knows that once he is at work they will evaporate and never come back. He has a dangerous job, though no more dangerous than the man standing next to him on the factory floor. It requires concentration. Safety guards look good as far as inspectors are concerned but they are an impediment to the work. They turn a ten-minute job into a twenty-minute job, and the boss can't afford that. Upper Lance hates it when the union comes in and talks about safety: he knows how to use this equipment and keep safe; he's not a child.

Debra isn't around and this idleness is starting to irritate him. She has gone into the church to pray for something or other. She likes to do that. He looks at the church door. It is closed. It is after six. Maybe he should go in and pray with her? No, he wouldn't know what to say. She asked him once if he had doubts about God, if that was why he wasn't very religious. He replied that he thought God had doubts about him. That was very clever; he always remembers it. He will use that line again if ever anybody asks him about his religious beliefs. So far, though, no one has asked.

No, maybe he will go to the pub and have two beers. That is his limit and Debra will be home by then, making dinner.

As he turns away from the church he sees Jim walking ahead of him, no doubt heading for the same place. By the time he walks in the front door of the pub, Jim is standing at the bar, throwing back some sort of spirit. Upper Lance is a little discouraged by the ease with which he drinks the spirit; as if it is water. As a boy Lance was taught by his mum to be wary of men who drank easily. His grandfather cut a swathe through his family life before he died of the drink. But in memory of his grandfather he walks up to Jim, says hello and asks to join him.

Lance's two beers turn into three as they talk about all manner of things. Jim is a good listener, Upper Lance thinks to himself, and I must be a good talker. As he finishes his third beer, the fourth is already on the coaster waiting for him.

Upper Lance looks around the bar at all the faces. He turns towards Jim as a ballet dancer would if he was offstage and heard his name called. It is a sudden movement. Jim steps back, a little shocked at the unexpectedness of it.

Upper Lance says, 'I was looking at the statue at the end of our street. That poor soldier. And all the names. I was thinking about him.' Lance grabs Jim's forearm. 'I don't believe he just stands up there on his own. No, all the secrets of the street—all the ghosts that have been pushed out of the houses, all the memories that have tried to be forgotten; all those thoughts that were believed and then suddenly not believed—all of those things are up there with him. Up there watching what goes on. No wonder he bows his head. All that weight on his back . . .' He releases Jim's arm and pauses to drink. The beer spills out of the glass and runs down his hand, under his sleeve.

'. . . And another thing. If his head was up, he would be able to see right down Currawalli Street. See who goes where, see what happens when no one is looking, see who keeps their curtains open when they should be closed, see who is knocking on whose door . . . God knows what he would see.

'Jim, you're a lot younger than me and I've learned a few things over the years. I'll tell you something: the main difference between then and now is simply this. Then, telling a lie and not telling the truth was exactly the same thing. But now you are able to not tell the truth without telling a lie. And in that,' he smiles at Jim, 'lies the destruction of the human race.'

'Oh,' Jim says, realising that the other man has passed his alcohol limit.

'And it will only get worse.' Upper Lance comes one step closer and lowers his voice. 'There are times when I wake up and I can clearly see what is happening to the world. But my clarity disappears within minutes. Sometimes at night when I'm at work, I get a chance to ponder things. I worry about my daughter's future. I also worry about being at work all night and not being with my wife. Whether she gets lonely . . . if you know what I mean?'

Jim thinks he does and decides that he doesn't want to go down this path with a man he hardly knows. But Upper Lance continues without waiting for Jim's response. 'Especially because our daughter has been away, so Debra is alone in the house. She says she likes it but I don't know . . . She used to have an appetite, if you know what I mean, but recently she doesn't . . . you know?'

Jim does know what he means. He shared a tent with a soldier from Sydney, roughly the same age as Upper Lance who wondered about the same things, and every time he came across a term or situation or emotion too uncomfortable to describe he would say exactly this: 'do you know what I mean?' Jim eventually learned that the issues being resolved didn't stop the *do you know what I mean*s; they continued unabated and ended up saying more about the man in the tent than it did about the woman in the house back at home in Sydney.

'Oh, I'm sorry.' Lance collects himself. 'I'm rabbiting on. I have a few nights off work and I'm a little excited.'

'Maybe we should go home now?'

'I'm not sure . . . I'm not sure if I can . . . walk that far.'

'I'll help you. We'll walk together.'

So Jim holds Upper Lance by the forearm and they step back from the bar with its hanging tin mugs and over to the door. The sun has gone down and the streetlights have come on. Jim anticipates Upper Lance's weaves and holds him tighter with each sudden movement. They walk past the unoccupied apricot tree (Jim is pleased Rodney won't be logging this in his book), past the honeysuckle on Jim's front fence, under the apostle bird tree and on up to number sixteen. Jim is going to leave Upper Lance at the letterbox, but when Jim releases his arm Lance overbalances, and so Jim walks him down the driveway and around the back. Through the kitchen window, he can see Debra at the stove. The two men walk in the back door and she looks up from the pan.

'I'm afraid I might have made him drunk,' says Jim. 'We got carried away talking.'

Debra turns off the stove and walks over to the table, pulling out a kitchen chair. Jim helps Upper Lance sit down.

'Oh Lance. Did you drink too much?' She looks up at Jim. 'He's not much of a drinker . . . thank God.'

'No, I can see that. I think he had four beers.'

'Two is his limit. Any more and he gets . . . like this. He will be alright after a couple of hours. What was he doing down the pub? He doesn't normally go.' She smiles at Jim as she straightens up. 'Thank you for helping him home. I bet he talked a lot. He loves to talk. As I bet you found out.'

'Oh well. I don't mind. I like to hear what people think.' Jim smiles back. 'I better be going. See you later.'

As he leaves he hears Debra call, 'Thanks again, Jim. Bye.'

He turns the corner of the house and begins to walk back down the driveway. As he does so, he sees Eve softly close the church door and begin to walk down the other side of the street towards her home. He doesn't call out to her.

❧ Chapter Twenty ❧

The last four steps before you reach the tree trunk are the most important. And they need to be deftly executed just at the point that your body starts to react to the panic rising in your throat. Enough momentum must be gained so that the impact on the bark of the trunk is minimal. Scratches and indentations are some of the things looked for when a tree sniper is known to be about. As with an athlete's preparation, it takes time and care to prepare oneself for the ascent, but Jim knows that this is an emergency—there is no time for mental preparation. He can hear the patrol as it makes its way through the rushes by the river. They are not far away and they are looking for him, that much he knows. Otherwise they would be keeping quiet and employing stealth. But when you are tracking a tree sniper you know that the panic provoked by the sound of voices is often the cause of an involuntary sudden movement. And that is the only give-away needed. Twenty metres ahead of the patrol will be a silent scout, the soldier who is noted for having the best eyes. It is he who waits to pick up any panicked movement. Then he makes one call and the patrol closes in.

Jim has heard of the things done to captured snipers and he always carries a pistol with one bullet should he ever be discovered. It is a tiny Chinese pistol made for ladies of the night in Shanghai to keep hidden in their clothing, in case they ever needed to protect themselves. Jim bought it in Saigon from a gun dealer as discreet as the pistol. The man told Jim that this was also a popular gun with high-ranking officers of the armies. Generals and colonels were never sure who they could trust among their support staff or for how long. And being in the High Command meant that you didn't know whether that pistol would eventually have to be turned on someone else or turned on yourself. Such was the instability of being a general.

Jim was pleased with the pistol's weight and size, which meant he could climb a tree unaffected. It didn't matter to him how accurate the aim was. And he carries it everywhere in his pocket as casually as he would a set of keys back in Currawalli Street.

As he tries to scale the trunk without marking the bark, Jim realises with a sudden shock that he doesn't have his rifle or his pack with him. He quickly looks down to check that he hasn't left them at the foot of the tree, sees he hasn't; then he has no more time to think about them and where they might be. He can hear the footsteps of the patrol now, and the scout must be closer again. He reaches for a strong branch above him and firmly pulls himself up onto it like a tree python. Steadily, so that no leaves are shaken by his movement. Deciding to keep climbing, he reaches for another branch above him, pulls himself up to this branch solely with his arms, keeping his legs still as if paralysed from the waist down. There are now leaves below him as well as around him and he begins to feel safer.

He has been doing this long enough to know that feeling safe in these situations is dangerous—this is when lethal blunders are made—so he stops breathing and scans the area around the base of the tree. He can now make out soldiers' voices more clearly but the sounds have little meaning. The scout may have already passed him by or he may be very close. Jim has no choice: he must climb higher. Sweat is beginning to run down his face and he wipes his cheeks slowly and delicately with his hand. This has the double advantage of rubbing off the dirt on his hand, making his face darker and ensuring that any loose bark he might touch will stick to his damp hands rather than fall to the ground below. Still, some drops of perspiration have run into his left eye; the salt stings and for a moment his vision is blurred.

He has no time to wait for his eye to clear; he must keep climbing. With his left eye squeezed tightly shut, he looks around him to ensure his next movement isn't going to brush against anything that could rustle or fall. Above and a little ahead of him he sees another branch, thicker than the one he is currently stretched out on. After quickly looking below, he reaches for it. As soon as his hands are clasped around it he begins to pull himself up, holding his legs out from the branch like a gymnast. Once he has pulled himself up to the branch and then pushed his chest and arms above it, he slowly draws in his legs.

Now he has to breathe. He is careful not to gasp even though his body is crying out for oxygen. He knows that if he lays his face down on the branch and forces his mind into another space, a similar space to the one he sinks into when waiting for a target, he can suppress his body's urgent need to gulp in air.

He looks about, moving only his eyes. He is completely surrounded by leaves and can no longer see the ground. The patrol is approaching; he can hear the clinking of each man's rifle and pack.

Stay still.

There is nothing more he can do.

Still.

Suddenly he hears movement on the branch beside him, jerky and unexpected. It is not the smooth movement of an animal or reptile for whom this tree is home. It can only be human. Holding his breath again, he continues to lie still.

'Why are you lying there like that?'

It is Rodney's voice.

Jim opens his eyes. There are three apricots hanging in front of his face.

'Have you come up to look at the pub's rose arch?' the boy asks.

'Um . . . I was just thinking about something from a long time ago.' Jim shakes his head to clear his eyes. 'Let's see what this rose arch looks like. Then we can go inside and design one.'

He holds Rodney steady as the boy squeezes past him. Even though it is a thin branch and they are up high, Jim can tell that Rodney knows he won't fall with Jim holding him safe. Jim suddenly sees this knowledge as something important.

From Rodney's observation spot, Jim looks up and down the street. It is the street where he grew up, and where once he knew every tree, bush and stone; the street that he was once pleased to leave behind so that he could touch new things. Yet, now he knows that what he was hoping to touch were just exposed treasures, which are only shallow imitations of hidden treasures, he is able to look about him with different eyes. That is what the memory of Mai's heart beating against his chest is. That is what this apricot tree is. That is what this street is. That is what home is. Hidden treasures.

He thinks a lot about the words scrawled in a man's handwriting on the back of the photo of his grandparents, Johnny and Kathleen. Some of the writing is indecipherable, and he looks at the photo every night, waiting for its meaning to become clear. But he can make out a few words. They read: 'the fine art of belonging'.

Jan looks up from his desk in the church office. Next Sunday's sermon is almost finished and so he allows himself a break from concentration. He looks idly at the last paragraph he has written, then leans forward, suddenly alert.

He then rereads the whole sermon. Most of it is alright. Just the last paragraph. It is almost a confession. That's how it reads. He doesn't need to make a confession. Who should he make a confession to? God? The Bishop? Sally? Of course not. He rubs his forehead and squeezes his eyes shut. All he can see is the blue light of her earrings from the other night. There is a knock at the door. He looks up at the clock and pauses before answering it.

*

And so, as they have always done, the clouds run across the big sky. When the wind blows one way it brings the smell of the bush; from the other way, the smell of the city.

Val no longer looks out her window for Thomas. She now gets tired at odd times and has taken to having a sleep in the afternoon.

People still meet on Patrick's platform—even people who don't live in the street come to sit there. Mary still makes her coronation cake, Patrick still checks his watch to see that everything is running on time, the apostle birds still hop and play with one another in their tree, dust and feathers blowing down the street still come together to give shape to a tiny spirit flying away, the Lances still conduct their rubbish-bin warfare, the reverend still waits in his office after six every night and pretends to work on church records, people still look up at the same sky and think about the future. Rodney no longer sits in the apricot tree; he is too busy working with Jim. They are now building a new front fence for some people around the corner on Little Road.

Parakeets still fly at ground level up the street, then lift themselves over the currawalli trees. And the smell of a distant bushfire is in the air.

🌺 Chapter Twenty-one 🌺

Jim has fallen for the second toe on Merryn's left foot. That doesn't make sense to him. It doesn't make any sense to her either. Whenever they are lounging together—as they increasingly seem to be able to find time to do—his hand invariably finds its way down her brown thigh, making the tiny blonde hairs stand up, sometimes lingering underneath her knee where the skin is softest, maybe a circle two times around the base of the ankle, jumping over the silver Moroccan chain that sits underneath that ankle and runs along the side of her foot to loop around her toes. As soon as he finds the toe he loves, he feels some tension leave his neck; he suspects that he is leaving the jungle a little further behind each time he holds this toe.

He doesn't tell Merryn any of this because he thinks she might find it too weird.

Today they are lying back on the grass next to the church, under the shadow of the silent soldier. Jim grew up playing around this statue but never climbing it, understanding without being told the significance of the soldier who stands with the butt of his rifle between his toes, his head bowed.

Merryn allows Jim to play with her toe and absently touches his forehead, sweeping his hair back. She reads aloud the inscription carved into the stone underneath the soldier: 'DEDICATED TO THE MEN AND WOMEN FROM THESE STREETS AND LANES WHO FELL IN THE GREAT WAR, 1914–1918.'

Jim listens as if he has never heard it before, and says wonderingly, 'I know every name written under that inscription. My friends and I memorised every word without knowing we were doing it.'

'Tell them to me,' Merryn says.

Jim stops running his finger over her toe and looks at her and then up at the blue sky. She takes her hand from his forehead. She sees Lukewarm coming up the street from number fourteen, carrying three apples and his camera. He told Jim and Merryn he wants to take their photo. She's holding a sprig of the honeysuckle in preparation for being photographed.

Jim finds it hard to link together what his life was before, as a child, and what it is now. In some ways Merryn is a type of conduit. She wants to find out as much of his history as she can. What his favourite toys were, what his mother's voice sounded like, what movie he took his first girlfriend to, when he met Lukewarm, why he keeps on the piano the old photograph of the two people.

For her, to hear him recite something that he memorised as a child is like finding a beautiful shell on the beach. Not that she would tell Jim that. She could tell Lukewarm, though; he understands things like that.

Jim sits up on one elbow and begins to recite the names. 'Brady, Albert AIF Gallipoli 1915. Conte, William AIF Belgium 1917. Covey, Alfred AIF France 1916. Cummings, Walter AIF France 1916. Dunold, Eric RN Atlantic 1916. Jones, Cedric AIF France 1916. Lloyd, Morrie AIF France 1918. Tierson, Janet WRAN France 1917. Tierson, Thomas RFC France 1917.'

'You missed one.'

'I don't think so.'

'You did!'

'Did I?'

'Yes. Oatley, John AIF France 1918.'

Jim smiles. It's a name he has never forgotten before. 'My grandfather. Fancy forgetting him.'

Merryn turns to look at him. 'Hey, that photo on the piano—that's your grandfather, isn't it?'

'Yep. Oatley, John AIF France 1918.'

'And the woman is your grandmother?'

'Yep. Kathleen. The photo was taken around the side of the house.'

'Your house?'

'Yep. Currawalli Street.'

Jim smiles, happy that this street is his home.

Always there has been this funny little hill. Always there has been a crooked path of some sort running along its crown. Sometimes it could not be called a path; sometimes it was just a break in the growth of the tree trunks where the wind had pushed them aside when they were saplings, like the part in a head of hair, for the wind always liked to run up this rise and sail over the crest; and it has always been a place to stop and be still for a moment. Wallabies climbed the gentle slope to reach the top and always looked around, for it was a good place to see if safety was still a companion. Dingoes used the top of this small hill to look back down the track in case there was anything small mistakenly thinking that it was safe to move. Kangaroos looked about from this spot to decide which way to go next; men stood here and looked for where there might be shelter. It isn't a big rise, not really a hill, but the illusion of height is fundamentally important to all animals.

❧ Acknowledgements ❧

I wish to thank Lyn Tranter, Stephen De Graaff, Helen Mountfort, Michael Hurwood, Howard Malkin and most of all, Claudia and Greta.

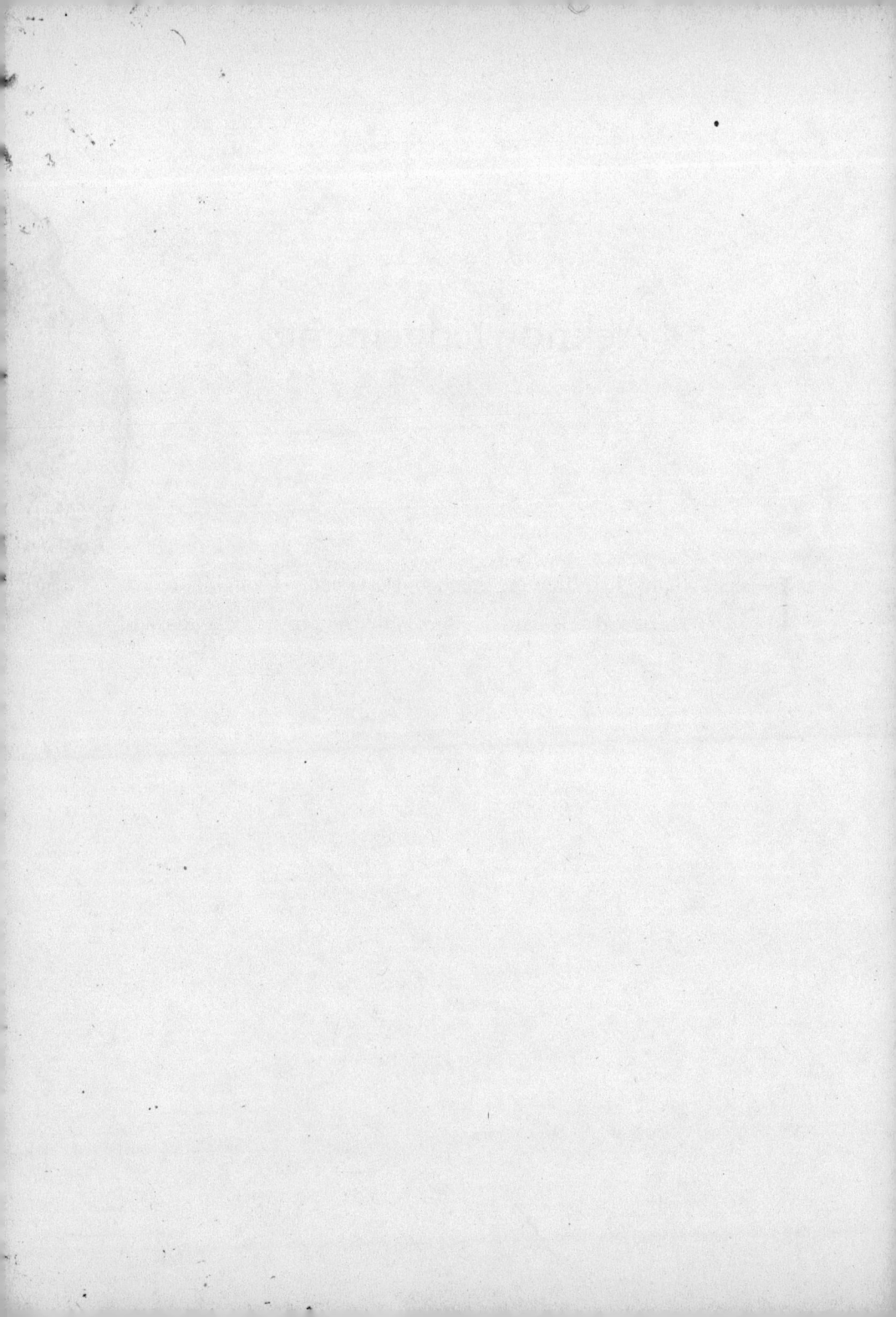